SH▮▮▮▮▮
OF THE
UNSEEN

MW01121916

Christine Steendam

*To Josh,
This one is Sans cheese.*

'15

ISBN-13: 978-0-9939259-4-8

This is a fictional work. The names, characters, incidents, places, and locations are solely the concepts and products of the author's imagination or are used to create a fictitious story and should not be construed as real.

Hazelridge Press

PO Box 21 Group 37
RR3
Dugald, MB R0E 0K0
www.christinesteendam.com

ISBN 978-0-9939259-4-8
Shadows of the Unseen
Christine Steendam
Copyright Christine Steendam 2015
Published by Hazelridge Press

Cover: Christine Steendam
Author Photo: Prairie and Pine Studio

First Edition/First Printing January 2015 Printed U.S.A.

HAZELRIDGE PRESS.

To Brenden, my brother and friend.

ACKNOWLEDGMENTS

I want to start this by thanking everyone who participates in NaNoWriMo (National Novel Writing Month). I am a yearly participant in this great event for a few reasons, one of which is that for just a month, it allows writing to be a social activity. Although writing is normally a solitary practice, it's good to remember that you're not alone in this crazy would of creating.

Thank you to Jacob, Brenden, Elissa, and Heather. My NaNoWriMo buddies. You guys are awesome.

Thank you to Andrew, Jessica, Elissa (again), Heather (again), and Mom for beta reading and taking precious time out of your own lives to give me feedback.

Thank you to everyone who got so excited about this book that you signed up to be an advance reader.

Thank you to Ellen, my publicist. I don't know what I'd do without you.

Thank you to my parents. I can't even begin to thank you for everything you do for me.

Thank you, Kyle. You're amazing and supportive. You always look out for me, keep me grounded, yet encourage me to shoot for the stars. I know I don't always seem appreciative, but I am. Thank you.

And last, but not least, thank you for picking up this book and reading it. I hope you enjoy it, and if you do, please consider leaving a review wherever you purchased it.

Christine Steendam

Part One   1
Chapter One   5
Chapter two   12
Chapter Three   21
Chapter Four   30
Chapter Five   35
Chapter Six   38
Chapter Seven   46
Chapter Eight   56
Chapter Nine   65
Chapter Ten   69
Chapter Eleven   72
Chapter Twelve   77
Chapter Thirteen   83
Chapter Fourteen   88
Chapter Fifteen   93
Chapter Sixteen   98
Chapter Seventeen   102
Chapter Eighteen   109
Chapter Nineteen   113
Chapter Twenty   126
Chapter Twenty-One   130
Chapter Twenty-two   137
Chapter Twenty-Three   142
Chapter Twenty-Four   149
Chapter Twenty-Five   156
Chapter Twenty-Six   162
Chapter Twenty-Seven   166
Chapter Twenty-Eight   174
Chapter Twenty-Nine   181
Part Two   191
Royce Williams   191
Chapter Thirty   193
Chapter Thirty-One   196
Chapter Thirty-Two   203
Chapter Thirty-Three   208
Chapter Thirty-Four   217

Chapter Thirty-Five	220
Chapter Thirty-Six	228
Chapter Thirty-Seven	237
Chapter Thirty-Eight	242
Chapter Thirty-Nine	246
Chapter Forty	252
Chapter Forty-One	259
Chapter Forty-Two	266
Chapter Forty-Three	272
Chapter forty-four	276
Chapter Forty-Five	278
Chapter Forty-Six	282
Chapter Forty-Seven	286
Epilogue	294
ABOUT THE AUTHOR	297

PART ONE

Royce Williams

Royce picked up the naked baby from where he rested in the incubator. The child's legs kicked out ferociously as the cool air hit his bare skin. The newborn's eyes fluttered open, his chin quivering with a threatened cry.

He carried him to a changing station and placed the baby on a warm mat. A wail escaped the infant's lips, but other than the man who clumsily held him on the table with one hand while his other hand fumbled for a diaper, the ward was empty, so the child's cries echoed in the vacant corridors.

Royce's hands were unsteady, unaccustomed to tending to the tiny human who kicked and screamed as he struggled to strap on the diaper and wrap him in a blanket.

"Hush," he whispered. "I know I'm no good at this, but your mother will take wonderful care of you. Every night you'll go to bed knowing people who love you are in the next room. Gentle hands will feed you, clothe you, and change you. Much gentler than my own."

Picking up the child again, this time resting him in the crook of his arm, tightly against his chest, he hummed as he walked. The wails of the baby diminished to a small whimper, then to steady, deep breathing as he fell back asleep.

Royce's journey through Frontier Industries paused at a stainless steel door in the middle of a pristine-white wall. His finger pressed a glowing button, turning it from blue to orange. He looked around to see if anyone was watching, but he was completely alone. The door whirred, then with a whoosh, almost like the sound of air being forced out of an enclosed area, it opened up to reveal a small, brightly-lit pod. Royce stepped in, pressing the button for his private parking pad on the roof of the building.

As the lift made its silent journey upward, Royce took a moment to look down at the sleeping child. He was perfect. Sabrina would love him as her own, and no one would be the wiser. Royce had already erased the records that the child had ever existed. As far as anyone would ever know, this child was his grandson, the heir to the Frontier Empire and next in line to serve as prime minister.

The door opened to reveal Royce's car sitting solitary and silent on the roof of the building. Placing the infant in the baby carrier strapped in the back seat, Royce fastened the buckles snugly around the baby, then got into the driver's seat. Starting the car, he punched the coordinates into the GPS and then sat back in his seat as the car lifted into the air and flew toward his destination.

Arriving at his destination, the car settled onto a concrete pad outside a luxurious single storey home.

Flowerbeds adorning the perimeter of the house and lush green grass filling the expanse of the yard spoke of the riches that funded it. A tall, cast-iron street lamp shone on the pathway leading to the front door.

Slipping his arm through the handle of the car seat, Royce carried the weight of the carrier in the crook of his elbow as he walked up the wide marble stoop. The steps tapered upward toward a frosted glass door with a family crest etched in the middle, revealing an abstract view of shapes and colors from inside the house.

Ringing the bell, he waited. He could see movement through the clear design, and then the door opened to reveal Kellan, his son-in-law. His face was haggard, dark circles were under his red-tinged eyes, and he couldn't seem to bring himself to offer even a polite smile, not that Royce blamed him— Kellan and Sabrina August had lost their first and only child just weeks ago. SIDS, they'd called it. A needless death was what Royce called it.

No one should ever have to feel the pain and sorrow of losing a child, especially his daughter. She was a princess in this world. She had never wanted for anything, and Royce wouldn't allow her to start now. With all his scientific advances, he couldn't save his grandchild. Maybe it was his punishment for creating the clones. He could use his creation to give her happiness again, though.

He slid the car seat off his arm and into his hand, stretching it out as an offering toward Kellan.

"What is this?" Kellan asked, a frown marring his face.

"He's mine. The only one of his kind. No one will know."

Kellan's frown deepened. "You can't just erase our Saber with a new baby," he hissed under his breath.

"I'm not trying to replace him. I'm trying to heal my daughter."

Kellan nodded, resigned, allowing Royce to enter. "His growth rate?"

"Hasn't been accelerated. He'll live a long, normal human life."

"If she doesn't want him, you'll take him away."

Royce set the seat down and removed the baby, handing him to Kellan. He gave the man no choice but to hold the child. He watched his son-in-law. Studying his movement, already tender and nurturing despite his insistence that this baby was not his.

The two men walked through the house, passing by a large dining room surrounded by four posts at each corner and then through the living room. A transparent glass door moved aside at their approach and allowed them access to the patio where Sabrina was sitting, reading with a cup of steaming tea beside her. She looked up, and her eyes immediately fell on the squirming bundle in her husband's arms.

The baby let out a cry, and Sabrina's hand flew to her mouth as she choked back a sob of her own. Royce could see the longing in her eyes, looking up at her husband wide and shining with tears.

Royce walked over, offering his arm to his daughter as she got out of her chair. She shook, but she walked to her husband with confidence and removed the fussing baby from his arms, placed him against her chest, and started bouncing up and down, humming a song as she patted his back.

Royce smiled, placing his hand on Kellan's shoulder. "His name is Saber. Saber August."

4

CHAPTER ONE

Saber August
Twenty-seven years later...

Saber smiled as his phone rang, and he rolled his chair across his small glass office. It was like working in a fish tank, his every move visible to whoever was working in the white lab just outside. Stopping at his desk, he tapped the phone icon that glowed on the glass surface and was met with the image of a smiling, red-haired woman.

"Hello, beautiful," he answered, his lips upturning slightly.

The woman's face took on a red shade, similar to the color of her hair, and her smile faded. "Prime Minister Williams has requested you come to his office."

"All business today, Pilar? Not even so much as a 'good afternoon'?"

"Just doing my job, *Sir.*" She emphasized the title of respect.

Saber offered a smile and nodded. "Please let my grandfather know I'll be right up." Pressing the end call button, the desk went blank.

This was not an uncommon exchange between Saber and Pilar. She was his grandfather's secretary, but it was all a game to Saber, one she had been wise not to get trapped in. Pilar was a clone, a race created by Royce Williams to serve the people. These clones were his claim to fame, what led him to ascend into riches and power, and eventually the seat of prime minister from nothing more than a struggling, penniless scientist.

Saber slipped off his lab coat and replaced it with a blazer. When his grandfather asked for him, he came as Saber August, not just another employee. In this world, he was a prince.

Walking down the halls, other employees smiled and nodded greetings. A few offered 'hellos' or stopped him to talk about a project. The clones always looked away, their eyes focused on the ground. They granted him a special kind of respect, moving to the far side of the hall when he approached. Not only was Saber the grandson of their creator and heir to the Frontier empire, but also next in line to serve as prime minister; someday their lives would be in his hands.

Entering the lift, Saber pressed his hand against the biometric scanner, allowing him access to his grandfather's office on the top floor. The lift whirred upward past 120 floors, and then came to a smooth halt. A ding sounded as the door slid to the side and admitted Saber into Royce William's large office. It was the only office on the floor, but a set of large, solid wood French doors separated the office from living quarters that could be opened to accommodate a social event or give Royce a

comfortable place to sleep if he worked late—
something that happened quite often.

It never ceased to amaze Saber how richly the
office was furnished. Things that should no longer
exist in this world filled the 120th floor. Huge white
curved bone accentuated one wall. Years ago, his
grandfather had told him they were elephant tusks, a
giant of the old world. Now those creatures were
nearly extinct, only the handful that took up residence
in a nature preserve remained.

On the floor in front of a gas-powered fireplace
lay the pure white pelt of a polar bear. Saber had
learned in school that these majestic beasts were also
nearing extinction. The expansion of cities and people
had made food scarce and their bitter fight for
survival nearly impossible.

He had leather couches made from hippo, a
surprisingly soft suede considering a hippo's
appearance, which filled the room with a rich, almost
earthy aroma. Real hand-scraped teak covered the
floor and ebony stained oak wainscoting made up the
perimeter of the office walls. Things that couldn't be
bought for any amount of money filled Royce
William's office, and his home was no different.
Royce spared no expense in life, nor was he ashamed
to show off the wealth he had accumulated over the
years.

Royce held up his hand to Saber to let him know
that he was busy, then shook his head to whomever
he was talking to on the phone. "No. I don't want
excuses. I want results."

Saber made his way to the bar, listening to his
grandfather's conversation as he surveyed the
decanters full of every type of liquor he could

imagine. Selecting the decanter filled with scotch, he poured himself a good two ounces of the amber liquid before taking a seat in the worn, soft leather chair across from his grandfather's desk. He sipped at his drink, enjoying the warm, cleansing sensation as it slid down his throat. The fumes from the strong drink traveled back up his throat with his exhaled breath and escaped out his nostrils.

Royce slid a wooden humidor forward and opened it, motioning for Saber to help himself.

"I want a report on my desk by tomorrow evening."

The voice protested on the other side of the phone, and Saber peered over to look at the desk, the image of someone he didn't know took up a good portion of it. Losing interest, he chose a cigar and then cut off the end and lit it, drawing inwards at the end to get a good burn before resting it in his hand on the armrest of the chair. The taste filled his throat, and the sweet smell of tobacco drifted through the room with the rising smoke. These were things that even he couldn't get unless he was visiting his grandfather. Cigarettes, sure, and alcohol was in abundance—but not the quality that Royce offered.

Royce hung up the phone, cutting off the protests from the other end, and looked at his grandson. He smiled, the crinkles around his eyes and mouth deepening. Saber swore he hadn't aged a day in all the years he had known him. Despite having long been gray, the man's hair was still full and thick, swept back more from the repeated habit of Royce running his hand backward through it than any real styling—a habit that Saber had inherited from him, lending them almost identical hairstyles.

"I'm told you're doing good work in the lab," he said, not making any segue into the conversation at hand.

Saber smiled with pride, then nodded. "I think I've made a breakthrough in my research. Time will tell. If we can suppress the genes that give the clones a sense of free will, it could solve our problem."

Royce nodded. "I want to know as soon as you receive results from your tests. If we can eradicate free will in the clones, we will erase any risk of an uprising."

Saber nodded. The whispers had started a year ago, talk of discontent and revolt. The whispers were quiet, almost non-existent, but Royce had eyes and ears everywhere. He had put Saber on solving the problem, relying on him to be discreet. The information was on a need-to-know basis.

"It'll take some time yet, even if I'm right, to find a way to suppress the gene activity in the clones already in existence."

"That's fine. And your mother? How's she been?" Royce changed the subject.

"Good. I was there Sunday. We missed you, by the way. She says you work too much and need to spend some time with your family before it's too late."

Royce chuckled. "I've been hearing that for years. Does it look like it's going to be too late anytime soon?"

Saber shook his head. "Regardless, you know the Sunday night dinners mean a lot to her."

Royce got up, walked to the bar, and poured himself a drink before returning to sit across from Saber. "I'll come this weekend."

They sat quietly for a time, Saber watching his grandfather curiously. There was more going on, words that he wasn't saying. "You didn't call me up here to talk about my work, did you? You could have gained that information from reading my reports."

"Can't an old man just want to spend time with his grandson?"

Saber grinned. "Sure, but knowing you, there's more to this than a social call."

Royce nodded and took a sip of his drink. Saber waited, puffing on his cigar. Royce had mentioned Saber's mother, so he could only guess it had something to do with her. The dinner on Sunday had been strained, to say the least. Sabrina and Kellan August had spent the evening berating him for his wild behavior and devil-may-care ways. His younger brother, Aaron, who lived the same lifestyle as Saber had not been singled out once.

"Your mother is concerned about you."

Saber scoffed, taking another puff of his quickly diminishing cigar.

"Do not make fun. You are nobility in this world, and I expect you to act as such."

Saber nodded. His mother had been lamenting his behavior for months now. It had only been a matter of time before his grandfather addressed it, especially after Sunday.

Saber fought back the urge to bring up Aaron, to bring his grandfather's attention to his younger grandson's similar behavior. It was petty—and unnecessary. All his life Saber had been the golden child, the one being groomed to stand in Royce's stead when the time came. There was more attention on him, more scrutiny, and more weight on his shoulders.

"You are to inherit everything I have created. Your actions must be beyond reproach, and right now they are not."

Royce touched his desk, bringing up a tabloid article screaming the headline: "Do you trust your future to this boy?" in big bold letters and a picture of him hunched and puking just outside a popular bar adorned more than half the page.

Saber looked away, sighing. The article was what had started the argument on Sunday.

"This," his grandfather said, indicating the article still glowing brightly on the glass top of his desk at Saber, "is an embarrassment to the family. To me."

Saber's face fell. He never could argue with his grandfather, nor handle his disapproval. "What do you expect me to do?"

Royce smiled, and Saber felt himself relax slightly. "I may be old, but I haven't forgotten what it is to be young. Be more discreet and hold it together. I don't want to see or hear anything like this about you again. Do you hear me?"

Saber swallowed his discomfort and nodded. "Is that everything?"

Royce nodded. "Yes. Enjoy your evening. I'll see you on Sunday."

Saber drained the last of his scotch, placing the glass down on the desk, directly on top of the tabloid article and took his leave, entering the lift and waving to his grandfather as the door whooshed closed. As the lift descended, Saber felt a weight lift from his shoulders. Conversations like that with his grandfather were anything but comfortable.

Heading out of Frontier Industries, he slid into his car and lifted it into the air, flying it toward his home.

CHAPTER TWO

Aaron August

Aaron lounged on the faux leather couch in the living room. It was stiff, and he had begged Saber to replace it on multiple occasions. But here it sat, and Aaron attempted to get comfortable on the couch that was much more suited to sitting on and drinking whisky than lounging in front of a TV.

The lift chimed, and the door whooshed open, revealing Saber. Aaron looked up, nodded at his older brother, then returned to watching the reality TV show that blared at him from the glowing screen on the wall.

Behind him, in the large, industrial-style kitchen, Aaron could hear Saber going about pouring himself a drink.

"Want one?" asked Saber.

Aaron didn't have to look behind him to know what Saber was offering. "A beer would go down great."

The only indication that Saber had heard was the clinking of a glass bottle being picked up off the fridge shelf.

Saber sat down beside Aaron and handed him the beer.

"I don't know how you drink that stuff, or why you waste your money on it."

"It's refreshing."

"You've been spending too much time at the university."

Aaron chuckled and took a sip. "You've just forgotten what it's like to be young."

"That's not what Grandfather said."

Aaron frowned, turned down the volume of the TV, and looked at his brother. He appeared annoyed, his face clouded by the heavy furrow in his brow. What did he have to be upset about? As the favorite of their grandfather, and the heir to the Frontier empire, he had the world at his fingertips.

Life had always come easily to Saber. Professors had called him a genius. Their parents had regarded him with pride, as he excelled at everything he turned his hands or mind to. And their grandfather, Royce Williams, would gladly give Saber anything he requested. Sure, Saber was no slouch, never had been, and was willing to work for everything he had, even though he didn't have to. But that didn't change the fact that Saber was given everything, and Aaron was overshadowed.

"Mom and Dad?" he asked.

Saber nodded. "Mom talked to Grandfather, and we had a *talk*. You know, disappointing him is way worse than dealing with Mom and Dad's anger. It was just a stupid tabloid."

Aaron shrugged. "At least they care about what you do. I might as well be invisible."

"Be thankful. I have my every move watched and scrutinized."

The boys fell into silence. Aaron sipped at his beer and waved his right hand upward in the air to turn the volume back up on the TV. Their conversation was done. There was nothing more to say.

A few minutes later, Saber got up and walked down the hall toward his room. Aaron glanced up to see him walk away, then returned his attention to the TV. His phone chimed, letting him know a text message had come. Picking it up, he read the message. He'd invited some friends from the university over later, but had forgotten to let Saber know. Oh well. He sent the reply to Trisha that she could come at nine, and then got up from the couch in search of dinner.

Saber and Aaron had a clone that came in during the day to tidy up and cook dinner. It could always be found in the oven, keeping warm.

Opening the oven, a wave of aromas instantly hit Aaron—the warm, comforting smell of pot roast, gravy, and Yorkshire pudding. As he reached inside to retrieve his plate, served, prepared, and warm, his stomach growled.

Just as he was mopping up the last of the gravy with his Yorkshire pudding, Saber joined him in the kitchen, his hair wet and messy from being towel-dried after a shower.

"You might want to get more presentable," he said around a mouthful of food. Swallowing, he continued, "I invited some friends over."

Saber nodded and retrieved his dinner plate from the oven, joining his brother at the island. "Just a few, right?

After my talk with grandfather, I'm not sure a party is such a great idea."

Aaron pressed his lips together. *He* had only invited a few friends, but that wasn't to say they wouldn't bring more people. "Yep, that's all I invited." It wasn't a lie, per se; it was just an omission of a suspicion. Besides, Saber might say he wanted a quiet evening right now, but Aaron knew that as soon as people started arriving, he would change his mind.

The rest of the night went by in a blur for Aaron. People had started to arrive, and before he knew it, the penthouse was full. Saber seemed to be having a good enough time, his arm draped around a pretty blonde as they sat on the couch, heads close together in conversation. Aaron, however, had his eyes on the girl who had just walked in.

He'd seen her a few times around the university, but didn't know her. She wore tight leather pants and a loose red blouse that flowed and rippled with every movement she made, but rested on all the right places. She was tall and her legs seemed to stretch on for miles before ending in a pair of strappy black heels. She'd pulled her blond hair, the golden color of wheat, into a ponytail, and it swung and danced as she conversed and laughed with a group of girls.

She looked behind her, her eyes meeting Aaron's, a shy smile curving the edges of her lips upward. She looked away again, returning to her conversation as if the moment they had shared hadn't happened, but Aaron knew better—and the brief moment of eye contact was invitation enough for him.

Walking up, he slipped his hand onto the small of her back and deftly separated her from the group of girls. "I'm Aaron," he said, removing his hand from her waist.

She blushed, but the smile let him know she didn't mind the attention. "Kristin," she replied, holding out her hand.

Aaron shook it, but didn't let go, letting their hands fall and relax at hip height. "Come with me. I have something to show you," he said, leading her through the packed room and down the hall to his bedroom. As the door to his room slid open at his approach, he felt Kristin hesitate, so he paused and turned to her with a smile.

"I promise I'm not looking to take advantage of you; we just have to go through my room to get to my private balcony. It's quieter out there."

That seemed to reassure her enough because she followed him through the doorway without hesitation. Once the door slid closed, he released her hand and walked to the mini fridge, pulling out a bottle of white wine and retrieving a couple glasses from the tray on top.

"This way," he said, motioning with his hand that held the glasses to the large glass door that slid open to reveal a balcony overlooking the city.

Kristin walked past him and found a seat on the sofa, making herself comfortable. He smiled, holding back a chuckle as he watched her kick off her shoes and sigh, leaning into the couch. "That's better," she said, looking at him. "What?"

"Nothing," Aaron said as he joined her on the couch, placing the glasses and bottle of wine on the table in front of them.

He loved this spot. It was his sanctuary. The beating music from inside was silenced out here, and all they heard was the whirr of the traffic and the sounds of the bustling city below.

SHADOWS OF THE UNSEEN

Aaron poured them each a glass of wine and swirled it around a couple of times before handing her the glass. She sipped it gingerly, and he watched her face, waiting for the moment of pure elation. It came. Her smile broadened, and she placed the glass down.

"Good?"

"Like nothing I've ever tasted."

"I live to impress."

"Apparently."

They fell into a comfortable silence as they both took another sip of wine.

"I've seen you around the university, what's your major?" asked Aaron.

"Political studies," Kristin replied. "And you?"

"Marketing and Public Relations. I've got a job waiting for me with my grandfather."

"Prime Minister Williams," Kristin stated.

He nodded. It was no secret who he was, or who his grandfather was.

"That's great. It must be nice to know your future is secure."

"It is, but I also don't have much choice in my future either. Family sticks with family, you know?"

Kristin offered a smile, but her eyes were distant, like she was reliving a memory.

"But enough about me. You probably know everything already," he said with a chuckle. "It's you I want to hear about."

Kristin smiled again, her wistful expression erased. She took another sip of her wine. "I don't know what you'd want to hear. I'm not a very exciting person."

"Tell me about your degree, your hopes, dreams, what you ate for breakfast. I don't care."

Kristin laughed, the musical sound overpowering all the background noise of the city and drawing Aaron's attention like a siren's song. She launched into talking about her degree, but quickly transitioned to current world issues and solutions. Her eyes brightened, and her hands waved in cadence with her words as she spoke, her passion apparent in every movement she made. Occasionally she would pick up her wine glass to take a sip, then set it back down to continue the conversation. Aaron responded when he could, but he was woefully unprepared for a discussion on world issues, so he stuck to nodding and one-word answers to let her know he was still interested.

Aaron watched her mouth as she spoke. He wanted to kiss those full, bright-red lips, but he shook his head, dislodging the thought and returned to the conversation at hand. "So you don't like the way this world is run?" he asked as Kristin took a break to sip her wine.

"I think the political system is good, if the election of prime minister hadn't been abolished with Williams' rise to power, and if he hadn't turned a democracy into an antiquated monarchy. Having the richest, most powerful man in the world *also* be the Prime Minster has created a dictatorship. The parliament is a face, a front, and means absolutely nothing. Your grandfather answers to no one, and that is a serious problem. We live in an autocracy and very few people seem to realize it. Those who do, don't say anything."

Aaron chuckled. "Should I be insulted?"

She shrugged and smiled. "If you like, but you don't strike me as someone who would be. I think you realize the power your grandfather holds, and you know it isn't democratic, but I doubt you care."

"It's not that I don't care, it's more that I've just never bothered to educate myself on the subject. But it doesn't seem to bother you much that I'm the grandson of your enemy."

Kristin laughed and put her hand on his arm, leaning in closer. The wine was going to her head; Aaron could see that by the glazed look in her eyes. "Maybe I'm trying to infiltrate the enemy camp," she whispered.

He chuckled, then wrapped his arm around her shoulders, pulling her against his side. She relaxed against him, resting her head on his shoulder and sighed.

"In all honesty, Aaron, I have no idea what I'm doing here. You and your family stand for the very things I'm against."

"Maybe I can change your mind about that," he whispered, resting his head to the right, on top of hers. He didn't want to think about his family, his grandfather, or her crusade. Right now he just wanted to live in the moment, drink in Kristin's scent, and hold her in his arms. He had never had this kind of connection with a woman before.

They spoke, off and on. Aaron told her amusing stories about growing up as an August, and Kristin told him about her various jobs that brought out chuckles and gasps on multiple occasions. As the night continued, the words passing between them became fewer and eventually Aaron felt Kristin's body relax and her breathing fall into the steady rhythm of sleep. Kissing the top of her head, he shifted into a more comfortable position, and he too drifted off.

When he woke the next morning, it was to her retreating back, sneaking out at the crack of dawn. Her shoes hung from her index and middle finger from their thin black straps. He didn't let her know that he was awake, didn't call her back or walk her to the door. He watched her glide through the door on tiptoes and then disappear from sight. He didn't even have her number. It was best this way.

CHAPTER THREE

Saber August

The streets were filled with people, walking by, pushing each other as they fought against an unyielding crowd. Saber stood up on his tippy toes, craning to see through or above the crowd.

"Mom?" he called.

No answer came through the noise of traffic and hundreds of conversations around him.

He turned around, trying to look in another direction. Something knocked him from behind, driving him to his knees. Pain soared up his legs, and instantly tears welled in his eyes.

"Mom?" he called out through sobs. "Mom?"

He placed his hands on the dirty concrete, bits of dirt and gravel digging into his palms as he pushed himself back up into a standing position and angrily wiped his tears away. Crying was for babies. He wasn't lost. He knew exactly where he was. It was his mom who was lost.

Pushing through the crowd, he managed to get out of the stream of constantly moving bodies. Leaning against the cool, smooth glass of the nearest building, he looked around again. He still saw no sign of Mom.

"How dare you!" exploded a voice to the left. Saber's head snapped to look at the large man.

"What did I do?" he squeaked out in a small voice.

"You dare touch me? Scum!"

Saber's eyes widened, and then he shut them, flinching away from the man's huge flying fist.

Smack!

He felt nothing. Opening his eyes, he saw a clone cowering beneath the man, holding her head between her hands.

"I'm sorry. It was an accident," she sobbed out.

The man responded with another fist to the side of her head, knocking her to her side on the cold hard pavement.

Saber couldn't look away as the horror unfolded. The man's foot connected with her ribs with a resounding crack that seemed to suppress all the noise around them. It was as if they were in a bubble and Saber was the only one who could see. Out of the thousands of people walking by, not one stopped, not one paused. The beating was invisible.

Blood seeped out of the clone's mouth and where her skin had split under the punishment being inflicted on her. She was silent. Unmoving.

"Stop!" he cried out, but the man didn't even look up. "Stop! You're hurting her!"

Still no reaction. Saber might as well have been invisible. He had to do something. He had to stop it. But his feet wouldn't move. He was frozen in place. "Help! Help her! Help her!"

* * *

Saber's eyes sprang open. His room was still dark and silent. Sweat drenched him, and his sheets were tangled around him, his blanket kicked away and hanging partially off the foot of the bed.

Sitting up, he rubbed his eyes and looked around again to assure himself that he was safe at home. *It was a dream, just a dream,* he told himself.

Climbing out of bed, he walked into the kitchen and opened the fridge. A soft glow from inside lit up the room, and he reached in and grabbed a bottle of water. Leaving the stifling confines of his apartment, he walked out onto the balcony that jutted off the living room. Cool air hit his bare skin, and he shivered, goose bumps stippling his flesh.

Taking a deep breath, he closed his eyes. The image of the dead clone woman flashed in front of them. He shook his head and opened his eyes again. He wouldn't be sleeping again tonight.

Taking a sip of his water, he went back into the apartment and retrieved a robe from his bedroom, slipped it on, and situated himself at his desk. Touching the glass top of his desk, it came alive, revealing a glowing keyboard and various windows he'd left open. The wall in front of him went transparent and revealed a screen.

If he couldn't sleep, he might as well work.

* * *

Saber sighed, resting his head in his hands. He'd been so close to a breakthrough. So close. He'd worked half the night, then had come to his office and worked all day, convinced he was nearly there.

But instead of a breakthrough, his research had just been sent two steps back. The latest test hadn't shown what he wanted and instead only introduced more questions.

Raising his head, he looked at the glowing numbers on his desktop, showing the time. It was well past the end of the day. His lab was abandoned, everyone else had clocked out and gone home an hour or so ago. But Saber had stayed to run one last experiment. Now he wished he hadn't. He could have gone home and relaxed, thinking that tomorrow he would be able to approach his grandfather with the news he had been waiting for. Instead, he would go home filled with disappointment.

Might as well get the report done and over with, he thought, getting up from his desk. He trudged the maze of halls in Frontier Industries until he made it to the private lift that led to Royce William's office.

Once at the very top, the lift door opened to admit Saber into the familiar office. Stepping in, he paused. Instead of seeing his grandfather, swallowed in a plume of smoke and talking on the phone, like he had expected, the room was empty. Frowning, he started to turn back to the lift, but paused as movement and a flash of color in his periphery drew his attention.

On the far end of the room, there was Pilar, his grandfather's assistant. Saber would recognize her red hair anywhere—differentiating her from the masses. Royce had insisted she appear different, so that he could tell her apart.

She appeared to be tidying up the office, cleaning out the ashtray beside one of the leather couches. He stood in silence, watching her until she looked up and smiled.

Unlike most clones—no, even a lot of humans—she didn't lower her eyes. She offered no real form of submission to Saber.

"Hello," she greeted. "Can I help you?"

"Uh," replied Saber, still unsure of the situation. "Is Royce around?"

"He had to go to a meeting. Saber, right? I'm Pilar. We've spoken on the phone."

"I know." She was different from the other clones, and not just because of her hair color. It was in the way she held herself. Maybe it was because of being groomed to serve the most powerful man in the world, but Saber didn't intimidate her, and he was used to being formidable.

"Can I help you with something?" she repeated her earlier question.

"I don't know," he responded, frowning. "I just came to . . . It doesn't matter. I'll let you get back to work."

She smiled, her eyes crinkling at the corners, and the room seemed to light up around her, relaxing Saber just a little. "I'm finished work for the day. If you're looking for someone to talk to, or just listen, I'd be happy to be of service."

Saber felt shock roll through him like a cold dose of water. Talk? To a clone? They weren't friends; they were there to serve.

Her face fell, and her smile weakened. Instantly, he felt as if she was in his mind, as if she had heard his thoughts and a moment of shame rose up.

"I know it's not my place—"

"No!" he quickly protested, walking forward. "I didn't mean it like that. I was just . . . I've never met a clone quite so . . . forward."

Her smile found its place back on her face.

"I could use a listening ear, if you don't mind."

"Not at all." She sat down on the couch she had been standing near and patted the empty spot beside her.

Saber forced a slight smile and walked toward her. He was in dangerous waters. He wasn't quite sure what he was thinking, treating a clone like a peer, but with so many conflicting thoughts going on, he couldn't help but feel that maybe she was the safest ear to hear him out. She was a clone, so she would never say anything, nor would anyone listen to her. And as his grandfather's assistant, she would be accustomed to being discreet.

On his way across the room, he stopped at the bar and poured himself a scotch and, after a moment's hesitation, poured one for Pilar. He brought it to her, and she smiled her appreciation, taking it readily.

"This isn't the first time you've had access to my grandfather's personal liquor cabinet, is it?"

"I'm good at listening," she responded. And that comforted Saber a little more in his decision.

"I don't really know where to start…"

"Start with what brought you here, and we'll see where it goes."

Saber felt his cheeks warm—something that hadn't happened since he was a young boy. He usually didn't confess his shortcomings to anyone. He was supposed to be confident, infallible, the future prime minister. He shouldn't fail—ever. But then again, Pilar wasn't human. He didn't have to impress her. She was something a little less than human, and humans demanded her respect. Perhaps that made confessing his sins to her a little less intimidating.

"I've been working on a project for my grandfather and I thought I had made a breakthrough, but instead I'm back to square one."

He paused, waiting to see if she had anything to say, but she remained silent.

"I don't know what went wrong, or why, but my grandfather is counting on this project to be a success, and I'm starting to doubt it'll work. I must have missed something. A chemical that is blocking the suppression agents…" he trailed off, lost in thought. Was that it? Was that the answer? That what he was trying to do *couldn't* be done, at least not the way he was going about things.

He looked at Pilar. "Maybe it's not that it can't be done," she said, as if she had plucked the thought right out of his mind, "But that it *shouldn't* be done."

Saber closed his eyes and sighed. "You know what I'm doing, don't you?" He opened his eyes and looked at her.

She nodded. "I'm a little more privy to your life than most. Good listener, remember?" She winked.

"And you don't hate me?"

She shook her head. "But I wish you'd stop."

Saber frowned, searching Pilar's face. She looked at him with wide eyes, almost pleading. Her hands clutched tightly in her lap, her knuckles white.

"Are you scared?"

"A little," she said, followed by a slight, nervous chuckle.

"Of what?"

"Of you. Of the power you have over me and my people."

A pang shot through Saber that he could only describe as guilt, and he sipped his scotch, looking away from the scared, yet bold woman sitting beside him. She shouldn't be making him feel guilty. She didn't deserve his pity. She was a clone, nobody. But he'd never experienced a clone in such a personal and human way. She refused to be invisible. How could he even think to take away her free will?

"What do I do?" he asked.

She smiled, her eyes still filled with sadness. "Follow your conscience. You know what's right."

Follow his conscience? What did that mean? That didn't give him an answer, just more questions.

Reaching forward to pick up his glass off the coffee table, his hand brushed hers briefly, but enough to make her flinch away. Her brown eyes lowered away from his face and focused on her lap. Picking up his glass, he took a sip.

In that one act of submission, she had once again dropped from human to clone. He felt strange and wrong, sitting here and talking to her about the future of her race. He drained the last of his glass and stood up. The illusion had been shattered, and there was no sense in sticking around.

"Thank you. You were most helpful."

She remained on the couch, staring into her scotch glass. Her eyes blank, glazed, like her mind was far away.

Getting up, he escaped into the safe confines of the lift and left her alone. She was a clone. She would be okay. She had it better than most, and this one instance would fade into the past. *They are cloned from humans, so they're gonna seem human*, he thought. *But they aren't like us. They're created by us. We're like gods, and they are our tiny little ants.*

Saber frowned at the description his mind fed him, but it rang true. He'd seen clones treated as lowly as ants.

When he was young, nine or ten-years-old, he'd seen a clone get beaten to death in the middle of the street. Even now, he sometimes woke up in a cold sweat due to the image of blood spattering the sidewalk. Even if Royce had created the clones, they lived and breathed like every other creature. If he could eradicate their free will, it would protect them. They wouldn't be able to do any wrong.

But he couldn't ignore the fact that he had felt a connection. And he couldn't just push that behind a master-servant relationship, no matter how hard he tried.

CHAPTER FOUR

Aaron August

"Aaron, can I talk to you for a minute?"

Aaron directed his attention to his professor, standing at the end of his row of seats.

"Uh, yeah. I'll catch up with you later, Rob," he said, sliding out of his row and following Professor Graham to the front of the lecture hall where he began gathering his papers.

"I'm concerned about you, Aaron. You aren't showing much dedication."

"Sorry, I have a lot going on."

"Every student in my class has a lot going on, but they try. You give me the bare minimum."

"You don't know that," Aaron shot back.

"Your work speaks for itself." Professor Graham picked up his tablet and pulled up a paper, covered in bright red markups and a giant 'D' circled. He handed it to Aaron.

Aaron looked. The red screamed failure at him. But his prof was right, he'd whipped off this paper last minute after putting it off for weeks. "What if that's the best I can do?"

"I *know* you can do better. If you want, I'll give you a chance to re-do this paper at no penalty. But only this once."

Aaron looked down again. The black words blurred together and the red comments like, 'this makes no sense, expound' and, 'be clearer. You're too vague' seemed to jump off the screen at him. He looked away and handed the tablet back. "No thanks. I'll take the D."

"Are you sure, Aaron? I'm not going to make this offer again."

Aaron shrugged. "A D is still a passing grade. I just gotta get through school, not be the best."

Professor Graham pressed his lips together in a thin line and nodded. "I'm sorry to hear that."

"It's not like hard work and dedication is going to get me any further in life than I already am."

Aaron turned around, walking up the stairs in the auditorium style lecture hall, and exited as the door opened automatically in front of him. Glancing at his phone, Aaron swore. He was late for his next class.

Taking off at a jog, he dodged various other students. Conversations echoed around the cavernous halls as he made his way through them. He needed to catch the tram to get to another building across campus for his next class.

Exiting the door, he saw the tram filling up, and he took off at a sprint, jumping on and scanning his wrist just as it was pulling away.

"Careful! You could get hurt," a girl in the front row said, glaring at him.

Aaron laughed, breathing heavily from his sprint. "I made it, didn't I?" Then he made his way down the aisle to an empty seat near the back.

The drive took a few minutes, stopping at two other buildings before reaching the one he needed.

Jumping down, he waved to the tram and the up-tight girl who was still sitting there. She glared back. Aaron chuckled and pulled out his phone, checking the time again. Now he was really late.

A laugh sounded, catching Aaron's ear, and he looked to see a group of girls standing on the quad a short distance away. The laughter had come from a girl whose back was towards him, but he'd recognize that laugh and that long blond hair anywhere. Kristin.

Do I go to class? Or go over there? He looked down at his phone again and sighed, shoving it into his pocket. He was so late there was no point showing up now. Heading toward the group of girls, he recognized Trisha standing amongst them. Good, he had a reason to join them then.

Trisha spotted him and waved, smiling. Aaron waved back, but he looked at Kristin. She glanced behind her, catching his eye for a minute, then looked away.

"I gotta go," he heard her say, as she left the group and walked towards the building, passing Aaron. He watched her go, his head turning to follow her movement until she disappeared into the building.

"You got it baaaaad," Trisha teased as he joined her and her friends.

"Huh? What?"

"Kristin. Don't think I didn't notice that she disappeared with you the other night. And that look you guys shared."

"There was no look," Aaron muttered, slinging his arm around Trisha's shoulder.

"Sure, sure. Aren't you supposed to be in Media Relations class right now?"

"Nah, I'm here with you, aren't I?"

Trisha giggled and slid out from under his arm. Planting a kiss on his cheek, she took the crook of his elbow in hand. "Walk me to class, then?"

"For you, of course."

He led her towards the building.

"You know, Kristin is a pretty serious girl. If you want to impress her, you should probably take your life a little more seriously."

"I'm not trying to impress her, Trisha. Just drop it, okay?"

Trisha let go of his arm and stopped, holding up her hands in surrender. "Sorry. I'm just trying to help. I think it's safe to say I know you well enough to know when you have the hots for someone."

"And I think you should know when to butt out."

The hurt that flashed in her eyes made Aaron immediately regret his words. "I'm sorry. I know you're just trying to help."

"Hey, what are friends for? Don't think a couple harsh words are going to scare me off."

Aaron smiled, putting his arm back around Trisha's shoulder. "Thanks."

"Just, uh, one more word of advice."

"What's that?"

"*If* you're interested in Kristin, and I'm not saying you are, you might want to dial down our relationship. There is nothing more intimidating to a woman than a man that already has a woman in his life."

Aaron laughed. "Trisha, you're the best, you know that?"

"I do."

"But I'm not going to forget about you."

"Sure you will. When you find love, I'll be left behind. That's just how it works."

CHAPTER FIVE

Saber August

Saber left his office for the day, shoving his cell into his pocket and scanning his wrist as he left, locking the lab up tight behind him.

"Night, Saber," a co-worker said as he passed by.

Saber nodded his reply. *What is his name?* He couldn't remember. He couldn't even remember meeting the guy, and maybe he hadn't. Frontier Industries employed thousands of people and probably every single one of them knew who he was.

The pristine, floor-to-ceiling white halls were a maze, but Saber knew them well and he walked confidently through them. He found his way to a lift and pressed the call button, waiting. A ding sounded, then the door opened. Looking up, he met the deep brown eyes of Pilar, her flaming red hair tied back in a braid.

"Oh, Saber. I was just on my way to find you."

"You could have called," he said, stepping into the lift.

"I did. You didn't answer."

Saber pulled out his cell and looked. 'One missed call' glowed up at him. He'd left his phone on silent.

"Well, what can I do for you?"

"I have something to show you."

Pilar reached forward, touching the 'B' button. The basement. What did she want to show him in the basement? There wasn't much down there besides storage.

Stepping out of the lift, Pilar led the way down more white halls. The basement looked no different from upstairs besides the fact that any outside halls didn't have any windows.

Pilar paused outside a room, a large glass window giving them a view inside. Saber looked. A group of maybe a dozen clones stood around the room, looking around at each other in what could only be described as nervous tension. Two armed guards stood near the door.

"What's going on?"

"They're here for termination," Pilar said in a barely audible whisper.

Saber frowned. "They look fine."

"They are. They've just reached their peak. Sixty in clone years."

"Only twenty in human," finished Saber.

Pilar nodded, tears shining in her eyes.

"When did this start?"

"About five years ago, when Royce realized that after sixty, clones began slowing down and costing more than they were worth."

"And if they don't slow down?"

"It doesn't matter. It takes time and resources to screen clones to see if they're physically fit to serve for a few more years. Instead, when they reach sixty years of maturity, they are collected and terminated."

"Why didn't I know this?"

"Some things Royce keeps secret, even from you."

"How do you know?"

"I'm invisible, remember? It's easy to see and hear things you aren't supposed to when no one notices you."

Saber watched the clones inside the room in silence. Some paced, others huddled together. Did they know what was happening?

A nurse stepped through a back door and into the room, saying something, and leading a clone away through the door. Saber flinched as the door slammed shut, the hollow sound echoing even through the thick walls and triple-paned window that separated them.

"Why are you showing me this?"

"Because you have power that no one else does." Pilar turned to face him. "And even if you try to deny it, you have kindness in you. I know you aren't heartless; I've seen a conscience behind your eyes. Maybe you want the world to think you don't care about anything, but you do."

"You don't know anything about me."

"I know you're haunted by something, and I know you have so much more potential than Royce has allowed to be realized."

Saber clenched his jaw and turned away. "Learn your place, clone. You're lucky I'm not going to report you for this."

He walked away, his footsteps echoing through the empty halls.

CHAPTER SIX

Aaron August

Aaron looked up as Saber walked into the apartment and immediately went to the kitchen. He frowned, watching his older brother reach for the scotch and pour himself a hefty glass, tossing it back in only a couple large gulps.

"Something wrong?" he asked, getting up from the couch. The TV shut off automatically as he walked away and left the apartment quiet. Too quiet.

"Rough day," Saber replied, refilling his glass.

Aaron watched the golden liquid sway and then settle in the crystal glass. This time, Saber let it sit for a few minutes before sighing and picking the glass up. He didn't drink it though, just walked away, down the hall and disappeared into his bedroom.

It wasn't unlike his brother to be moody like this, but it was unlike him to drown whatever was bothering him in alcohol, which meant it had to be something pretty big.

Aaron looked down at his phone and pressed the screen to unlock it. A text glowed at him from Trisha.

Here's Kristin's contact. You're welcome ;)

He didn't know why, or what prompted the unsolicited text that he had received a couple hours ago, but it wouldn't leave him alone. He was supposed to forget about Kristin, but having means to contact her was making it all the more difficult.

What have I got to lose? he thought, still staring at the glowing digits, his thumb hovering above, wavering slightly in indecision. He sighed and removed his thumb from the ready position, and went back to the couch, slumping into the stiff leather seat. Holding his phone up once again, he pressed the reply button to the text.

He couldn't bring himself to call Kristin, but he could arrange a group meeting. If Trisha invited her, it would seem like random chance, not like he was chasing after her. That, or she'd see right through his ploy and think him pathetic.

The response came quickly from Trisha. Nothing more than a time and place, but it was the confirmation that Aaron needed. His heart rate picked up immediately upon reading the words. What if it was awkward? What if she wasn't the girl he remembered from Friday night? What if he wasn't the guy *she* remembered?

Getting up, he walked down the hall to Saber's room. The sound of a guitar drifted through the door as Aaron raised his fist to knock. He paused, listening for a moment. His brother was an accomplished guitarist, but tonight he was playing a classical piece. The music was sorrowful, almost conflicted. He was playing to sort out what was bothering him, and

Aaron realized there might be more going on than just a bad day at work.

Knocking, the music stopped and Saber called out, "Come in."

The door whooshed open on Saber's command, and he looked at Aaron from the far side of his room, beside a window that spanned the entire wall from floor-to-ceiling.

"What's up?" he asked.

"Gonna go out tonight, meet Trisha and some of her girlfriends. Wanna come?"

Saber hesitated, his lips pressed together and his brow furrowed in thought, then nodded. "Sure, why not. What time?"

"In an hour at Karpov's. We should eat something first."

Saber put his guitar aside and stood up. "I'm going to take a shower."

"'Kay."

Aaron retreated from the room and back into the large living area. Looking around, he sighed. Something was going on with Saber. Aaron often heard him wake up in the middle of the night and wander around the apartment. He had nightmares. He had ever since they were young, but Aaron thought they stopped in their teenage years, back when Saber had attended months of therapy upon their grandfather's insistence, and pocketbook.

Recently, though, they had returned… ever since he had started working at Frontier Industries on whatever top secret project their grandfather had him heading up.

Aaron retrieved his food from the oven and brought it to the couch.

"TV on," he said around a mouthful of food.

Waving his index finger upwards like it was a magic wand, the channel switched. He repeated the motion until he stopped on a sitcom, and continued eating his dinner. At least this would distract him from Saber's problems.

A short while later, Saber came out, dressed in charcoal gray dress pants and a deep red shirt. The collar was left unbuttoned, and he had on leather lace-up shoes. Aaron looked down at what he was wearing—jeans and a polo shirt—and felt significantly underdressed. *And seriously, when did I drop food onto my lap?* How could he be expected to get Kristin's attention with Saber beside him? And looking like a slob.

Putting his empty dinner plate on the coffee table, he got up to change.

"Can we take your car?" asked Saber as Aaron started walking out of the room.

Aaron paused and turned back. "Maybe we should go separately—" The smug look on Saber's face stopped him mid-sentence.

"By Trisha and a few girlfriends, did you mean that pretty blond you were hanging out with Friday night?"

"No idea," Aaron tried to cover. "Trisha invited me. I didn't ask who she was bringing."

Saber grinned, his bad mood apparently forgotten for the time being. "Sure, sure. Okay, I'll take my own car. Wouldn't want to ruin your game, little bro."

Aaron scowled and walked away, turning his back on Saber, who was still chuckling.

Standing in the middle of his huge walk-in closet, only a quarter of the available space used, Aaron surveyed his options. Normally, he found his wardrobe more than enough, but today it seemed woefully empty. *This must be what girls feel like when they say they have nothing to wear,* he thought, scowling over the idea that he was turning into such a feminine dolt. *Yeah, that'll really impress Kristin.*

Grabbing a clean pair of jeans and a teal dress shirt, Aaron changed quickly and looked at his feet. Shoes…

He looked at the shelf that contained various styles of footwear and picked up a pair of dressier tennis shoes and slipped them on. Satisfied with his appearance, he joined Saber out in the living area.

Getting up, Saber walked to the lift. "Ready to go?" he asked, pressing the call button to open the door.

Aaron nodded and stepped in behind his brother, turning around as the lift started to go up the one floor to their private parking pad. By the time he was facing the door again, it opened to reveal their vehicles.

Aaron walked to his car; the door lifting open for him as he approached, recognizing the chip in his wrist that identified him, and started as he slid into the faux leather seat. He looked at Saber, who was mimicking Aaron's movements. For a moment, he felt a little jealous as he watched his brother get into his car. It had been a gift from their grandfather upon graduating from university last year and accepting his position at Frontier Industries, and it was a beauty. One-of-a-kind, custom-made vehicle. The car that Aaron sat in was a gift from their parents— and although a luxurious vehicle in its own right, it was nothing compared to Saber's.

"Hello, Aaron," his car said in a soft, feminine voice as the door lowered and latched with a hiss of hydraulics. "May I have your destination?"

"Karpov's."

"Destination set. Trip commencing."

Aaron's phone chimed and he turned to the video panel set in the dash of his car. An image of Saber grinned at him.

"Answer," he said as his car slowly lifted from the rooftop beside Saber's.

"Race you," challenged Saber as the image was replaced by a video feed of him.

"Dee, set the car to manual," he instructed. Dee was the name of his car—they all came with names these days.

"Manual engaged," came the response, and the steering wheel unlocked under Aaron's hands. He looked at the video screen and nodded. "Ready or not," and he punched down the gas pedal.

Saber was right behind him, zipping in and out of traffic, around buildings, through airspace that was not meant to be public streets. The blinking red dot in his windshield indicated their final destination.

Saber's face reappeared in the dashboard screen and he laughed manically. "You wanna do this?"

"Oh, do I ever," Aaron replied with a grin that stretched at the sides of his face.

"Eat my dust."

He laughed and punched the gas even harder, but Saber came zipping up behind him and cut in front in a split second.

"Where did you come from?"

"Shortcut." Saber laughed. The look of enjoyment on his face lightened Aaron's mood. *This is the Saber I know*, he thought as he wove back and forth, up and down looking for an opening to slip into the lead.

Sirens and flashing lights filled Aaron's review mirror and he laughed. Screw the cops, they couldn't hope to keep up with these cars.

"Crap!" Saber exclaimed through the phone connection. Aaron knew the last thing his brother needed was to create more public fuss for his grandfather to diffuse.

"I think the stakes of this race just changed," Saber continued. "Follow me."

Aaron stopped trying to pass his brother and fell in behind him, keeping pace as he watched his brother's car for a change in route. Saber's car suddenly surged forward and Aaron punched the gas down harder, matching his speed. He whooped as buildings and cars whizzed by, nothing more than passing blurs.

Horns blared at them, but they sounded like distant shouts of anger as Saber and Aaron left vehicles far behind within seconds. Suddenly, Saber whipped his car left, hitting an oncoming car's buffer zone and sending it spinning out behind them. Aaron dodged to the right as the car started spinning toward him, and then looked in his rear-view mirror to see the havoc it left in their wake. It was messy, but relatively harmless; more a huge game of bumper cars than anything.

Aaron laughed as he saw the police car that followed them careen off in another direction as it collided with another car's buffer zone.

"Looks like we lost him," he said, slowing his car down to a slightly more manageable speed.

"Should we make an entrance?" asked Saber.

Aaron looked forward to see their destination approaching, and grinned. "Lead the way."

They slowed down their pace considerably, but they still flew hot. Approaching the bar, Aaron could see the balcony full of people, some sitting at tables, others leaning against the perimeter barrier that shimmered in the setting sunlight. His grin spread widely across his face,

SHADOWS OF THE UNSEEN

and he waited for Saber's instruction. Revving up his engine just a little higher to pull beside his brother, he looked at Saber through his side window, meeting his eye. They flew straight for the balcony, not slowing their speed.

"I'm breaking right," sounded Saber from the car's speakers.

"Left," replied Aaron to confirm.

They could see the people on the balcony starting to notice them, and pointing. They were getting concerned, which quickly turned to a panicked scattering. Saber burst out laughing.

"Right when you see the whites, you alter course," Aaron whispered to himself, as he broke to the left at the last second. He looked behind him to see that Saber had successfully made a mirror move. He laughed, adrenaline coursing through him.

"Let's park these things and find your friends," said Saber.

CHAPTER SEVEN

Saber August

Saber slowed his vehicle down to a crawl, and aimed it up toward the rooftop parking. He pulled into the parkway by the lift, and stepped out of his car. Pulling the valet key from out of his pocket, he tossed it to the waiting clone and smiled when he noticed the clone's slack-jawed awe over the vehicle. Normally, he wouldn't give a clone even a second thought, but his talk with Pilar that afternoon left him feeling a little kinder towards their race.

"Enjoy the ride," he said with a wink. "There's a five credit note in the cup holder. It's yours."

Aaron walked up, and by the look of confusion on his face, he'd witnessed the exchange between Saber and the clone. His head swiveled as he watched the clone climb into the car and fly it away.

Falling into step beside Saber, they entered the lift together and Aaron finally spoke. "Why did you do that?"

Saber shrugged. "I don't know. I felt like giving the guy a little bonus."

"He's a clone, he doesn't need a bonus."

Saber shrugged again and smiled. It certainly wasn't in his character, or how he had been raised, but something about seeing those clones, huddled in a room for termination like nothing more than sick dogs, planted a seed of doubt, and made him see them with a bit more humanity. They were, after all, the children of humanity. They deserved more than simple termination due to cost.

Shaking his head to clear his thoughts, the lift doors opened and his senses were bombarded by loud music and a hazy, sweet smelling vapor from E-Cigarettes. Walking in, Saber nodded at a few people who waved a greeting, but he followed Aaron across the bar to a table where his friends were already seated.

The girls were all seated in the semi-circle booth on one side so Aaron slid into the other, stopping next to the girl that Saber recognized from the weekend. He held back the smirk that fought to be released. So, she was here, and Aaron looked as pleased as ever about it. He slid in next to Aaron, taking the seat nearest the end.

Saber offered greetings to the girls, then fell into silence as he allowed the others at the table to control the conversation. He listened half-heartedly, his mind back on Pilar and his research. He shouldn't have come out tonight. He should have gone to see grandfather instead of trying to distract himself from the problem at hand. But the problem was too large for a little bit of distraction to erase from his mind.

A clone waitress approached the table, her eyes downcast to the floor. "Can I get you all anything?" she asked, refusing to meet a single person's gaze.

"I'll have a Vodka Martini, and you can start us a tab, please," Saber ordered.

"I'll need your credit info," she replied, almost robot-like. Saber held out his wrist to be scanned and she looked at the small, hand held computer for verification. As the screen beeped, her face paled and her pasted-on smile sunk. Her eyes finally looked up at who she was serving, but, Saber noticed, somehow she still managed to avoid eye contact. "You . . . I have . . . VIP . . ." she trailed off, and Saber smiled kindly at her.

"It's okay. We're good here."

She nodded and left, forgetting to take the rest of the drink orders. Then spun on her heel and returned, apologizing profusely.

"Well, that was strange," said Trisha after the waitress left.

Aaron shrugged. "Not so strange. Saber gets reactions like that everywhere since he was named Royce Williams' heir."

Saber rolled his eyes. "It's just great having people forget how to speak when they recognize me," he grumbled.

"I don't know," said Kristin, "you should be embracing the power and opportunity you've been given to make some changes for the better."

Aaron chuckled. "For the better? This is hardly the place to discuss politics."

Saber looked between the two. They had been sitting comfortably together a minute ago, but now they shifted into an icy silence. Kristin's back went stiff and straight and her jaw clamped firmly closed. Aaron seemed oblivious though, as he laughed with Trisha and Claire about some politics professor at the university.

Saber's attention was riveted on Kristin, though. She was visibly upset, and looked to be holding in an angry comment or two.

"Would you like to go to the patio with me?" Saber asked, directing his question to Kristin. The conversation didn't even pause around them. "I could use some fresh air."

Kristin nodded, her face relaxing as she tapped Aaron on the shoulder. "Excuse me."

Saber slid out, allowing Aaron and then Kristin to exit the booth, then offered his arm to her as Aaron slid back in. Aaron frowned, giving his brother a questioning look. He offered a reassuring smile to Aaron and hoped he understood that Saber wasn't trying to hone in on his territory.

He led Kristin through the busy bar to the patio. Once out, he could hear the buzz of people still talking about the stunt he and Aaron had pulled, and he chuckled.

"What's so funny?" Kristin asked.

"Nothing."

They found a table near the edge of the balcony and he pulled out a seat for her, then made his way to the vacant seat opposite.

"A gentleman," she commented with a raised eyebrow. "There aren't many of you around these days."

"I guess my mother raised me right."

Conversation stopped and Saber waved over a waitress, ordering another vodka martini and allowing the waitress to scan his wrist.

"They're talking about the two maniacs that scared the living daylights out of everyone a few minutes before you and Aaron walked into the bar," she said.

Saber's attention returned to her. "I'm sorry?"

"That's what everyone out here seems to be talking about. And what you chuckled at when we walked out."

Saber shrugged in a way that he thought was innocent. "It was amusing."

"You wouldn't happen to know who was involved, would you?"

"I'm not sure. Would you describe me as a maniac?"

"Honestly? I really don't know what to think of you, Saber August. You and your brother…" she trailed off.

"We have to remain unreadable. When you're in the spotlight all your life, it's the only defense you have."

"And Aaron? How am I supposed to know who he really is? Last Friday he was kind, respectful, and intellectual. Tonight it's all fun and games. He brushed me off as if what I had to say didn't matter. The guy I talked to last Friday wouldn't have done that."

Saber smiled, leaning on the table and meeting her eyes. "The guy you met on Friday is the real Aaron. The one in there," he motioned to the doors that led back into the bar. "That's a front, a façade that keeps him safe and impenetrable. He can't talk about political reform in public."

Kristin nodded. "But you can?"

Saber smiled wryly and scoffed a little. "I have to be careful, but not as careful as Aaron. I'm the favorite."

Silence fell upon the two of them and Saber sipped at his drink, thinking of what else to say to keep the atmosphere from growing awkward.

"But you know what the hardest part of all this is?" he blurted out, not really sure where it was coming from.

Kristin shook her head.

"The lack of connection, you know? There aren't many people in the world I can call friends. People hang around me because of who I am, but few of them are true friends."

"Maybe because you keep them at arm's length. You can't expect them to become true friends if you don't offer them a modicum of trust."

"I'm trusting you, aren't I?"

She smiled. "I have a feeling this isn't a common occurrence."

Saber nodded, but Kristin was the second person he had opened up to in the last few days. It left him feeling uneasy, but he pushed the thought down. He shouldn't be revealing himself and his problems to perfect strangers.

"You going to sit out here all night?" asked Aaron, approaching the table.

Saber looked up at his brother and shook his head. "I guess it's time we went back in." He gave Aaron a look and nodded his head toward Kristin. Apparently, he understood the unspoken suggestion, because Aaron walked to her chair and slid it back as she stood, then offered her his arm.

"Apparently both August brothers are gentlemen tonight."

"I try," replied Aaron, grinning widely. Saber almost rolled his eyes at how pleased Aaron looked to have Kristin on his arm.

Back inside the dimly lit and loud bar, Saber instantly felt tense again. His step faltered for a minute, and he paused.

"You okay?" asked Aaron, stopping and turning to look at Saber in concern.

Saber regained his footing and nodded. "Yeah, fine. Just tripped."

Aaron shrugged and turned to continue back to their table where Trisha and Claire waited.

"I'm going to go hit the head," said Saber, not quite ready to rejoin the group. He needed a moment alone to regroup.

Kristin's arm slipped out of Aaron's. "I'm going to do the same," she said, following Saber across the crowded room.

The hall to the restroom was quiet and abandoned.

"I hate the restrooms here," Kristin muttered. "This hall is so sketchy. I didn't want to walk alone."

He'd never thought of it like that, but he could see how the dimly lit hall that ran beside the kitchen could be intimidating. It was cut off from the rest of the bar by a large industrial door. Anything that went on down here would never be heard in the bar, and clones manned the kitchen—if anything happened between two humans they would never step in. To raise their hand against a human, even one committing a crime, would be to sign their own death warrant.

"Don't worry, I'll protect you…" Saber's words trailed off and he frowned, stopping.

"What is it?"

He held up his finger to quiet her, and listened. He heard it again: a scream. It sounded close by, but muffled by a wall or doorway and almost overpowered by the loud music from the bar. This time Kristin must have heard it because she paled a little and looked up at Saber with wide eyes. "What do we do?"

Pilar's words came back to him and his jaw set firmly in determination. Follow his conscience. Well, his conscience said he couldn't allow screams of pain to continue without intervening.

He walked briskly down the hall, right past the doorway to the bathroom and didn't even pause as he pushed his way through the kitchen doors. A group of clones huddled together near the door that Saber burst through, but he didn't give them so much as a second glance, his eyes riveted to the scene in front of him.

The sound of something solid hitting flesh met his ears, followed by a whimper. Images plucked from Saber's nightmares flashed before his eyes, and reality mixed seamlessly with the past as the clone before him took another blow from a solid titanium baseball bat.

Red filled Saber's vision, and he leapt forward, grabbing the man's arm mid-swing.

"What do you think—"

"Leave him alone," growled Saber, his mind not entirely on the moment, switching back and forth between the man's arm and the convulsing, bloody corpse of the clone so many years ago.

"Get your hands off of me. This is my clone, I can punish it as I please."

"You wouldn't treat your dog this badly," Saber ground out through clenched teeth.

"Saber," came Kristin's voice from behind him, but it barely registered. The sound of his heart pounding wildly made her words little more than white noise.

"Get off or I will have you thrown out."

Saber twisted the man's arm and he screamed in agony, letting go of the bat. It clattered to the floor, and he let go of the man's hand. He stood there for a moment in shock and Saber knelt down next to the clone.

"Are you okay?"

The clone groaned in response and barely moved his head. He was alive, but badly stunned. Blood poured from a head wound. The clone needed to get to a Frontier Industry doctor, and fast.

"Saber!" Kristin screamed.

His vision exploded in spots of bright light and he reeled, catching himself with his hands braced against the cold tile floor. Getting up, he pulled himself to full height and stared at the man who had just hit him, who had beaten a clone senseless. A growl escaped from his throat, more animal than human in nature, and he leaned down, picking up the bat that had fallen earlier. Swinging back as his opponent pulled back his fist, he put all of his strength behind the forward swing, connecting with a loud crack against the man's arm. Silence filled the room, and then a guttural scream followed as the man fell to the ground, clutching his useless arm against his side.

"You broke it! You broke my arm!" he cried, but Saber barely heard him. He hit the writhing man again and again, not even aware of where he was hitting him or when the man stopped screaming. This man had to pay for what he'd done. For hurting this clone, for the one he'd witnessed murdered so many years ago…

Hands grasped his arm and stopped his swing, tugging him away from the man that lay silent and still on the floor, a pool of blood growing beneath him.

His vision slowly cleared and he turned to face Kristin.

"What did you do? What did you do?" she cried through sobs, tears streaking her face and smudging her makeup.

Saber looked around. The clones who had stood huddled together when he had entered stared at him in shock, unmoving.

"Get out of here. Go get Aaron and have him help you get this clone to Frontier Industries," he said to Kristin, dropping the bat with a loud, echoing clatter.

"Saber—"

"Get out!" he hissed.

Kristin backed off, then turned and ran out the doors, which swung back and forth a few times before finding their resting place.

Saber walked to the clones. "Anyone asks, she wasn't here. Okay?"

A series of nods answered him and he walked briskly out of the kitchen. He needed to get out of here before the cops showed up. He needed to find his grandfather.

CHAPTER EIGHT

Aaron August

"So this guy just looks at me, jaw dropped..." Aaron trailed off when Kristin fell into the booth next to him. Her shoulders shook from the sobs that wracked her body and tears that covered her face, leaving her make-up smudged.

Trisha and Claire looked at each other and then at Aaron, and he could tell they were all thinking the same thing—what had Saber done?

Aaron placed his hand on Kristin's and she immediately clasped it tightly.

"Kristin, what's wrong?" he asked, trying to convey a calm that he didn't feel. He was fuming—Saber had something to do with her state and, family or not, if he had hurt her Aaron would defend her.

She took a few deep breaths before speaking, swallowing back tears and wiping at her eyes with her free hand, streaking black make-up across her face. She looked at Trisha and Claire hesitantly.

"Why don't you guys head out?" he said to them. "I'll make sure she gets home safely."

The girls nodded and got up, swiping their wrists across the scanner near the door on their way out to pay the balance on their tab.

"There's a clone in the kitchen, he's hurt," she said in a shaky voice.

Aaron nodded. "How did it happen?"

"We were in the hall when we heard a scream... Saber intervened..."

Sobs took control again and Aaron waited quietly, allowing her to regain her composure on her own terms.

"Okay, Kristin," started Aaron, moving so that he could angle his body towards her. He still held her hand, but with the other, he reached forward and directed her face to look at him. "You need to tell me what happened. Did Saber hurt you?"

She shook her head and relief flooded Aaron. As long as Saber hadn't hurt her, he figured he could handle whatever came out of Kristin's mouth next.

"There was a clone being beaten and Saber just... lost it."

Aaron closed his eyes. *The nightmares...*

"He asked me to get the clone to Frontier Industries."

"Okay," Aaron drew in a deep breath as a plan formulated. "I want you to call the cops. Report that you heard moaning when you went to the bathroom and found them like that. I'll help you with the rest. Do you think you can do that?"

Kristin nodded and pulled out her phone, dialing the emergency number. .

"Hi, I'd like to report an emergency," she said with a shaky voice. Aaron had to commend her for her composure though, as she held back her tears.

"A human and a clone are badly hurt. I found them in the kitchen of Karpov's."

"Yes, I can wait here. I'll wait in the hall outside the kitchen."

She hung up and turned to Aaron. "They're on their way."

It didn't take long for the police to show up with paramedics in tow. They marched directly to Kristin. "Are you the one that put in the call?"

She nodded.

"They're just in there," said Aaron, pointing to the kitchen doors as he put his arm around Kristin, trying to appear to the police as a comforting friend.

"We need you to stick around, we might have some questions," the one said before they disappeared into the kitchen.

Aaron and Kristin waited outside for what seemed like ages. How long had it been since Saber had left? Was he safe? And the clone...? Saber had requested they get him medical attention. Why? It was common practice to just terminate an injured clone. For some reason his brother had not only defended this clone, but also wanted to help. It was insane, but if it meant something to Saber then he'd do it.

Finally the police emerged, the paramedics still inside. One of the cops pulled out his phone while the other addressed Kristin.

"We'd like to ask you a few questions. My partner here is going to record our conversation. Is that alright?"

Kristin nodded mutely. She hadn't said a word since the cops arrived and the tears had stopped. She was shutting down.

"What made you go into the kitchen?"

"I was walking towards the bathroom when I heard loud moaning, so I went to check on it."

"The clones inside say it was a young man, mid to late twenties. Did you see anyone like that?"

"There is a bar full of young men that fit that description," cut in Aaron. "Ask the right person and they could pin it on me."

"Yes, but were you back here?"

Aaron shook his head.

"Miss Pierce, did you see anyone who could have done this?"

She shook her head. "No, no one. There were just the clones when I got here."

"Okay, thank you. Here's my card," the police officer handed Kristin and Aaron each his contact information. "Please call if you remember anything. Even if it seems small and unimportant, we need to know about it."

Kristin nodded.

"Excuse me, Officers, but I'm Aaron August. The clone is property of Frontier Industries and should be returned there."

The cop nodded. "Of course. You can go speak to the paramedics. They'll see to it."

As the cops walked away, Aaron turned to Kristin. "You should wait out here. I'm going to go talk to the paramedics."

Once again, she nodded, but stared blankly past him. Aaron sighed. He'd deal with her later.

Walking into the kitchen, he was hit by the metallic scent of blood, mixed with the smells of cooking food. His stomach churned, and threatened to expel its contents as he saw the gory sight. How had Saber been capable of this? The human man lay, unrecognizable, beaten, a bloody bat lying next to him. The paramedics looked up and then drew a sheet over the body.

"Can we help you?" asked the one—an older looking man.

"I'm Aaron August of Frontier Industries. I'm here to take custody of the clone."

The paramedic chuckled. "We didn't even have to call in a termination unit and you're here already. You must have trackers on these things."

Aaron cringed. Why would Saber want to prolong this clone's suffering? It was lying on a stretcher, moaning in its unconscious state. No pain medicine had been administered to him, broken bones hadn't been set. It appeared as if they had just loaded him on the stretcher and then turned their attention to the dead human. The kindest thing to do would be to call the termination unit.

"No problem. Actually, you wouldn't mind dropping him off at Frontier, would you?"

The paramedics looked at Aaron and then at each other and shrugged. "The other guy is dead, so I don't see why not. You didn't come with a van or something?"

Aaron smiled sheepishly. "Honestly guys, I was already here having drinks when the call came in. This isn't usually my job."

"Yeah, no problem. We'll meet you there once we get these two loaded."

Aaron walked out of the kitchen, not wanting to be around the broken and beaten bodies any longer. He didn't even pause as he stepped out to meet Kristin, just took her hand in his and continued his journey down the hall and as far away from the kitchen as he could get.

By the time the valet brought his car around, the paramedics were loading the clone. They loaded the dead body of the human first, now zipped up in a black body bag.

The drive was made in silence, Kristin staring out the window blankly. Aaron glanced at her from time to time, but he really couldn't blame her—he was feeling lost himself. The scene he saw was not something he ever thought his brother could, or would, be capable of. But the evidence said that he was. Something had changed in Saber, he had snapped, and it scared Aaron. If he could barely handle it, how much worse it must be for Kristin, who had witnessed it?

Finally, they pulled up in front of the huge building that made up the headquarters of Frontier Industries. It was a monolith among skyscrapers—easily the largest one in the world. And it should be. It was Royce Williams' legacy, his throne room.

Aaron parked his car, not even caring that it was in a no-park zone. No one would dare tow him. Kristin stood right behind him as the ambulance pulled up and stopped, the back door opening. Aaron ran into the building, the doors sliding open at his approach. Parked near the medical ward, the nearest entrance was the free clinic. The entry was full of people.

"Hey, you!" he called out to a couple orderlies.

"Yeah?"

"Grab a stretcher. I have a clone coming in."

The orderlies looked at each other, then shrugged and retrieved the requested stretcher, following him outside where the paramedics had unloaded the clone and waited.

"Thanks guys, we can take it from here."

The two orderlies slowly lifted the clone from the one stretcher and slid him onto the Frontier stretcher. The clone continued to moan in pain, and it occurred to Aaron that they wouldn't have administered IV painkillers—not to something that was just going to be terminated.

Following the orderly as he pushed the stretcher into the building, Kristin walked beside him. Aaron kept an eye on the clone, watching its chest rise and fall in a steady, if slow and shallow rhythm.

The pristine white halls all looked identical, and at this time of night, they were abandoned. But as Aaron approached the glass door that led into the medical wing, it whispered open and admitted them into the sterile, hospital type ward.

"Can I help you?" asked a nurse, not at all kindly.

Aaron put on his most charming smile, wishing it was as charming as Saber's, and responded calmly. "Yes, you can. Saber August sent me. This clone has been badly hurt and is in need of medical attention."

The nurse scowled and beckoned to a doctor.

"Yes?"

Aaron repeated what he'd just told the nurse, and the doctor looked equally as unhappy. "How is this my problem? I look after minor injuries, not termination cases."

"When Saber August says it's your problem you better make it your problem," replied Aaron.

The doctor's scowl just deepened across his already unhappy face, and he moved closer to the clone, inspecting him and taking his vitals.

"Alright, I'll take it from here."

Aaron stepped back, taking Kristin's hand. Whether the doctor actually treated the clone or not was not his problem. He'd done what Saber asked.

Walking out of the building and back to his car, he held Kristin's hand tightly, drawing on her for some sort of comfort. Exiting the building, relief filled him to see the car still parked where he had left it.

Leading Kristin to the passenger's side, he opened the door for her and helped her in. She smiled her thanks, but her eyes still held a quiet sort of terror; like she was reliving the evening in her mind.

Moving back around and entering the car on the driver's side, he took her hand again. "Let's get you home. Can you enter your address in?"

Kristin nodded and reached toward the screen, quickly punching the address into the GPS. The car spoke to Aaron, but he barely listened. He put the car into manual, needing something to keep his mind busy, and lifted the vehicle into the air, following the red dot on his windshield as it directed him.

Minutes later, they arrived outside an older apartment building near the university. He parked the car in her two-vehicle carport and shut it down. Without a word, he helped her out, walked her to the lift, and they both entered. She didn't protest, or send him away, and he wasn't willing to let her out of his sight until she stood safely in her apartment.

Once at her apartment door, they stopped.

"This is me."

Aaron nodded. "I'll call tomorrow, okay? If you need to talk to anyone about tonight… a counselor… my grandfather will pay for it."

"Thank you."

Kristin unlocked her door with a press of her thumb to the scanner and Aaron turned to walk back down the hallway they'd come up.

"Wait!" she called after him.

He paused and turned back. Exhaustion took over him and left him too tired to think about what her call to him might mean. He just waited for her to continue.

"Would it be too forward of me to ask you to stay? I don't want to be alone."

"I don't really want to be alone either."

CHAPTER NINE

Saber August

Saber parked the vehicle outside his grandfather's front door and jumped out. His hands tremored, as he stated his name at the front door through a shaky voice. The door slid open, allowing him access to the lavish house.

Royce Williams came strolling out of his office, meeting Saber halfway down the hall. They both stopped a few feet away from each other, and Saber waited quietly as his grandfather looked him up and down.

"In my study. Now."

Saber mutely followed his grandfather, who practically marched down the hall and through the large double wooden doors that opened to his home study.

"Sit," commanded Royce, taking a seat behind his desk.

Saber lowered into the chair and looked down at his hands, unable to meet his grandfather's eyes. Dry blood covered his hands. Saber hadn't even noticed until now... what a mess he must look.

"Do you care to explain this state you're in, Saber?"

He looked up slowly, clasping his hands together in an attempt to hide the crimson stains that told their own story. "I made a huge mistake."

"I can see that. But I can't help you unless you tell me exactly what happened."

Royce's voice had calmed somewhat, and when Saber met his eyes, they were softer, kinder. Saber took a deep breath. "Can I wash up first?"

"I think that's best."

He got up and left the stifling, dark room, and breathed deeply. He needed to get this blood off of him. It stank of copper, death and guilt, and clouded his thoughts. Every time he breathed in and the smell reached his nose, his vision faded and took him back to a time that he'd rather not remember.

Taking the stairs to the second floor where the bedrooms were situated, Saber made his way down the right wing of the house and into the bedroom that was reserved for him when he stayed. The closet was stocked with clothes and personal effects to make him feel like this was his home away from home, and it had been for a good portion of his life.

Walking straight into the large bathroom, he discarded his clothes and stepped under the stream of hot water coming from the shower. The water that ran off his body had a pink tinge from the blood that it carried with it, but soon it ran clear, and Saber's mind calmed. He stood in the shower longer than he needed to, trying to wash off more than the dirt on the outside, trying to wash away the childhood nightmares that had become a reality.

A wave of nausea rolled through Saber, and he fell to his knees in the tile shower, retching violently until there was nothing left in his stomach. Laying down slowly on the wet tile, water still cascading down on him, he let out a sob. Tears mixed with water as he cried for the death of the human, the cruelty to the clone, but most of all the death of whom he had once been.

If the hurling cleansed his body, the tears cleansed his soul.

When Saber finally made it back to his grandfather's study, over an hour had passed. He wasn't sure if Royce would still be waiting up for him, a quick glance at the clock telling him it was nearly 1 am. But Royce still sat there, behind his desk, as stalwart and unmoved as ever.

He looked up from reading the screen when Saber entered.

"Good, you're back. Have a seat."

Saber did so, and waited for his grandfather to initiate the conversation he dreaded.

Turning the portable tablet around on his old-fashioned wood desk, Royce pushed it towards Saber. He looked down, reading the headline. 'Human dead after unknown assailant defends clone'. He looked up at his grandfather.

"I take it this unknown assailant isn't so unknown?"

Saber nodded mutely.

Royce sighed, covering his face with his hands and slowly drawing them down. He seemed older suddenly, and weak. And, as Saber studied his grandfather, looking for the strength he needed, he saw fear—something he'd never seen in Royce Williams before.

"I think it would be best if you left for a little while. Stayed out of the public eye."

Saber nodded.

"They have no reason to suspect you now. Let's keep it that way."

CHAPTER TEN

Aaron August

Aaron lay on Kristin's bed, staring up at the plain white ceiling with nothing to look at besides a few dead bugs and cracks in the drywall. He'd been awake for a while now, just listening to Kristin breathe deeply, still sound asleep beside him. His clothes felt uncomfortable. He'd slept in his jeans and dress shirt, flat on his back on top of the blankets. He'd been a perfect gentleman, letting her curl up under the blankets.

Kristin's breathing changed cadence, becoming shallower, and her body shifted slightly. He looked at her and watched as she blinked her eyes open and stared at the wall, away from him. After a minute or two of lying there in silence, as if absorbing the fact that she was awake and no longer dreaming, Kristin rolled onto her back and stretched her arms out, her right hand connecting solidly with Aaron's chest.

Pulling back in surprise, she jumped out of the bed, dragging blankets with her and tripping slightly.

Aaron sat up and leaned against the headboard, smiling. "Good morning."

"What are you doing here?" she asked, her eyes wild and unsure.

"You asked me to stay…" he trailed off, waiting for her to remember.

She seemed to study him, looking him up and down, rubbing her right arm with her left hand. Slowly, she nodded. "Thank you for staying with me, but you need to leave," she said, barely above a whisper.

Aaron's smile disappeared and he got out of the bed, standing up, leaving the large bed between the two of them. "I'm sorry, I didn't mean to overstep my bounds. You fell asleep—"

"It's fine. Just, you need to go. You caught me at a vulnerable time last night and I just need to be alone."

Aaron nodded and walked away, not saying anything, leaving Kristin standing in the bedroom. Stopping in the kitchen, he grabbed the portable tablet off the kitchen table and wrote down his name and number, then let himself out of the apartment. This time she didn't call him back.

He made his way down to where his car was parked in the carport, and drove home in silence, clicking off the radio when it blasted out at him at his preferred volume.

This was the second night he'd spent with Kristin— both times completely innocent, and yet, the first time she'd snuck away like a thief in the night, and the second time he was sent away to do the walk of shame. He would have thought after last night, after the trauma they had both gone through, after he had been there for her, held her while she cried on his shoulder and watched her as she slept because she'd been too afraid to sleep alone, that they would have moved past whatever was holding them back.

But no. Something was still holding Kristin back. And if he had to judge by her reaction this morning, Aaron would have to guess it was fear.

CHAPTER ELEVEN

Saber August

The sun was high in the sky and birds sang loudly through the open window when Saber awoke the next morning. He groaned, stretching out his limbs before rolling into a sitting position and cracking his neck from side to side.

Glancing at his phone resting on the nightstand, he saw the time read 11:15 am. His grandfather, if he was even still home, would not be impressed. Royce Williams despised slothfulness above all other sins.

Saber shuffled across the plush carpet and into the bathroom, the heated tile floor offering a gentle transition from the soft flooring of the bedroom. He turned on the shower and, after removing his clothes, slipped under the stream of hot water. His grandfather had waited this long, he could wait another few minutes for Saber to freshen up and get presentable before discussing what future, or little future he had.

72

Despite his attempt to not care, Saber rushed through the shower and got dressed quickly; grabbing the first pair of jeans and button up shirt he laid his hands on. He remained barefoot, his feet slapping against the hardwood floor as he made his way down the hall and the stairs in his journey to the dining room.

When he walked in, he saw Royce Williams sitting with his tablet on the surface of the huge wooden table, and a cup of steaming coffee in his hand. A red-haired woman sat with her back towards Saber, but he didn't have to see her face to recognize Pilar. Her presence didn't really surprise him. She was Royce's personal assistant, but Saber had thought his grandfather would have wanted to keep their conversation private.

"So kind of you to join us," said Royce, not looking up from the tablet.

As Saber made his way around the table to sit across from Pilar on his grandfather's right hand side, he noticed her look over his shoulder, her eyes following him. He offered her a smile and took his seat.

Now that he sat across from her, he had a clear view of the woman that had first caused him to question his life. He could study her. She sat, back straight in the chair. She held her head high, and she met Saber's gaze evenly, seemingly not intimidated by him. She was the same strong woman he had met in his grandfather's office only last night.

A clone walked into the dining room, carrying Saber's breakfast and placing the plate loaded with eggs, pancakes, sausage, hashbrowns, and fruit in front of him.

"Coffee, Sir?" asked the clone, her eyes downcast.

Saber nodded, even though she couldn't possibly see the motion since her eyes were staring directly at her feet. "Yes, please," he added.

The clone disappeared, only to return again a moment later with a steaming cup of coffee.

Despite being carbon copies, the clone serving him, and his grandfather's assistant couldn't have been more different. Sure, their faces were the same, but Pilar's business attire and bright red hair set her apart. Add in the confidence that Pilar exuded, while this clone could barely take her eyes off the floor, made it hard for him to even consider Pilar to be on the same level as the serving girl.

"Thank you," he said as the clone made a quick escape back into the kitchen.

He glanced up, meeting Pilar's amused look. His politeness towards the clone hadn't gone unnoticed by her. If Royce had noticed as well, he didn't show it—the tablet in front of him retained his attention. Finally, with a touch, he shut the screen off, rested his elbows on the table and steepled his fingers in a thoughtful manner. Saber continued to eat, but he granted Royce his attention.

"I've spent the morning reading every news report regarding the incident. It seems they have no idea it was you. A rough description was released, but it could be anyone."

Saber breathed a sigh of relief, and his whole body relaxed. He hadn't even realized how stiff he'd been holding his shoulders until he'd let them slump. "That's good news."

Royce nodded. "But it's too soon to say you're in the clear. We will move forward with our plan for you to leave for a while."

Saber frowned, but nodded. "I'll book a flight."

"No need. Pilar has already taken care of it. She will be accompanying you."

Annoyance jolted through Saber. "You don't trust me?"

"I think a lot has happened in the last twelve hours, and I need to protect you—from others, and from yourself. There will be no argument."

Saber nodded and looked back at Pilar. She grinned, her eyes dancing in amusement. *At least someone thinks this is funny,* he thought, stabbing a piece of cantaloupe with his fork and popping it into his mouth.

"Your flight leaves in two hours."

Saber swallowed. "How long will we be gone?"

"Until I deem it safe for you to return."

"And if it never is?"

"It won't be safe on a tropical beach then either."

Saber shivered and quickly shoveled the last of his food into his mouth. Once he swallowed, he scraped the chair back and got up.

"I better get home and pack."

"No need," said Pilar, speaking for the first time this morning. "I already went to your apartment and packed for you."

Saber stared at her, then looked at his grandfather. This woman, no, *clone* had gone through his things, packed his clothes, his toothbrush, shoes, and underwear while he slept. She'd gone through his home. She booked him a flight, and would be watching his every move from now on. Saber almost *wished* he was on the run. Then at least he wouldn't have his grandfather controlling his life.

No, then you'd have fear controlling your life, his logical side interjected, stopping that train of thought cold.

"Thank you."

She smiled, this time tight-lipped and almost apologetic, as if she knew his discomfort with the situation.

"You best get going," said Royce, picking up his tablet again. "Security will take a while."

Saber nodded mutely, and walked out of the dining room and back up to his room to slip on some socks and shoes. He moved slower than he should, but he needed a few minutes to absorb everything that had happened this morning.

A knock sounded on his door and then it opened a moment later to admit Pilar.

"Are you ready?" she asked, standing just inside the room.

Saber nodded and walked by her, but as he passed, he felt her warm hand brush his arm. Pausing, he turned to face her, a frown furrowing his brow, asking the question he didn't voice aloud.

"You aren't alone," she said, a blush creeping up her otherwise pale face, her eyes wide. "We know what you did, and you have friends on the other side."

Saber stared at her, mutely, and then nodded once. He continued out of the room and towards the front entrance. He didn't want to talk or even acknowledge what had just been said. He just wanted to get out of here and forget everything for a little while.

CHAPTER TWELVE

Aaron August

Aaron paced just outside of Kristin's apartment. A huge bouquet of flowers rested in the crook of one arm with the other hand supporting it.

Walking to the door, he stopped and stared. Then turned, and walked back down the hall towards the exit.

Stopping again, he shook his head, sighed, and turned back around. This time when he reached Kristin's door, he immediately reached forward and pressed the doorbell before he had a chance to change his mind.

He could hear the chime sound inside and then footsteps approaching the door. His stomach flip-flopped and he licked his lips, adjusting the flowers in his arms. His heart beat a steady, yet faster-than-normal pace as he waited for the door to slide open. Was she watching him through a video feed right now, and deciding if she was going to admit him?

I'll wait thirty more seconds, he thought, counting out the seconds in his head as he stepped from one foot to the other with every new number that ticked by.

He reached thirty and sighed. The door hadn't opened. *Guess she doesn't want to talk to me.* Turning to leave, he took half a dozen steps before he heard a door whoosh open behind him. Stopping, he waited for her to say something.

"Well, are you going to just stand there, or tell me why you're here?"

Aaron smiled and turned around, walking to her with a long and energetic stride. "I wanted to talk to you. Can I come in?" he asked, presenting her with the flowers.

Kristin didn't take them. She just stared, then looked up at him, her body standing firmly in the doorway. "No, Aaron. You need to leave."

The bouquet sunk in his arms, and Aaron felt a little ridiculous holding it, unaccepted by the woman he was trying to woo. "Please don't send me away, Kristin."

"Look, Aaron, I'm sorry, but you can't come around here unannounced and think you're gonna win me over with flowers and a smile. I'm not going to fall for that romantic crap."

Aaron's face fell, but he nodded. "That's fair. But romantic crap aside, I just want to talk. I could really use a friend right now, and as much as you say otherwise, I think you probably could too."

He bent down and put the flowers at her feet, then turned around and walked down the hall. Pausing for a minute, he didn't look back. "You didn't have to open the door," he said, just loud enough that she could hear, before continuing down the hall.

He knew he probably looked dejected, his shoulders slumped and his walk slow and laborious.

"Aaron . . ."

He stopped, unsure if he'd heard her or just imagined it. Deciding to take a chance, he turned around yet again. There she was, still standing in the doorway, her hands on her hips in a commanding sort of way. He smiled and walked back, his long and excited stride covering the distance between them twice as fast as it took for him to create it. She reached down and picked up the abandoned flowers, the sweet aroma wafting between them as she stepped aside and let him through the door.

"Just friends," she reiterated as he passed her.

He chuckled and leaned in to plant a kiss on her cheek. "Just friends."

Kristin smiled and shook her head in silent laughter, shooing him away with the flowers that filled her arms. "Aaron, I'm serious. I can't handle a relationship right now."

"So am I."

Aaron plopped down on the couch and kicked off his shoes in the middle of her living room. His socked feet found a home on her glass coffee table, and he watched as Kristin's face went from surprised, to annoyed, to resigned. Walking to her kitchen, she busied herself preparing the flowers to go in a vase while Aaron sat in silence, watching her. Once she finished looking after the flowers, she opened the fridge and pulled out a couple beers, cracking them open and handing him one.

Sitting down on the far side of the couch, she curled her legs up under her, draped her left arm across her stomach in a protective manner, and sipped her beer.

"So. . ." she started, obviously unsure of the situation. "Have you heard anything about Saber yet?"

Aaron shook his head. "I haven't been able to bring myself to ask anybody. I went home this morning and tried to distract myself for a while, then decided it wasn't working, got flowers, and came here."

Kristin didn't reply, she just glanced at the flowers sitting on her counter, then her eyes returned to her beer. The silence that hung in the room spoke volumes. She was scared and unsure. He could see that, and she'd said as much last night. He should go talk to Saber, or their grandfather. Then at least he could come to Kristin and let her know that she was safe, that no one knew she had been there, that Saber would never bother her again. Instead, he was too scared to face his own brother.

Aaron broke the silence. "He hasn't been home since last night and I don't want to be there when he does come. I'll go see my grandfather tonight.

"I don't know what all happened last night, but I know that he murdered someone. I'm scared, Kristin. Is that wrong?"

She shook her head, tears welling up in her eyes and spilling over, creating wet paths down her face in single streams. "Be glad you didn't see it. I don't know Saber that well, but the man I saw back there wasn't the man I thought he was. It was . . . scary. It was like Saber checked out and someone else was using his body."

Aaron chugged back his beer and sat a little straighter on the couch, his feet finding their way back to the floor from the coffee table.

Now that she had started speaking about that night, it all came pouring out. The emotions, the tears, and the words. "I just stood there, Aaron. I stood there and watched him beat a man to death. The screams . . ."

Aaron moved over on the couch and gathered her in his arms, his beer forgotten on the coffee table. He didn't want her to speak. He didn't want to imagine that his brother was capable of such violence. But he'd seen the result, and he knew that keeping her from speaking would do nothing to erase what he'd seen.

"It's okay, Kristin. It's not your fault," he spoke gently, stroking her hair as she nestled in closer against his strong chest.

"I should have stopped him sooner," she sobbed.

"Don't say that. You had no idea how he'd react."

"I could have gone for help."

"It's not your fault," Aaron reiterated more firmly. "Saber snapped, and there was nothing you could have done about it."

"I'm sorry, I'm sorry," she continued to sob out, her tears soaking Aaron's chest.

Aaron didn't know what to say anymore, so he just held her close and hoped she found comfort in it. Suddenly, the sobs stopped after one large intake of breath, then her hands found hold on his chest and she pushed. He relaxed his arms, letting her go.

"What's wrong?"

"I can't do this. I can't be your friend."

Aaron stood up, his stomach once again flipping and flopping as hurt and confusion filled him. He crossed his arms on his chest, as if to protect his already bruised heart, and stared at Kristin, anger burning in his eyes. "Don't play games with me. I asked to be your friend. You can't handle that?"

He could see the tears swimming just on the edge of her eyelids, threatening to spill, but somehow she held them back. She bit her lip and shook her head, not even giving him as much as a verbal response for the sudden change of heart.

"Why not? What have I ever done to hurt you?"

"Get out," she muttered.

"What? You're sending me away because I tried to comfort you? Thanks a lot, Kristin."

"You don't know what you're talking about," she replied, a red tinge of anger filling her face.

"Really? Cause I'm pretty sure you're just too afraid to let anyone in. Do you have any close friends, Kristin? Or do you keep everyone at arm's length cause it's safer that way?"

"Get out! You have no idea what you're talking about!" she screamed.

Aaron laughed bitterly, throwing his hands up in the air in mock surrender. "You're right, I have no idea what your issue is," he said, watching her sink to her knees, sobs so much more violent than the ones she'd shed because of Saber racked her body. Turning, he left, leaving her to deal with whatever had her chasing him out.

CHAPTER THIRTEEN

Saber August

The airport bustled with activity. Saber walked in, bag in hand, Pilar next to him, as they fought through the crowds. It didn't take long for people to notice, though, and attention turned in Saber's direction. Paths opened in front of him like water parting before a ship.

Saber's heart pounded, waiting for someone to call him out. *Murderer*, echoed in his mind as he made his journey through security alone. Pilar stood nearby, in the line designated for clones.

"Hey, you're Mr. Williams grandson, aren't you?" asked one of the security guards.

Saber nodded slowly, swallowing back his nervousness. "That would be me."

"Why aren't you flying in a private jet or something?"

Saber chuckled, relieved that news of his crime hadn't emerged… yet… "They keep the private jets for the important stuff," he said with a wink, continuing on through the checkpoint and ending the short conversation.

Pilar already waited on the other side, smoothing her blouse and pants and attempting to look collected. But Saber could see she was shaken.

"What happened?"

She looked up and blushed. "Nothing, I just hate security. I'll never get used to the strip searches and pat downs," she said, followed by a laugh that sounded hollow and shaky, as if it was covering up threatening tears.

Saber frowned, but didn't pursue the subject. She was obviously uncomfortable with it, so he sat down in a chair to await the boarding call.

"I'm going to go to the rest room and straighten up," she said, giving up on fixing her hair.

Saber nodded, pulling out his phone to start surfing the Net.

The click, click of her retreating heals were quickly swallowed up by the noise around him, and Saber looked up to see her through the crowd, just slipping into a bathroom. He hadn't realized how invasive clone security was. Pilar had been shaken and disheveled, and she was no stranger to flying—as Royce William's personal assistant, she would have travelled with him. She didn't have shock or surprise from an unexpected experience. She had the quiet fear of someone abused, but resigned to it. Saber's stomach churned and he closed his eyes, drawing in a deep breath to calm himself and the anger that was slowly building up. Now was not the time to get self-righteous or defender of the weak. Right now, he just had to get on a plane, and go on vacation until everything blew over, or he had to run.

"Attention, we are now boarding first class passengers of flight two-two-nine en route to Aruba."

"That's you," said Pilar, walking up. She looked much calmer and put together. Her clothes straightened out, her hair rearranged, and her demeanor once again confident.

Saber stood up, slipping his phone back into his pocket once standing, and walked with Pilar to the gate. He stood in line, Pilar beside him.

"I'll be in the back of the plane if you need me," she said.

Saber nodded. "I'll be fine. This isn't the first time I've flown."

"I know, I'm sorry. I'm used to looking after everything for your grandfather."

"I'm not Royce."

Pilar nodded and smiled softly in understanding. "I know. I'll see you when we land."

She walked away, leaving Saber to enter the plane on his own. She would board last, among the few other clones that were traveling.

"Excuse me, Sir," said the guard at the entry to the plane. Saber looked and realized he was next in line. Walking up, he held his wrist to the scanner, and got the nod when his information matched the passenger manifest.

Traveling was very streamlined these days. Saber had read about antiquated means of travel and security, involving checking into flights and carrying paper boarding passes and identification that expired. These days, everything anyone needed was in a chip in their wrist. Credit, bank, identification, it was all there.

Saber took his seat in the large passenger pod that sported his name on the LCD screen just outside of it. Inside, he found a large plush chair, that reclined fully into a bed, and a TV. A curtain could be closed for privacy, but Saber kept it open. He preferred not to be completely enclosed.

"Can I get you anything to drink, Mr. August?" asked a clone flight attendant, identical to Pilar aside from her brown hair.

Saber nodded. "Scotch, please."

She smiled. "I'll be right out with that. Anything else I can get you?"

He shook his head and turned his attention to the TV, flipping through channels, trying to find something that would keep him entertained for the couple hours aboard the plane.

Finding a documentary that looked somewhat interesting, he sat back and waited for his drink. Just as it arrived, he saw Pilar walk past to her seat. She glanced, making eye contact with him and smiled. He smiled back, accepting the drink from the flight attendant, whose face was a carbon copy of Pilar's. Even their smiles were the same. Saber frowned; it was like seeing double, but he *knew* he wasn't.

He shook his head and looked back at the TV. It was strange, living amongst the clones all his life and never really noticing them, never feeling ill at ease by seeing so many identical faces around him every day. They were white noise in life; ignored and faceless. But now that he had seen the humanity of clones, he couldn't seem to *stop* noticing.

"All the passengers are now aboard. Please fasten your seatbelts for take-off. We will be on our way shortly," came the voice of a flight attendant through the loud speaker.

Saber clicked the metal tab into its housing and secured himself to his seat, then sipped his scotch. The plane slowly moved, accelerating and pushing him into the back of his seat as it took off.

Saber sighed. He should feel relaxed, leaving the center of attention. But instead, the closer he got to Aruba, the more he felt like he was running from a problem he should be facing.

CHAPTER FOURTEEN

Aaron August

Wanting to put Kristin out of his mind, Aaron drove to Frontier Industries, stopping at the front desk in the huge, lavish foyer.

"I'm here to see Royce Williams, can you page him?" asked Aaron, leaning on the desk and smiling down at the receptionist.

She looked back up at him, a smile plastered on her face that he could tell was there automatically. It was an accessory, something she wore all day, every day. It was just another part of the uniform.

"Do you have an appointment?"

"I don't need one."

"Everyone needs an appointment with Mr. Williams."

Aaron sighed. Saber never would have had to deal with this. Then again, everyone knew who Saber was. "Do you know who I am?"

"Should I?" Her smile remained plastered on, but Aaron could see just the slightest bit of doubt hidden behind her eyes.

"Just page him and tell him Aaron August is here to see him."

Recognition dawned on her face and her smile faded. "I'm so sorry, Mr. August. I'll page him right away and see if he's free." Her words came out in a hurried jumble, nervous and apologetic.

"Thank you."

He waited as she pressed a button on her display desk and then spoke into an earpiece. "Oh, Mr. Williams, Sir, I didn't expect you to answer—"

She went silent for a moment, nodding, although no one could see her.

"Yes, Sir. Aaron August is here to see you—"

Cut off again, she snapped her mouth shut as if on a spring-loaded hinge, and listened.

"Of course, I'll send him right up."

Pressing a button on her display desk again, she looked back up at Aaron, a little paler than before and a shaky smile on her lips.

"He'll see you. You know the way?"

Aaron nodded and tapped his knuckles on the desk. "Yep. Thank you," he said, making his way to the private lift behind the desk.

The door slid open at his approach, and the minute he stepped inside it closed again. He didn't have to press any buttons, just rode it to the only floor this particular lift journeyed to: Royce Williams' office.

When the doors opened, Aaron strode out, pausing to look around. He'd only been up here a few times, and each time he felt bombarded by the overwhelming scent of leather and wood. It was old, reminiscent of ages past, and lacked the crisp sterility Aaron was used to being surrounded by.

"Are you just going to stand there, or are you going to sit down?" asked Royce, always a formidable presence, even when seated behind a desk.

"Just admiring the decor," Aaron replied, walking to the desk and taking a seat.

"And I can't help but sense disapproval of my choices."

"Not my style, that's all."

"Saber likes it."

"Saber and I have never been that similar."

"Let's cut to the chase, shall we? As much as I enjoy visits from you, I have a lot on my plate today."

Aaron nodded, but a sting of jealousy engulfed him for a moment. His grandfather never would have rushed Saber out. Saber, the chosen one. Saber, the favorite. But Saber had messed up this time. If he could not be forgiven, would Aaron take his place? He stifled a grin that threatened to emerge.

"I, uh, wanted to ask about Saber."

His grandfather's face turned somber, and he crossed his arms. "So far the situation seems to be contained. I've sent him on a vacation to get him out of the public eye for a bit."

Aaron frowned. "And if it becomes uncontained?"

"I'll deal with it."

Aaron nodded, getting up from his seat. Questions hadn't really been answered, but at least he knew what was going on, sort of, and that he didn't have to worry about running into Saber anytime soon. Maybe ever.

As he turned to leave, his grandfather's voice stopped him. "Aaron."

He didn't turn around, just waited for his grandfather to continue.

"I don't think I have to tell you that if it does leak, you'll be the first person I look at."

Aaron's shoulders squared against the threat, and anger rolled through him. "He's my brother," he replied through clenched teeth, still not turning to face the man.

"History doesn't put much stock in the relationship between brothers."

Aaron closed his eyes, and breathed deeply, trying to refrain from saying something he'd regret. Instead, he placed one foot in front of the other until he entered the lift. He didn't turn around until the door slid shut, then he let out a ragged breath. Leaning forward, he pressed the stop button on the lift, pausing his journey down, and leaned against the wall. His hands covered his eyes, his elbows resting against his knees, as he took a moment to collect himself and his thoughts.

How could he think that Saber's misfortune might be his rise into favor? His grandfather thought him capable of betraying his own flesh and blood, and maybe he was. The thought had crossed his mind.

He trembled, as he sucked in a deep breath. *What have I got myself into?* The most powerful man in the world just issued him a veiled threat. His family name meant *nothing* in this instance.

He'd been turned away by Kristin, he'd been turned away by his family time and again in favor of Saber, and today his grandfather turned him away. He made it more than clear that, no matter how badly Saber screwed up, he would never fall from grace. And Aaron could never, ever hope to rise into his grandfather's graces.

Wiping angrily at his tears, Aaron straightened up and pressed the button to allow the lift to move again.

It wasn't like any of this was news to him. Aaron grew up being overshadowed by Saber in everything and with everyone. He'd just hoped that someday he would be noticed.

CHAPTER FIFTEEN

Saber August

Pressure building in his ears brought Saber out of a deep sleep. Sitting up straight, he arched his back and rolled his neck to relieve the tension that had built up. As comfortable as the seats were, they were not a replacement for a bed.

Yawning, the pressure in his ears released and he looked out the window to see they were making their descent into Aruba. *Maybe I'll be able to consider this a vacation after all,* he thought. But the slight unrest to his stomach, and the way he couldn't keep himself from looking around or checking the news, told him that he wasn't here to relax.

Amongst the first to disembark, Saber hurried through the throngs of people in the airport to the baggage carousel where he waited for Pilar to join him, and their luggage to make its way around.

Pilar joined him shortly, looking tired, but more relaxed than before.

"Have the bags come yet?" she asked.

Saber shook his head. "Hello to you, too. How was the flight?"

"Good, if you consider no food, no drink and being packed in like sardines in the back an enjoyable way to travel."

Guilt shot through Saber and left him not knowing how to reply. Could he apologize for something he had very little control over?

"I'm sorry. That comment wasn't fair," said Pilar, taking him off the hook. "There are our bags." She pointed to a couple bags just coming around the corner on the conveyor belt, and Saber stepped closer to the carousel. He grabbed first one, then the other as they came by at a leisurely pace.

With their bags collected, they strode through the airport and outside where Saber was approached by a male clone.

"Mr. August, I'm Frank. I'm to drive you to your grandfather's vacation home, and be available to you for the duration of your stay."

Saber held out his hand. "Pleased to meet you, Frank."

Frank stared at Saber's outstretched hand, then looked up at him. He gingerly reached forward and clasped his hand, shaking it once, and then letting go like he had been touching hot coals. Rubbing his hands on his pants, he walked to the car and opened the door for Saber. Pilar climbed in behind him, and Frank shut the door.

Saber watched out the window as Frank gathered their bags and stowed them in the trunk, then climbed into the driver's seat and lifted the car into the air, flying off to their destination.

"Don't take it personally," said Pilar, looking at him.

"What?"

"The handshake. Clones aren't used to human contact."

Saber smiled and reached beside him, taking Pilar's hand. A jolt of electricity went through him as her small, warm hand was engulfed in his. He placed his hand over hers, all the while holding eye contact with her, and watching her reaction go from instinctual wide-eyed fear to a nervous happiness that reflected his own.

"And you?"

"I'm getting used to it," she whispered.

"Good."

He didn't let her hand go as they drove. Her pulse thrummed a steady beat in her wrists that told him she was just as human as he was. If it wasn't for Pilar, he'd probably be going insane right about now. She seemed to keep him grounded and controlled. She instilled in him a quiet resistance, a will to live, and a desire to do better than he had in the past.

He couldn't let that go.

***

That evening, Saber sat under the stars on a beach chair, listening to the waves lap the shore. Pilar reclined in a chair next to his, her eyes closed.

"You awake?" he asked.

"Mmmhmmm."

"Have you ever experienced anything like this?"

Pilar opened her eyes and rolled onto her side, looking at him. "Been out here? Once, with your grandfather, for a business trip."

"No, been on vacation."

Pilar laughed. "Clones don't get vacations."

"I thought maybe you had special privileges," Saber replied, hoping she couldn't see his blush.

"I do, but a vacation isn't one of them. So many clones never leave the confines of the Outer system. A very small percentage of us get to commute to a job in the Central system. I consider myself very fortunate for what I've experienced in life."

"But it's not enough."

"Is life ever enough? Look at the humans that surround you every day, and tell me that their lives, with all the freedom they enjoy, are enough. People will always want, Saber. It's in our nature."

Saber nodded. Not too long ago he would have argued that clones didn't share a nature with humans, but now he knew differently. Pilar was every bit as human as he was.

They fell into a comfortable silence again, but only for a short time before Saber looked at her. This time she stared back at him and met his eyes.

"What?" he asked.

"You could do great things."

Saber scoffed and smiled slightly, getting up and sitting on the reclining beach bed with her, taking her hand.

"You said that I'm not alone, earlier. That there are sympathizers."

Pilar nodded, stroking the outside of his hand with her thumb. Her boldness grew all the time. She stared up at him with wide, adoring eyes. "There is a resistance movement amongst the clones."

Saber closed his eyes and took a deep breath, feeling her thumb slide effortlessly against his skin in a pendulum motion. Releasing the breath, he opened his eyes again and looked at her. "I want to help. Can you take me to them?"

A smile grew on her face. "Tomorrow."

CHAPTER SIXTEEN

Aaron August

Aaron holed up in his apartment for twenty-four hours. He spent his time drinking beer, playing video games and sleeping. He got offers to hang out with people, attend parties, and join study groups, but he turned each one down. He wasn't in the mood to see anyone.

He knew he was moping, but he didn't really care. He couldn't stop thinking about Kristin, and she seemed to want nothing to do with him. His grandfather had threatened him, and his parents hadn't checked up on him even once since all this went down. How could they be so unconcerned? *Because grandfather fed them a lie*, he thought, taking a sip of beer and directing his player in the first-person shooter game over to a group of bushes for cover.

Aaron had never felt so alone in his entire life. People had always surrounded him. They knew his name, and the power it meant, so he'd never lacked for company. It hadn't been until he was much older that he realized people didn't hang around him because they wanted to know him, they just wanted to know his wealth and power.

He'd never let it bother him before. He'd always embraced his life, and the revolving door social life that seemed to come with friends that didn't stick around long term. It meant he didn't have to open up too much to anyone. He was in it for a good time, so was everyone else, and then everyone moved on.

But it wasn't enough anymore. Aaron was sick and tired of being overlooked by his parents, of being unimportant to his grandfather, of being overshadowed by his brother, and of not having a single person in the world who actually cared about him.

Except for Saber.

Saber always cared. He'd always looked out for Aaron and included him. Aaron had taken the camaraderie between the two of them for granted. But now, Saber was gone. Grandfather said it was only temporary, but Aaron had seen a change in Saber lately, and then what he'd done... that wasn't something you came back from. No, even if Saber could come home without any repercussions for the crime he committed, he'd never be the same. But Aaron didn't think he would come back. Grandson of the most powerful man in the world or not, Saber would be found out sooner or later, and when people realized the murder was in defense of a clone, there would be a cry for blood.

Royce Williams would have to concede.

Aaron's phone chimed from where he'd left it in the kitchen. He looked behind him, at the phone sitting on the counter, blinking its notification, then turned back to face the TV. He didn't really care, and he didn't feel like turning down yet another invitation.

His stomach growled angrily, and Aaron realized, upon sipping the last of the beer out of the bottle, that he needed something beyond his liquid diet to satiate his hunger. Turning off the game to a few shouts of disappointment and annoyance of other team members over the Net, he got up and walked into the kitchen.

He walked to the oven and opened it, the aromatic smell of chicken, potatoes, and corn wafted up to him. *When did the clone come?* he thought, reaching in and removing the single plate of food. Apparently, the clone had been informed of Saber's absence as well, since the usual second plate was missing.

Taking his food to the island, Aaron sat on the barstool. It felt less lonely to eat at the counter, rather than at the table amongst three empty chairs. He shoveled food into his mouth slowly, large bites being consumed at turtle speed with thoughtful chewing.

He had been home all day, which meant the clone had been here at some point while he played video games. How had he not noticed? How did the clone's presence not even register with him? It wasn't as if he'd been busy. He had been bored all day, playing video games on the Net, snacking, and drinking beer. Pausing in his consumption of food, he looked around, surveying the large penthouse apartment. It was spotless. It hadn't been this morning. Beer bottles had littered the coffee table, crumbs had surrounded the couch, and last night's dishes had sat in the sink waiting to be washed. All that had been cleaned up at some point.

The clone cleaned all around me, likely right in front of me, and I never noticed.

Aaron pushed the plate of food aside, no longer feeling hungry. If he felt alone and ignored in the world, how must worse did a clone feel? They passed through life seemingly invisible.

Aaron sighed, reaching for his phone that sat blinking on the counter. At least he wasn't invisible. People actually wanted him around. People actually noticed him. Just not his family.

Opening the message, he saw Kristin's name glowing at him from the screen. He blinked once, then again. He pressed her name to open the text. He hadn't expected to hear from her—especially not this soon. He planned to give it a couple of days before he approached her yet again, but instead she reached out to him.

Let's not get ahead of ourselves, thought Aaron. *She could have texted to say she never wants to see me again.*

He looked down at the screen, his heart pounding, betraying his nervousness.

"We need to talk."

Aaron's heart slowed down and he breathed a sigh of relief. Those words could be good or bad, but talking was better than silence. Pressing the button to reply, he began to type.

CHAPTER SEVENTEEN

Saber August

They drove to the meeting in silence. They left after dark, climbing into Royce Williams' private heli and taking it to the mainland. Once there, a rental car was waiting for them. Pilar arranged everything.

Saber flew the car, following Pilar's directions rather than a GPS. She hadn't allowed him to enter in the location. Maybe she was being paranoid, but Saber appreciated her caution.

The longer they flew, the higher the tension seemed to grow inside the vehicle. He couldn't define the feelings warring inside him. Excitement? Fear? Apprehension? Pilar seemed nervous, though. She played with her hands in her lap. Folding them, then running them through her hair, then inspecting her fingernails. She didn't say anything beyond giving the occasional direction.

They headed into the Outer system, which only added to Saber's mixed feelings. He'd never been to the Outer system. His grandfather, who did make occasional trips in, had always told him it was no place for someone of his standing. There was no need for him to travel into clone territory, and without proper protection, it could be dangerous.

For a moment, Saber wished they had gotten a less conspicuous rental. The car stuck out like a sore thumb. What would happen if he left it parked somewhere?

Pilar spoke up once they were quite far out of the Central system. "Pull in down there." She pointed.

Saber followed her directions and lowered the car down to the ground gradually.

"You can park there."

"Will it be safe?"

She nodded. "There are human patrols that come through. You didn't think the government would leave us clones up to our own devices, did you?"

Saber shrugged. "We had to go through the border, maybe they don't care what happens on this side."

She smiled ruefully. "They care. We're property. An investment. No one leaves their investments unattended."

Saber parked the car, feeling only slightly less uncomfortable. He turned off the engine, but didn't get out of his seat.

Pilar opened the door. "Coming?"

Saber shook away his apprehension, and exited the car, smiling at Pilar in an attempt to bolster his nerves. He followed her confident stride into an old warehouse, and through dark, dank halls that echoed with every footstep and plunk of dripping water. It was eerie, perhaps fitting of an illegal revolution. Like something out of a movie or a story. He never expected to walk down halls like these. Saber August walked down halls of gleaming metal, marble, or granite.

Then again, if he went to prison, he'd be seeing similar surroundings to this for the rest of his life.

"What is this place?" he whispered.

"An old factory. I'm not too sure what it manufactured, but it's been long shut down."

"Is it safe?"

Pilar shrugged. "Structure wise? Who knows? It hasn't fallen on us yet. I'm pretty sure they build these things to withstand the test of time."

Finally, there was a light at the end of the tunnel. They approached a room where the soft glow of candlelight and oil lanterns flickered through the open door. It was archaic, from a time long forgotten, but it was almost fitting in a place like this. The Outer system itself was a completely different world from the Central system. But the room told Saber something else. *They're scared*, he thought. *Meeting in secret like this.*

Entering the room, two male clones stood waiting. They turned to look at Saber and Pilar when they entered, their faces grim and serious. They nodded greeting to Pilar, but looked Saber up and down like a bug they were going to dissect. It made his skin crawl, but he kept his face impassive and unreadable.

"Mark, Tyler, this is Saber August."

They nodded in his direction, studying him with interested, yet wary eyes, and they didn't move from where they stood when he held out his hand to shake.

Saber let his hand fall uselessly by his side and looked at Pilar for some kind of reassurance. She smiled at him, and for a moment, his heart stopped pounding, but only for the briefly before it started again. He was sure the other clones could hear it.

"Why don't you turn on the lights in here?" asked Saber, looking for any way to break the unnerving silence, challenging them to admit their fear.

The one that Pilar introduced as Mark let a slight smile break his stony face, more an acknowledgement than a smile of happiness. "If we draw electricity, they'll know someone has been here. We'd rather not leave a trace."

There it was. *We'd rather not leave a trace.* They needed to leave more than a trace if they hoped to get anywhere with this.

"Let's get right to it, shall we?" interjected Pilar. She immediately commanded the small room, which looked like it had once served as an office.

The men nodded and she walked to the center of the room. "Saber has agreed to join our cause."

"A human, join our cause?" muttered Tyler.

Pilar frowned and shook her head. "Don't talk like that. You don't know him, I do. I'm vouching for him, and that should be enough."

Mark seemed to accept it, but Tyler shook his head, obviously the stronger willed of the two. "I don't trust him. What if he uses this as leverage to keep his position as *prince* of the world," he spat out the word prince as if it left a bad taste in his mouth.

Pilar flushed and her eyes hardened. Saber had never seen her so close to losing it, not that he'd known her long enough to have experienced her range of emotions, but he was starting to learn that she was a firecracker.

"Are you questioning me? Really? Without you, you wouldn't have a hope. You want freedom? You want children of your own that the government doesn't abort? Do you want to live past fifty? You jump when I say jump, and you trust when I say trust."

Abort? Saber didn't even realize that clones were capable of reproduction. How many millions of abortions occurred to keep the clones from having their own offspring? Abortion had been abolished years ago. With the human population reducing at a scary rate, they had been on their way to extinction. In a desperate act, the government of the time had forbidden abortion. It created uproar among the younger generation, but contraception had advanced to 100% prevention if used correctly. If you didn't want kids, you were careful. If you ended up pregnant anyway, it was fate.

Saber realized he was missing the argument that was occurring between Pilar and Tyler, a power struggle over him. Stepping forward, he put his hand on Pilar's arm. "Tyler, you have all the power here."

"Just knowing who we are is dangerous," growled Tyler.

Saber raised an eyebrow and looked at the clone. "Really? I'm pretty sure no one can identify you by your name, and if I went to a sketch artist and had them draw you, you'd be just another face."

Pilar snorted, trying to hold back her laughter, and Mark chuckled. Tyler didn't take the personal jab quite so well. "You don't think the humans would round up anyone they suspected and terminate them?"

Saber sighed. Tyler was right. Closing his eyes, he pictured the crime that had landed him here in the first place, and drew a deep breath, letting it go as he opened his eyes again. He knew what he had to do to gain this clone's trust, but the risk terrified him.

"I murdered a human in defense of a clone two days ago. I'm sure news of the murder made it to you, now you have the confession of the killer. I can't turn on you—if I do, you can take me down with you. Mutually assured destruction."

He felt Pilar's hand grasp his and squeeze, but he refused to look at her for the assurance he craved. Instead, he met Tyler's eyes in a silent battle of wills, waiting for the man to decide whether he would give Saber a chance. Finally, he nodded, and approached him, grasping Saber's hand in a firm handshake. "I'll give you a chance. Don't screw me."

Saber smiled and stepped back, closer to Pilar. She looked at him and nodded, the slightest upturning of her lips showed her approval.

"Can we go over the game plan now?" she asked.

Nods of approval came from the three men.

"Saber is opening doors for us that we didn't have access to before. We have direct access to Royce Williams. He is not only very important to Royce, but to the entire human population. They see him as their prince. If he speaks in our favor, it will open eyes."

"Royce Williams won't just let us go because his grandson asks nicely," said Tyler.

Saber stepped forward; it was his turn to talk. "Royce will listen. Maybe we can start negotiations."

"And if he isn't willing to hear you out?" asked Mark.

"Then I threaten with revealing my crime."

Pilar nodded. "Royce Williams doesn't want to lose his grandson and heir. If Saber can use himself as a hostage of sorts, we could end this war before it even begins."

"And if he calls your bluff? Then what?" Tyler pointed out.

"It's not a bluff. I will confess, if I have to."

"And go to prison?"

"He'll run. Here. For now, let's concentrate on the first step. Saber will speak with Royce, and we'll meet again in a week. If there is no hint of progress, we'll discuss our next step.

"I'm tired of waiting around. Things are going to start happening."

Saber watched Pilar as she spoke with confidence and power. She was an Amazon, a war queen. Her red hair shone like a battle cry in Saber's mind, and he would follow her anywhere. He wasn't just signing on to save himself and free a race, he was signing on to a war, and this was just the beginning. It would only get uglier and bloodier as time went on.

SHADOWS OF THE UNSEEN

CHAPTER EIGHTEEN

Aaron August

Aaron drove to a popular 24-hour café near the university and parked. After he messaged Kristin back earlier, she'd apologized for the mixed messages she'd been giving and the way she'd sent him away yesterday, then she'd asked him if they could meet. Part of him had wanted to refuse. Everything about her told him that getting close to her was a bad idea. She was damaged. But despite the objections his logical side presented, he pushed them away and accepted. Something about Kristin made him feel like he needed her. He wanted to hold her and never let her go. He wanted to know what had caused her to be so afraid, so damaged, and he wanted to fix it. He wanted to make her happy.

Agreeing they needed to take things slow, they settled on meeting in a public setting. Hence the café.

Ordering two coffees, and having his choice of tables, he chose one in the farthest corner and waited for Kristin to arrive. He didn't wait long before she walked in. She scanned the café, searching, looking tired, and a little lost. He stood up and waved. Immediately she looked more sure of herself, but no smile came across her face, and Aaron's heart sunk a little.

"Hi," he said.

"Hi."

She took the seat opposite him and he pushed a coffee towards her. They sat in silence for a few minutes. Kristin opened her mouth a couple of times to speak, but then closed it and looked back down at her coffee, her hands clasped around it as if she was leeching courage from it.

Finally, Aaron spoke. "I don't know what happened the other day, but I want you to be okay with me."

Kristin nodded slowly, like someone who had just been chided. "We are okay. You didn't do anything wrong. It's me . . ." she trailed off and glanced up at Aaron for just a moment, then her eyes fell. Why couldn't she look at him?

"I want to understand."

Her shoulders shook. Was she crying?

"Why are you being so nice to me after everything that has happened, and how I pushed you away?" Her voice shook with tears and Aaron's heart ached. He wanted to reach across the table and comfort her, but he didn't know how it would be received, so he reached for his own forearm and squeezed it tightly.

"People are nice to you all the time, Kristin," he replied softly. "The woman I met last weekend is incredible, *you* are incredible. Don't forget that, Kristin. I feel honored that you would even spend time with me."

She laughed a little through her tears, and looked up at him through red, puffy eyes. "You haven't given me much of a choice."

Aaron smiled. Even though she was sad, her smile lit up the room. "I want to be with you, Kristin. If that means being your friend, then I'll be that."

She reached across the table to stroke his hand and looked at him with wide, scared eyes. But she smiled and he knew that whatever would come out of her mouth next would be hard for her, but good.

"I want you in my life, Aaron. I don't know to what extent, but I do want you here. I'm a mess. I know that. I was long before this whole thing happened with Saber. But I want to heal, and I think maybe you're the person to help me do that, if you're willing to be patient with me."

Aaron nodded and removed his hand from his arm, placing it on top of her hand, sandwiching it between the two of his. "I'll wait forever if that's what you need."

She giggled, her tears dry. "You're funny, Aaron. I like it. How come you don't get all the girls?"

He wiggled his eyebrows and winked. "Oh, but I do. I'm just giving up my womanizing lifestyle for you."

She burst out laughing, and he stared at her, a hurt expression on his face. "What? You don't believe I could have any girl I want?"

She stopped laughing, but her smile went from ear to ear. "I believe you could, but you're not like that. You're a romantic."

Aaron shrugged. "Guilty as charged. I believe in fairy tales and happily-ever-afters."

"And if I don't?"

"Then it's my personal mission to show you that dreams do come true."

Kristin's laugh entranced Aaron. They talked for hours, until nearly dawn, and drank way too much coffee. Not once did it cross his mind that he wanted to go home to his comfy bed. He wanted to spend all night talking to this beautiful, pragmatic woman. She was so vibrant and alive. She spoke with passion about her beliefs, and it made Aaron want to believe in them too.

When the pink of the rising sun began to tinge the horizon, Aaron yawned.

"We better go home," said Kristin, looking outside.

Aaron smiled, tired. "But I hate to leave you."

"Separation is healthy. Remember, I need to take things slow."

"I'll walk you to your car."

They got up, but Kristin put her hand on his arm once they exited the café. "We part here. Don't call or message me today, okay? I need time to digest everything."

"How about you call me when you're ready?"

"Perfect." She leaned in and planted a kiss on his cheek, then walked away.

As he watched her leave, he couldn't help but think that she was walking away into the sunrise with his heart. He chuckled to himself, as he climbed into his own vehicle—how romantic and cliché, but an apt illustration of their relationship nonetheless. They were backwards. Instead of a sunset, like all the stories, it was a sunrise. Instead of the man walking away, it was the woman. Instead of her heart on the line, it was his. But maybe it would make a good fairy tale after all.

CHAPTER NINETEEN

Saber August

Light just barely touched the horizon as Saber walked out onto the balcony of his grandfather's beach house in bare feet and loose cotton pants. A light, cool breeze from the ocean woke up his senses better than the mug of hot coffee clutched between his hands.

"It's beautiful, isn't it?"

Saber startled slightly, and looked over his shoulder to see Pilar walking up. His coffee sloshed, spilling a drop over the edge that traveled down the side of the mug until it met the barrier of his index finger. Removing his hand and wiping it on his pants, he nodded. "It's almost enough to make me forget why I'm here."

Pilar stood next to him, looking straight out to the ocean, but Saber watched her. Her hair blew in the wind, loose and disheveled. She wore no make-up. She looked innocent and human. Reaching, he placed his arm around her lower back, and drew her close. He could feel her stiffen under his touch, so he released the pressure and allowed her to pull away if she felt the need. But she stayed, slowly relaxing into his arm and resting her head on his shoulder.

They stood in silence, Saber listened to the waves crash on the shore and just enjoyed being with Pilar without any worry about the possible major changes his life could take on at any moment. Or even the changes that had already occurred.

"What would you like to do today?" asked Pilar, lifting her head up and looking at him.

Saber smiled, kissing her on the forehead. "I want to stay in, laze on the beach, and continue to forget about life, if that's okay with you."

Pilar nodded. "For now. But we'll have to face real life at some point. That meeting last night was very real, Saber. You signed up to free a slave race. That isn't a hobby or something to piss off your grandfather. Lives are at stake."

He nodded, all sense of relaxation forgotten. It was too early for this. He clutched his coffee mug tighter as he fought down his annoyance caused by Pilar's apparent lack of confidence in his dedication—though his reputation certainly would have done very little to instill her confidence in him. Breathing deeply to dispel his anger, he released his hold on her, and stepped in front to face her. "Give us today here in paradise to just be. We can book a flight back home for tomorrow and I'll meet with Royce."

Pilar nodded. "Fine. Today we can have."

* * *

Saber paced the length of the living room as Pilar dialed Frontier Industries.

"Hi, I'd like to be transferred to transportation services," she said when the face of who was likely a receptionist filled the screen.

The screen blinked out and was almost immediately filled again with the image of a man. "How can I help you?"

"I need to order a private jet pickup in Aruba for tomorrow morning. Mr. August is finished vacationing and would like to return home."

"And this has been authorized by Mr. Williams?" asked the man.

Pilar smiled. "Would I be calling you if it hadn't?"

"I'll have the plane waiting by 8 am. Anything else you'll need?"

"A car to pick us up when we arrive."

Saber watched as Pilar conducted herself with confidence and poise on the phone. Neither Frontier employee had even questioned her authority, yet they were humans while she was nothing more than a clone. Her word was an extension of Royce's. Even Saber couldn't have secured a chartered jet. His grandfather had never granted him that authority.

Unlike when they flew out, they wanted their arrival back home to go unnoticed. Saber didn't know what would be waiting for them when they arrived, and he wanted to find out on his own terms.

When the phone conversation ended, Pilar reclined on the couch and picked up a small tablet to read. Realizing he would get no attention from her, Saber wandered off to another room. He paced the beach house like a caged tiger, randomly picking things up, inspecting them, then setting them back down. When he made it back to the living room, he started the process again in there, inspecting everything, looking for something to do.

"You're driving me crazy," said Pilar, from where she sat on the couch reading.

"Sorry," he replied, standing still. "I don't know what to do with myself."

"I can see that." She set down her tablet and stood up, walking to him and pulling him into an embrace. "What do normal couples do?"

Saber chuckled, "Is that what we are? A couple?"

Pilar's cheeks flared red. "Well, I don't, I thought..." she trailed off and looked down at the ground.

Lifting her chin so that her eyes met his, Saber kissed her. "I'd really like that, despite the fact that it probably breaks so many laws."

"It won't be the first one, or the last."

"But that doesn't solve what we do with our time. I'm not normal, Pilar, I want to give you better than normal while I still can."

"Have you ever stopped to think that maybe normal is what's real?"

Saber shrugged. "Not for me. I've always been more into the storybook romances."

"All the stories and movies about romance and grand gesture are just that; stories. I'd rather have every day normalcy that I see walking down the street, hand in hand, long after the excitement of new romance has died out."

"What if I want more?"

"We'll have our chance for an epic story. Right now is our last chance at normal for a long time, maybe ever."

Saber watched her as she spoke; her eyes alight with passion and fear. Reaching forward, he brushed her hair behind her ear, his hand pausing there. Despite their multiple intimate moments in the last few days, his heart still began to pound wildly, and by the increased speed of the rise and fall of Pilar's chest, he'd guess she was feeling it too.

"Pilar, may I take you out for lunch?"

"That sounds just about perfect."

* * *

Pilar grinned, her face lighting up as they walked into the dimly lit restaurant. "I don't think I've ever been taken out to lunch before."

"Not even by other . . ." he trailed off, unsure of what to say. He didn't really feel comfortable calling them clones. It felt racist and wrong.

But Pilar finished for him. "Other clones? I guess so. But this seems different."

"It shouldn't be. We're all just people."

"But no one else sees it that way," she said, touching his arm and looking up at him.

A hostess walked up, looking Pilar up and down as if she was a rodent. *She's human,* he thought. *Most restaurant employees are clones.*

"Can I help you?" she asked.

"A table for two, please. Somewhere close to the back, and a little more private, if you can," he instructed.

She nodded, her long black hair swinging with the movement. "Right this way."

She led them through the restaurant to a secluded booth in the back, and waited for them to take their seats. She pressed her thumb down on the table and pulled up the menu on the glowing tabletop, then left without another word.

Saber perused the menu, looking up at Pilar occasionally to see if she was done or not.

"Something wrong?" she asked, after a few minutes.

"No, why?"

"You keep looking up at me like you're checking to make sure I'm alright."

Saber smiled and reached across the table for her hand. "Is it wrong that I want to protect you?"

"No. It's… nice, if unnecessary."

Saber nodded. "Are you ready to order?" he asked, changing the subject.

"Sure, what are you having?"

"They have fantastic sushi here. Do you like that? I can order some for us to share—"

Pilar laughed, cutting him off mid-sentence. "It slips your mind, doesn't it?"

"What?"

"That I'm a clone. That I haven't had the same privileges or luxuries as you. I don't even know what real meat tastes like, much less something like sushi."

Saber could have kicked himself. Of course she'd never had sushi. Meat was a rarity, a luxury reserved for humans, with a large price tag attached.

"I'm sorry…" he trailed off, not sure how to continue.

"Don't be. I don't mind, really. And I'd love to try sushi. I was looking at this menu just completely overwhelmed by the options and the costs. I'd actually feel a lot better if you took the decision away from me," she said, followed by a nervous chuckle.

"I'm not taking the decision from you, Pilar," he said, hating that she resorted to her inferior role when she was uncomfortable. Her shoulders curved inwards, stiff. Her whole body seemed to hunch in on itself, as if she was trying to make herself less visible.

"You can have whatever you want. Price isn't an issue."

"I know that. I'd like the sushi. Really."

"Okay." He returned his attention to the menu and began selecting dishes, then pressed the large 'order' button on the upper right hand corner of his menu.

"Would you like some wine?" he asked, opening the drink menu file so that it glowed in front of the both of them.

"I, uh . . ."

Saber laughed. "I'm going to order a bottle. You can have some if you like."

He clicked beside the bottle of red cabernet and once again pressed the order button.

"You know clones aren't allowed to drink, Saber. It's against the law. I could get in a lot of trouble."

"You're with me. You'll be fine. But if you aren't comfortable, you don't have to drink it."

She nodded, falling silent. Saber studied her as she fidgeted with a set of chopsticks in her hand, and looked around the restaurant with wide eyes. Her movements were choppy and nervous, as if she wanted to look and watch, but feared she would get in trouble for even raising her eyes to look.

Within minutes of placing the order, a tall, thin, model-like woman walked up with the bottle of wine in hand.

"Good evening, Sir," she said, not even casting so much as a glance towards Pilar. She might as well be invisible. "You have excellent taste in wine. Would you care to try it?"

Saber nodded. "Please."

119

The waitress poured a small amount of wine for Saber to try, and waited for him to taste it and give her the go ahead to serve more.

He looked at her; she angled her body away from Pilar, her entire attention on Saber. She hadn't acknowledged Pilar's presence in even the slightest gesture.

Picking up the glass, he made a quick decision and handed it to Pilar, winking at her.

She paled a little, but accepted the glass and swirled it around—she must have seen Royce do it before—then took a sip.

The waitress finally turned to face Pilar, and stood there, a look of shock scrawled across her face.

Pilar glanced at Saber, and he nodded towards the waitress, hoping she understood. He wanted her to feel power, to feel in control of the situation, to feel like this human's equal. If she wanted to lead a rebellion, she needed to believe she deserved to stand on the same ground as this woman, and every other human being in the world who would look down their noses at her.

Pilar still hadn't said anything, the air thickened as the waitress looked back and forth between the two of them, searching for an answer.

"The lady seems to approve," said Saber. "The wine is so good it has her speechless."

The waitress responded with a nervous laugh, then leaned to top off Pilar's glass first, then Saber's.

"Is there anything else I can get the two of you?" she asked, placing the bottle on the table.

"No, that's it. Thank you," replied Pilar before Saber could even open his mouth.

He smiled at her. "You did it."

"Did what?"

"Took control, there at the end. That's what I wanted you to do with the wine."

"You blindsided me, Saber," she retorted. She hadn't so much as reached for her glass since the initial tasting.

"But did you see her face? She was shocked."

"Can you blame her? She has never experienced anything like that before. If she reports me—"

"I told you, you'll be fine. No one will question me."

"Are you forgetting that you could be a wanted man?" she hissed, leaning forward so that no one else would hear.

He shrugged. "Right now I'm not. I'll protect you. I won't let anything happen to you."

"Really? How? By killing another human?" she snapped.

Saber stared at her, blinking a couple of times. Where did that come from?

"I'm sorry—"

"No, you meant that."

Her eyes flashed and she let out a huff of air. "Well, if you would just stop pushing me."

"It's not about me pushing you, Pilar. You lashed out with words you've been thinking all along. Do I scare you?"

She shook her head, now reaching for her glass and taking a sip, the red wine staining the cracks of her lips.

"But you think I was wrong?"

She nodded. "I don't think murder is ever the answer. If we start killing humans, how are we any different from them?"

"It was a mistake. An accident. I lost control..."

"I know. I'm sorry. I do understand, sort of. As much as I can, anyway. I don't think you fully understand it yourself."

Just then the plates of food arrived, served by the same woman who had brought their wine. She placed the tray of sushi rolls and sashimi in the middle of the table and took a step back. "Soy sauce is on the table, wasabi and ginger is on the plate there. Is there anything else I can get you?"

"A glass of water, please," replied Pilar, looking up at the woman with a smile on her face.

Saber had to hold back a laugh. She looked the woman straight in the eye, feigning confidence in the moment. Her discomfort only apparent by the way she continued to hold her body tense and turned inwards.

"Of course. I'll be right out with that."

Pilar gave him a triumphant smile once they were alone again. "Confident enough for you?"

"I'm sorry. I shouldn't have brought you here."

"Why do you say that?"

"There are no clones here. Normally you would be served by your own kind, but here..."

Pilar smiled, reaching for his hand and stroking the top of it with her fingers. "It is intimidating, but I kind of like it. I feel... special. For once I feel a little human."

Saber turned his hand and held hers tightly. "You are human. And we're going to do whatever it takes to make the rest of the world realize that."

* * *

Saber and Pilar spent as much of the day doing normal things as they could. They finished lunch, then went for a walk along the pier. Saber took her shopping, enjoying the sight of her utter wonder over all the materialism that surrounded her.

He even caught her staring inside the window of a jewelry store, her hands and nose pressed up against the glass like she was a little kid looking in on a candy shop.

When they arrived back at the house Saber barbequed for her, or rather ordered in barbeque, and they sat on the deck eating steak—Pilar's very first steak.

Lounging outside at the end of the night, on a blanket spread over the sand, Pilar snuggled in close to Saber as they watched and listened to the waves crash against the shore.

"Saber?"

"Mmmmhmmm?"

"Where do we go from here?"

Why? Why couldn't they just forget everything for one entire day? "To see Royce."

"No, after that."

"I don't know."

She sighed. "This is just the beginning, isn't it?"

He nodded slowly, but she wouldn't see as she stared out at the water, her back leaning against his side. "Are you ready for what comes next?" he asked.

She stayed silent, and although he couldn't see her face, he knew she was frowning. The little frown that furrowed her brow just slightly when she was thinking.

"I'm really not sure. Are you?"

"If I'm not, it's too late to turn back now."

Saber felt a thrill of fear course through him, but he pushed it down. No, he wouldn't think about what he was starting. He needed this one day, this last night of normalcy before his whole world imploded.

"I'll keep you safe," he whispered, kissing the top of her head. He felt her body move, shivering—it was too warm for it to be caused by the temperature. *Did I cause that?* Or did the new chapter of their lives that they were about to enter do it?

"I know."

With his left hand, the one that wasn't wrapped around Pilar, he reached into his pocket and pulled out the delicate gold necklace that he purchased earlier that day while Pilar had been using the restroom. He had seen her staring at it through the window of the jewelry store, and he couldn't help but get it for her.

The necklace was a delicate white gold chain with a small pendant, the shape of a dove soaring. The eye of the dove was a tiny diamond.

Removing his arm from around her, he gently guided her into a sitting position.

She turned to look at him. "Are you okay?"

Saber nodded. "Here, I have something for you."

He unclasped the necklace and draped it around her neck, moving her long fiery hair to the side to clasp it in place.

Her hand reached up, and she gently touched the pendant with her fingers. She looked at him again, her eyes wide, her hand not leaving the base of her neck.

"You shouldn't have," she whispered.

"I wanted to."

She closed her eyes and leaned back against him, her head resting on his chest right above where his heart sat.

After a little while, he felt her breathing steady and deepen in sleep. Slowly, carefully, he moved her off him, stood up, and lifted her into his arms, carrying her towards the house. She stirred slightly in his arms, but didn't wake-up, just snuggled in close to his chest.

Once inside, he laid her on the bed and draped a blanket on her. Sitting down, he stroked her cheek, moving her hair away from her face and behind her ear.

Her face was calm and serene, her hair fanned around her like a sun. She looked so innocent in her sleep—so relaxed. There wasn't a blemish or imperfection, not a line of worry, or a trouble in the world. Just pure, childlike innocence.

Saber's heart ached. She was so beautiful and alive, but she wouldn't stay this way. She wouldn't come out of the impending war unscathed. No one would.

CHAPTER TWENTY

Aaron August

Aaron woke up to a pounding on the door. Getting up, he stretched, then listened to see if the pounding continued. It did.

He walked out to the main area of the penthouse apartment, shuffling his bare feet against the heated tile of the front entrance. The banging came from the lift door.

Aaron pressed his palm against the wall next to the lift and the wall went opaque, revealing a video screen and a feed of the interior of the lift.

There stood Saber, looking straight up at the camera, one hand wrapped in a fist, resting on the door. The other sat on his hip. He glared at the camera, then banged on the door again.

"I know you're there, Aaron. Open the door before I break it," he called, the sound carrying through the video feed.

"Saber, settle down. Threats probably won't convince your brother to do anything," came a softer, more feminine voice. Then a redheaded clone stepped into the picture and rested her hand on Saber's shoulder, as if to try to calm him.

Sighing, Aaron pressed the admittance button, and the lift door opened with a whoosh.

"About time! Why did you change the code?" asked Saber without so much as a hello as he walked in. "You do realize this is my apartment, and I only let you stay here out of the kindness of my heart, right?"

"Nice to see you too, my dear brother. And no worse for wear, I see. Grandfather must have set you up nicely."

"I certainly can't complain," replied Saber, falling down on the couch and throwing up his feet. The clone followed behind him dutifully, then gently sat beside him, leaning against his side just enough for Aaron to notice that something wasn't quite right between the two of them.

"And Grandfather loaned you his assistant for the week?"

Saber frowned, looking at Aaron, who still hadn't moved from his spot near the lift, where he was observing the two people that had just walked into his— well, technically Saber's—apartment like nothing at all was wrong.

"It's not like that, Aaron. Pilar is... a friend."

Aaron scoffed, then walked into the kitchen to get a coffee. It was too early in the morning to be dealing with the return of his prodigal brother without caffeine.

"Right, because it's completely normal to be friends with a clone."

"Her name is Pilar. Use it," Saber snapped back.

Aaron looked at his brother, confused. This wasn't the Saber he was used to. Then again, he had been doing many things that were out of character lately.

"I'm sorry. I didn't realize we are now treating clones as equals."

The flush that spread across Pilar's face, and the way she cast her eyes downward, her whole body shifting inwards, didn't go unnoticed by Aaron. Good. She needed to realize that just because Saber was confused, that didn't mean things had changed. She was still a clone. She was still inferior, even if she was Royce Williams' assistant.

Saber's face flushed as well, but for a different reason. His eyes snapped in anger and he stood up, walking to Aaron and pulling himself up to his full height. Aaron always forgot the small, two-inch height difference between the two of them. But when Saber stood like this, the two inches he had on Aaron made him seem like an imposing giant. The only other person that Aaron knew to do that was their grandfather—though he could do it without even leaving his chair.

"Don't you ever talk like that again. Things are going to start changing around here. Just you wait."

Aaron shrugged, retrieving his coffee, prepared just the way he liked it with two creams and two sugars, from the dispenser and walked to the counter, taking a seat at the tall barstool with his back to where Pilar remained seated on the couch.

Saber followed him, his hands planted on the countertop opposite Aaron.

"I'm serious. And regardless of what the norm is, this is my house, and if I bring Pilar in here and say she's an equal, you'll treat her as such. Got it?"

Aaron shrugged again, sipping his coffee. "I'm not a child, Saber. You could just talk to me and explain things as an adult."

"And you would handle things any better if I did?"

"Maybe. Maybe not. Think of things from my perspective for once. You went and murdered someone in defense of a clone, then disappeared, and the only person who knew where you went was Grandfather—"

"The less you know, the better."

"Now you show up, banging on the door, unannounced, no warning, with a clone on your arm, demanding that she be treated with respect. You know I'm not a bigot, but all this is a little much for me to take in."

Saber's face seemed to soften and his body relaxed a bit. At least he wasn't in defense mode anymore. "You're right, I'm sorry. I have to go see Royce, but when we're back, we'll talk. Okay?"

Aaron nodded. *Do I want to talk to Saber? I at least owe it to him to hear him out before judging him.* "Okay."

CHAPTER TWENTY-ONE

Saber August

Saber walked with Pilar through the front door of Frontier Industries. He'd never before seen the large building as imposing or foreboding, but as he drove towards it today, he noticed the huge shadow it cast over the city. His grandfather's legacy: a shadow over a world that had so much potential, so much brightness just waiting to shine through.

Saber didn't bother approaching the front desk. Long ago, he'd been given access to anything and everything his grandfather did.

He chuckled as he scanned his hand on the biometric scanner and the door slid open to admit him and Pilar. Stepping in, the door shut.

"What's so funny?" Pilar asked.

"I just realized my grandfather's greatest mistake."

"What's that?"

130

"He gave me access to everything. He created in this world his equal. If he hadn't made me who I am, there would be nobody to stand up to him."

Pilar smiled, but Saber noticed it was half-hearted. In fact, all confidence she used to have seemed to have fallen away, and she replaced it with that of a meek clone—a slave.

He turned to her, and cupped her chin in his hand, forcing her to meet his eyes. "Hey, hold your head up, okay? You work here, you belong here, and Royce Williams has never intimidated you before. Don't let him start now."

She pulled her head sideways and out of his hand, then nodded. She clasped her hands in front of her, all business, but at least she held her head high and her shoulders square now.

"Let's keep this business, Saber," she whispered. "We're here to talk to your grandfather as representatives of the clones. Now is not the time to flaunt our relationship."

Saber nodded. She was right, of course. Pilar had a habit of being right more often than he'd liked to admit.

The lift chimed to warn them that they'd made it to their destination, and then the doors slid open to reveal Royce Williams standing by a large window, his back towards them, a puff of smoke rising up and around him every few seconds as he smoked a cigar.

Two men sat at his desk, but as the lift door opened, they turned to see who had arrived. Royce didn't.

"Gentlemen, this is my grandson, Saber August," said Royce without turning around.

Pilar walked a few feet behind Saber, and found a place to stand off to the side as the men stood and greeted him.

Royce now turned and walked to his desk, tapping the end of his cigar on an ashtray.

"Saber, this is Senator Collins of the Northern division, and Senator Hendricks of the North-west division."

"Pleased to meet you," replied Saber, shaking each man's hand in turn.

"Please, take a seat in the sitting area. We're just finishing up."

Saber complied, for once not helping himself to the expensive liquor at his grandfather's disposal. Pilar followed close behind, and stood behind the large wing-backed chair that Saber chose.

"You know what you're going to say?" she asked in a whisper. Saber glanced up and behind to look at her. She set her eyes straight ahead, staring at the large window that made up the entire opposite wall. If he hadn't heard her, he wouldn't have guessed she'd spoken.

"I think so. I know well enough to get us started, anyway," he replied, just as quietly as she had.

He felt her hand brush his shoulder, ever so slightly, as if to reassure him and let him know she was there, supporting him in spirit, if not in word. Here, she had no power. This was Saber's playground.

True to his word, Royce finished his meeting quickly, shaking hands with the two senators and walking them to the lift before turning his attention to Saber.

"I don't recall telling you to come home," he said, approaching them, his cigar trailing smoke behind.

"You didn't. I made a decision."

"I thought we discussed that it was in your best interest to stay out of sight for a while."

"In my best interest, yes. In the clones' best interest, no."

Royce frowned, holding his cigar out and allowing it to smolder while he studied Saber.

Saber felt like a bug under a microscope as his grandfather watched him. He felt Pilar's fingertips gently brush the back of his neck, where Royce wouldn't be able to see, letting him know that she was still there.

"What do you mean by, 'in the clones' best interest'? They're clones. Their well-being is not your concern. Their entire purpose is to serve us, Saber."

Saber stood up, unable to feel the confidence to face Royce while sitting. Standing, they were equal in height and held themselves the same way—with authority.

"Have you ever stopped to consider how you treat them? They're your creation. You should care for them and love them, not abuse them and then recycle them. They are just like us; they're the same, right down to their DNA. I've spent hours pouring over what makes them the way they are, and you know what I found? They aren't any different from us. We just treat them like they are."

Royce let out a sound that Saber could only akin to a growl.

"We are nothing like them."

"Why? Because they were grown in a lab?"

"You know it's more than that."

"Because they are genetically identical to each other, to their original? We all take pieces of our parents, why are they any different?"

"Because they're just copies, nothing more."

"That's why it's okay to abort their children?"

"Clones can't reproduce."

"They can. I know it, and you do too. Do you want the world to find out?"

"*If* it gets out, I will deal with it."

133

"If you want to save face, your own neck, you need to start changing how clones are treated and perceived. Otherwise, when the world finds out, you'll have a coup d'état on your hands."

Royce began pacing, agitated. He walked back and forth, then halted and strode to Pilar, grabbing her arm and forcing her to face him. He drew her so close they were likely breathing the very same air.

Saber rushed to her, just close enough that he could defend her if needed. She held her chin up high, though, and met Royce's eyes with a boldness that made Saber's heart swell with pride.

"You," Royce ground out. "You fed Saber these lies? You turned him against me?"

"I did no such thing."

Saber watched Royce warily as the man clutched Pilar's arm. Slowly, his hand relaxed its grip, but then, suddenly it shot out and grabbed her neck, pushing her, forcing her to backpedal until she slammed against the large window. Saber rushed after them.

"Grandfather, stop! You're hurting her!" he yelled, grabbing his grandfather's arm and attempting to pull it off her, but his grip was unrelenting.

Pilar's face began turning red, and her mouth hung open, moving slightly in a vain attempt to draw in air. Her hands grappled at his, clamped firmly on her neck, as her fingers fought to pry them off.

"Grandfather, let her go," he seethed.

"After everything I did for you. I treated you well. I gave you more freedom than any other clone, and this is how you repay me? By corrupting him? By turning him against me?"

His hand released her neck and she fell down, leaning against the window and gasping for breath. Saber immediately fell to his knees beside her, and pulled her into his arms.

"I see it now," said Royce. "You think you love her." He spat out the words like sour milk, then crouched in front of them. He reached forward, this time his hand moving slowly and nonthreatening. His fingers picked up the dove resting on Pilar's throat, and he turned it around slowly between his thumb and forefinger, studying it.

"Yes, it all makes sense now. She is beautiful, is she not?"

He didn't wait for Saber's reply. Instead, he let go of the necklace and stroked her cheek. Saber could feel Pilar stiffen in his arms at the unwanted touch, her heart pounding wildly. She still breathed heavily from her near strangulation.

"I created her to be this way, to be beautiful. Her original was chosen from among many women, but she was the most beautiful. I should have known better. A beautiful woman can be even the greatest man's undoing."

His hand left Pilar's face and he got up, walking back to his desk.

Saber took the moment of reprieve to help Pilar up and lead her towards the lift, his arm protectively around her shoulders. So this is where he got his temper from. As he pressed his hand against the biometric scanner to call the lift, Saber looked back at his grandfather, who was once again standing at the window, looking out at the world that he owned, his back towards them. Should he say something? Or get out while he still could? He had no idea what Royce was capable of—even though he liked to think he was immune from harm, Pilar most definitely was not.

"What are you waiting for?" asked Royce.

"I'm thinking about what to say to you. But I can't think of anything beyond what I've already said."

"Then you had better leave. If you want me to take you seriously, you'll speak to me without her. Come to me as Saber August, heir to Frontier Industries, not as a representative of some clone movement."

The lift opened, and without another word, Saber ushered Pilar in. The door seemed to take an eternity to close, but when it finally did, he let out a whoosh of air that he hadn't even realized he'd been holding.

He turned to Pilar and stroked her cheek. "Are you okay?" he asked, his voice soft as he pressed a kiss down on top of her head.

He could feel her slowly nod and he drew away to inspect her. Her hand strayed to her neck to touch the ugly red mark that held the imprint of Royce William's vice-like grip.

"I'm so sorry. I didn't think he'd react like that."

Pilar smiled, allowing her hand to fall. "It's okay. I didn't think so either. He's always been... kind to me," she said, her voice raspy and weak.

"His kindness only stretches so far, it seems."

Pilar nodded and drew away from him as the lift chimed its warning, and then the doors opened to the main lobby.

They walked through, Pilar a few paces behind him, acting as if nothing was wrong. But everything was wrong. Everything had changed.

CHAPTER TWENTY-TWO

Aaron August

The lift door opened and admitted Saber and Pilar. Aaron held back his annoyance at their presence and offered Saber a greeting, ignoring Pilar for the most part—that was the easiest way to handle the situation. But one look at her made him stop what he was doing to study her in concern. She looked awful. Her hair was disheveled and her eyes were rimmed in red, like she'd been crying. The ugly red mark on her neck, which was beginning to bruise a deep purple, only helped to complete the look.

Who had done that to her? It was obvious by the way she held Saber's hand, seemingly unwilling to let go, that she looked to him for protection from whatever, or whomever, had done this to her. But he had to admit that the thought did cross his mind, if only briefly. Saber had a temper...

For a moment, he felt an urge to protect her swell within himself, but he pushed it down. *It's nothing more than instinct*, he thought. *It's natural to want to protect a woman.*

Saber led Pilar to his room, and moments later walked back out. In the kitchen, he opened the fridge, pulling out a beer.

"Want one?" he asked.

Aaron lifted an eyebrow. "Isn't it a bit early in the day for that?"

Saber closed the fridge door just enough to see the glowing screen on the front where the time would be boldly displayed. He shrugged. "It's after three. How is that early?"

He was right. Three really wasn't *that* early. "Sure, bring me one. Then maybe we can talk about what has been going on... and maybe what happened to the..." he trailed off. "To Pilar."

Saber grabbed another beer and walked to Aaron, passing it to him and sinking into the couch.

"Well?" asked Aaron, sitting down beside him.

Saber sighed, cracking open the beer with a pop and a hiss as the compressed beverage let out steam that had nothing to do with heat. "It was Royce."

Aaron blinked. "Grandfather?"

"That man is *not* my grandfather. That man is a liar, a tyrant, and plays at being god. He did that to Pilar. Her neck, did you see her neck?"

Aaron nodded mutely, waiting for his brother to finish his outburst.

"He strangled her, and if I hadn't been there..." he trailed off.

"It's no secret Grandfather—Royce—isn't the kindest, most caring, or forgiving of people. But there is more going on, and no one has told me anything. Are you going to?"

"I think my eyes have been opened. The clones, they're human."

Aaron choked on his beer, sputtering and struggling for breath. Banging his fist against his chest to try and force the liquid out of his lungs, he finally, painfully, managed to draw a breath in. "Could you warn a guy before springing that little bit of craziness on him?" he croaked out, his throat sore.

"It's not crazy, Aaron. We've been lied to, brainwashed into thinking that they're little more than animals. But look at them, they're just like us."

He frowned, taking a sip of beer to keep from having to reply right away. He repeated the words again and again in his mind. His brother, really and truly, had lost his mind.

"And you're what? Their ambassador?" just saying the words felt ridiculous.

Saber nodded. "I am. Sort of. I don't know. It's all so confusing."

"And the human you murdered?"

"I lost it. You know the nightmares. It was like I was back in it. I couldn't stop. I think it has something to do with Royce... the man I saw today... he could have murdered someone too. I saw myself in him."

Aaron's phone chimed, distracting him for a moment from the conversation—though bombshell would probably be more accurate.

On my way. See you in 5. -Kristin

He set the phone aside. He'd forgotten she was coming, and as much as he wanted to be happy about it, he worried. Saber wasn't exactly the easiest subject for her. To be face-to-face with him again… should he warn her?

"Kristin's on her way." Aaron watched Saber's face for a reaction.

"That's great. How is she doing?"

"She's been better. She…" he trailed off.

"I scare her."

Aaron nodded.

Standing up, Saber smiled and swallowed back the last of his beer. "No need to say anymore. I'll go to my room, check on Pilar."

"How is she?"

"Sleeping. It took a lot out of her, but she'll be okay. I think she's stronger than we realize."

Saber started walking down the hall to his room.

"Saber?"

He paused and turned back.

"Thank you for understanding. Do you mind if I try to explain things to Kristin? She sympathizes with the clones… maybe she'll be more accepting of you if she realizes—"

Saber's shaking head cut him short.

"Why not?"

"The less she knows, the less she's involved, the better. Things are going to be changing, Aaron. And change never comes smoothly."

Saber's words left a chill in the room as he turned and continued walking away. Aaron sat, lost in thought, until the lift chimed in a request for access to the apartment. Getting up, he walked to the door and opened it, wrapping Kristin in a hug before she could even offer a greeting.

"What's all this about?" asked Kristin, pushing him away.

"Sorry, I had a rough day."

"We agreed to take things slow."

"Friends hug."

"And that's all this is? A friend hug?"

Aaron held up his hands in surrender "Of course." Though he certainly wouldn't have minded it being more.

Kristin's musical laugh filled the apartment, and seemed to dispel the chill in the air that Saber's presence had left.

CHAPTER TWENTY-THREE

Saber August

Bang, bang, bang! Saber groaned, sitting up on the couch he had fallen asleep on last night. He looked to his bed where Pilar still slept, curled on her side, her shoulders rising and falling at a slow, steady cadence.

The pounding continued, another three in a row, urgent and insistent. "Saber, you need to get up. Now," came Aaron's muffled voice through the door.

Pilar began to stir, and another series of bangs had her sitting up and rubbing her eyes, looking around the room in sleepy confusion until her gaze fell on Saber.

"What's going on?" she asked, her voice raspy from sleep and yesterday's trauma.

"I'm up!" Saber called, shrugging in response to Pilar's question.

Getting up, Saber walked to the door and opened it, putting him face to face with his brother. Aaron still wore the clothes he had on last night, bags under his eyes, and his hair disheveled.

"You look terrible," Saber chuckled. "Up all night?"

"I just walked Kristin to her car. We talked. But that's not really what's important right now. You need to go."

Saber frowned. Aaron looked agitated and scared. Pilar walked up, resting her hand on his shoulder. "What's wrong, Aaron?" she asked. Just hearing her speak with her scratchy, pained voice had rage rising up in Saber again.

"There are cops below; they'll be on their way up any minute. You need to go."

Saber's heart pounded, and he nodded mutely, repeating the words in his mind a few times until they sunk in. They were here for him. Jumping into action, Saber started running around the room, grabbing a suitcase from his closet and throwing it on the bed, then tossing various clothes in, and other items he felt he might want or need.

Pilar had walked out onto the balcony, presumably to look below, but returned to the room within seconds. "No time," she said, grabbing Saber's hand and leading him out of the room. "They're heading in."

Saber followed her obediently, Aaron walking beside. At the lift, she pressed the call button, and they waited anxiously for the doors to open. Saber's heart beat in his chest like a war drum, fast and loud, and his blood rushed through his ears like a torrential river. All he could think was that the lift could be carrying up his potential captors right now, and he'd be playing right into their hands.

The whole thought process only took a second, and the lift chimed, opening up to reveal an empty pod. The air escaped his lungs in one big whoosh.

Pilar immediately entered the lift, pulling Saber along with her, then they turned to face Aaron. Saber pressed the door-open button. The cops couldn't get here while the lift was in use—they had a few minutes before an override would force it down.

"Thank you, Aaron."

"For what?"

"For warning us. With everything that's been going on—"

Aaron cut him off. "We're brothers, Saber. No matter what you do, I'll look out for you."

He dug into his pocket and held out a car key. "Take my car. It'll be less conspicuous than yours."

Saber accepted the gift and handed his own key and cell phone to Aaron. He wouldn't take it with him. "You just want my sweet ride," he joked.

Aaron laughed. "You figured me out."

He stepped forward, pulling Saber into an embrace. Saber stiffened, surprised, then relaxed into his brother's arms and returned the gesture of affection. The hug was quick, just enough to convey the love they both felt, then they stepped apart, Aaron backing out of the lift.

"Whatever happens, stay out of it, okay? Keep yourself distanced from Grandfather. Things are about to change, and change doesn't come without pain. I don't want you getting hurt."

Aaron nodded. "I'll be careful."

Saber let go of the button that had been telling the lift to keep the doors open, and they now began to shut. Aaron held up his arm in farewell, then the doors hissed shut and the lift rocketed upwards.

He brushed a tear from his eye, and took Pilar's hand. This could very well be the last time they ever spoke. Did Aaron realize that? If he didn't, he would soon find out.

He felt Pilar squeeze his hand, and he squeezed back, silently letting her know that he was okay.

The lift opened seconds later to reveal the dim carport where Saber's and Aaron's cars were kept. He strode through the concrete room, his footsteps echoing, but paused at his car. Touching the smooth metal exterior of the hood, he brushed his fingers along it.

"We have to go," urged Pilar in a soft voice. Saber nodded, walked the rest of the way to Aaron's car, and climbed in. There was no time for chivalry; Pilar walked around and opened her own door, joining him.

The instant the door clicked shut, Saber began lifting the car and directing it towards the still opening hatch where a patch of dark sky could be seen.

Once out, he punched the gas and sped forward. The skies were mostly abandoned at this time of the morning, and a quick glance down at the dash told Saber it was only 5:30 am. The sun was just beginning to peek over the horizon, giving the sky a soft pink glow, but the moon could still be seen, dimly holding on to its place in the sky for a few moments longer.

It seemed strange to Saber that the police would raid so early in the morning—which could only mean Royce sent them. He told them that Saber had committed the murder, and he would have been the one to tell them to go before the sun was even up. Was that his way of running Saber out of town? Or did he truly want him behind bars where he could be controlled?

"What about the border?" asked Pilar, speaking for the first time since they'd gotten into the vehicle.

"They don't check people going out, just coming in," he replied, sounding a whole lot more confident about the situation than he felt.

She nodded and turned back to stare out the window at the buildings streaking past at light speed.

Satisfied that she had nothing more to say, Saber returned his gaze ahead, his attention anywhere but on driving. It began to hit him what all this meant. He'd never return to this thriving metropolis. Instead of a prince, the rebellion was getting a fugitive. He'd walked away from his job, his family, his status, and now they were about to get locked out of the Central system.

Not just locked out, run out. And he had to hope and pray that Royce hadn't sent a bulletin to the wall calling for his arrest.

Minutes later, they pulled up to the huge gate—which was actually a force field—that stretched higher than every building, except for Frontier Industries. Frontier had at least fifty feet on the wall, and the building cast a shadow across the force field.

Lowering his altitude to about midway up the wall, Saber pulled up to a platform and rolled down his window. The platform was attached to a guardhouse, built directly into the wall. Identical checkpoints could be found all along the wall at regular intervals.

A guard walked up, staring down at his tablet as he read what was likely the vehicle information for Aaron's car.

Saber's heart beat wildly in his chest, and he hoped it was just his imagination that made it seem so loud.

"What's your purpose for visiting the Outer system?" the guard asked, reciting off the line he probably gave hundreds of times a day, without even a glance up from his tablet.

"Just dropping her back off at home," replied Saber with a wink.

The border guard looked up for the first time since he'd walked over, and peered in at Pilar—looking every bit the part of a humble clone.

"Isn't she cute?" asked Saber, smiling and stroking her hand.

The guard chuckled, tapping away at the tablet again. "Aren't they all? Go on through, Mr. August, and have a great day," he said, making one last motion on the tablet that caused the force-field to shimmer and open a section just large enough for Saber to drive through.

He tipped his head and pulled slowly forward. Once through, the force field snapped back in place, cutting them off from the Central system. Saber heard Pilar let out a breath of air, and he took her hand, squeezing it.

"Home free," he said, much more jovially than he felt. Despite his relief, he felt a sense of loss over leaving everything he knew behind.

"I can't believe you let that guard think I was an escort," growled Pilar.

He shrugged. "Easiest explanation. It's not like he knows who you are."

Saber looked around. The Outer system was a darker world. The last time he'd been in here, it had been at night, and he hadn't been struck by the dreariness of it all. But now, as the sun rose steadily, the depressing nature of the clone's world became all too apparent. Where the Central system was made up of sleek angles, vibrant colors, and shining lights; the Outer system was covered in a layer of smog from the factories, the only color to be seen was gray, and the only shapes were sharp, hard squares. Immediately, a weight fell on Saber's shoulders, and a sense of desperation filled him. All sense of hope was checked in at the gate, and he was left with only a deep and foreboding emptiness.

"Take a left here," Pilar directed, as Saber approached an intersection.

She directed Saber down a maze of dark streets, finally pulling in front of a three-storey brick building.

"This is my place."

Saber held the car steady, hovering in place. "What do I do with the car?" He didn't want to park it on the street, that was just asking for it to be robbed or vandalized— not to mention giving Royce a big 'X marks the spot' for Saber's location.

"I'm going to give Mark and Tyler a call; we'll meet them at the old factory and stash your car there."

Saber brought the car down to rest on the pitted and potholed pavement outside her building. Pilar unbuckled her seatbelt and looked at him, reaching out and stroking his face.

"I'll be right back."

She leaned forward and kissed him, her soft lips melding with his. But he couldn't find it in him to kiss her back. *I've destroyed my life, and Pilar's,* he thought.

He could see the hurt and questioning in her eyes as she pulled away, but she didn't say anything as she got out of the car and entered the building, disappearing from sight.

She was only gone a handful of minutes before she burst out of the doors at a jog and approached the car.

"Let's go," she said, climbing in.

CHAPTER TWENTY-FOUR

Aaron August

Aaron watched the lift doors close on Saber and Pilar, then went to the kitchen and sat at the table, waiting for the police to make their arrival. A sense of loss filled him, and left him feeling empty. *This isn't goodbye,* he thought. *Saber will return once he's cleared. Grandfather isn't a monster; he'll come through for Saber.*

Aaron counted down the seconds. Pilar and Saber would have made it to the carport by the time Aaron sat down at the table. Since then, five seconds had passed. It took ten to get from the 49th floor down to the lobby. Give a generous ten seconds for the police to load into the lift, and another ten to get up. Thirty measly seconds from the time Aaron sat down, to when the lift door would ding to announce the arrival of the police. Like clockwork, the chime filled the apartment, and was followed by the steady cadence of marching feet pouring in the apartment and spreading out, surrounding Aaron.

Aaron stood up slowly, and walked towards the one that wore the captain's hat and insignia. "Can I help you?"

"We have a warrant for the arrest of Saber August."

Aaron looked around, gesturing with his hands at the dozen or so cops that filled the room. "And you felt the need to take the entire department to pick up a playboy scientist?"

By the frown on the cop's face, Aaron could tell he had no interest in putting up with his smart attitude.

"Is Mr. August here, or not?"

Aaron smirked. "Depends who you mean by Mr. August. I have been referred to as Mr. August on occasion. Am I the man you're looking for?"

The cop growled. "Don't be smart with me. Your grandfather authorized me to take you into custody should you prove less than cooperative."

Aaron frowned, but quickly hid it with a smile of false bravado. The cop must be bluffing. Grandfather would never authorize his arrest.

"I'm afraid you just missed him. He's off flying into the sunrise with some pretty redhead. You know how he is, always impressing the ladies. I'm sure you've seen the tabloids."

The cop took a threatening step forward, and Aaron felt a thrill of fear pass through him. Maybe he'd pushed him too far. "I don't know where he went," he added, before the cop could ask.

It must have been what he wanted to hear, because without a word, he put his hand in the air and motioned for all the other uniformed men and women to follow him back into the lift. They crammed in like a can of sardines, and Aaron had to hold back his laughter until the lift door closed.

As soon as he was alone, the amusement of the situation faded and he felt suddenly more alone than he ever had in his life. Pulling his phone out of his pocket, he walked back to the couch and sat down, dialing Kristin.

"Miss me already?" her voice carried through the airwaves and into Aaron's ear. "I just walked through my door."

"My grandfather tried to have Saber arrested."

"What?" she asked, her voice turning from teasing and happy to confused and scared.

"He's okay, he had to run, though."

"I'm already heading back out the door. I'll be right there and you can give me the whole story."

Aaron didn't need to go further into detail until she got here. Kristin couldn't handle Aaron being there for her, but she rushed over to be the supportive friend, and the shoulder to lean on, without a moment of hesitation.

He paced restlessly, starting in the living room and then going up the hallway to his bedroom, outside, then back in again. He never thought of the apartment as small before—quite the opposite, it was huge—but right now, it felt cramped and confining.

Finally, the lift dinged and Aaron pressed a button on his phone, granting her access.

Walking in, she strode straight for him and wrapped him in a hug. She didn't say anything.

He reveled in the comfort of her arms wrapped protectively around him. Thoughts of Saber, his confusion and loss slowly drifted away, as if squeezed out by Kristin's arms. Only she filled his mind. The fruity scent of her hair, the way it tickled his lips and chin just a little, her head fitting right under his chin like a puzzle piece. He could feel his breathing sync with hers. *This is the woman for me*—no one else could affect him like Kristin Pierce.

She pulled out of the hug all too soon, and stepped back, putting some distance between them. Probably wise, because at the rate Aaron's thoughts were going, he was only seconds away from thinking it was a good idea to kiss her.

"Are you okay?" she asked the one question that Aaron had no answer prepared for.

His thoughts returned to him, his feelings caused by the morning's events crashing back like the Red Sea walls that Moses had held back. Slowly, he shook his head. No, he wasn't okay. He hadn't been okay since this whole mess started.

Walking into the living room, Kristin following close behind, he sat down on the couch. He tried to swallow back the emotion that threatened to overcome him, but now that the walls had been broken down, they weren't going to leave him alone until he talked about it.

Kristin sat next to him on the couch, close enough for their knees to touch. She brought her legs up and curled them beneath her, getting comfortable.

"What happened?"

Aaron explained everything, from Saber coming home yesterday with a clone, and not telling Kristin that they were here last night, to his grandfather's attack on Pilar, and finally dealing with a dozen cops filling his penthouse. Now that he reiterated it, he realized how crazy the last 24 hours had been.

"So he's gone? Not just taking a break like he did after the… incident?"

Aaron didn't blame her for avoiding the word murder. He nodded. "I don't know to where, but I don't think he'll be back. Not for a long time anyway."

"Maybe that's a good thing, putting distance between him and your grandfather, and giving it time to settle down."

She was right, if Saber had any intention of allowing things to settle down. "I don't think settling down is going to happen. Something else is going on, something big. Saber warned me to stay out of whatever would happen next."

"What does that mean?"

"I don't know. I almost wish Saber would just disappear and live a quiet life somewhere far away. I know I shouldn't think that way, but…" he trailed off and Kristin took his hand, squeezing it.

"It's not wrong to feel that way."

"He's my brother."

"And you just want what's best for him."

They fell into silence. Aaron didn't know what else to say. Words wouldn't make him feel any less guilty, nor could they take away the pain of his brother leaving.

Finally, Aaron spoke, his thoughts leaving Saber and going back to Kristin. "What happened to you?"

He tread dangerous ground, after the way she'd reacted to him trying to make a connection before, but he needed to know. He wanted to know what he was getting into, and most of all, he wanted to help. She'd sat here and listened to his pains and struggles. He wanted to do the same for her.

Her face clouded and her eyes looked into the distance, as if watching memories on the wall behind

Aaron. She didn't look at him while she spoke. Instead, she continued to look past him, squeezing each finger on her right hand in turn, again and again.

"I grew up in a decidedly middle-class family. We had what we needed, but we never had more than enough. It was a good life, I can't really complain." She paused, and Aaron could see her eyes were far away, in a place he'd never visited.

"My dad walked out on us when I was sixteen. My mom expected me to step up and help. I guess, in my adolescent selfishness, it was too much to put on my shoulders. Looking back now, though, it was a necessity.

"I turned to boys, usually older or in more powerful positions, for the escape I needed. I've worked hard to leave that life behind, Aaron. I don't want to look for an escape anymore. I want to be able to live life as me. And you... well, you fit the pattern of power."

Aaron refrained from reaching out to her, knowing it would not be a welcome contact at the moment. She'd never gone through anything traumatic like he expected, but she carried a lot of bitterness towards her parents, and herself.

"That's why you won't let me get close to you?"

"Men walk out. Maybe now, maybe twenty years from now. Love isn't real, and it most certainly doesn't last." Kristin spat out the words with such vehemence, such anger, that Aaron could see the scars running deep under her skin.

He couldn't help but reach out for her. He moved closer, wrapping his arms around her and pulling her up against him. "I won't do that."

"You will," she cried, tears running down her face, makeup washing away with it.

"I will never walk out on you, I can't," he whispered against her hair.

He wanted to take her pain away. He wanted to make her trust him. He didn't want to fix her; he wanted to make her whole.

She pulled in closer to him, and cried against his chest. She didn't push him away, and that was a start. He wouldn't ask anything more of her today, not when she'd already given so much. So he held her, held her when his legs grew numb and his arms ached from holding her. But he refused to let go, refused to falter and prove to her that men always fail, even in the smallest things. He would be the one man in her life that would be there for her. He would give her the happily ever after that she deserved.

CHAPTER TWENTY-FIVE

Saber August

Saber drove the shadowed city streets to the old factory where they met Tyler and Mark only a few nights ago. They pulled up outside a large shipping door. The alley was dark despite the sun hanging high in the sky.

Pilar leapt out of the car and walked to the shipping door, opening it by using the chain hanging beside it. She moved it up inch by inch until Saber could park his car inside.

Stepping out, he joined her in the vaulted concrete room.

"You okay?" she asked.

No, I'm not. Everything he knew had been ripped away in a matter of days. *Am I that obvious?*

"I'm never going back, am I?"

She put her arm around him and pulled him close, resting her head against his chest. She said nothing, just held him, all the confirmation he needed in that one move.

"We better get to the back room," she said.

They walked down the long hall they'd travelled only a few days ago, their footsteps echoing in the empty, cavernous building.

"Why can't we just meet at someone's apartment instead of this creepy abandoned building?" grumbled Saber, listening to the drip, drip of moisture falling off cold steel pipes and forming puddles on the musty concrete floor.

"It's all Tyler's idea. He's . . . paranoid."

Saber snorted. "He's a lot of things."

"Don't say anything too loudly, he could hear you."

"There is no way he beat us here—"

"He lives two buildings away."

"Oh."

Saber fell silent, but he caught the edges of a smile playing on Pilar's lips. At least she still managed to keep a little lightness in a situation that was steadily becoming darker and heavier.

Stepping into the abandoned office, they found Tyler and Mark already waiting. Mark leaned against the wall, smoking a cigarette.

"Nice of you to join us," said Tyler, a hint of bitterness in his voice.

"The situation has picked up a lot faster than we thought."

"And what exactly does that mean?" asked Tyler, pacing the room, his agitation apparent. "What did your boyfriend do to mess everything up so quickly?"

Mark continued to smoke. Saber watched his face. He stood impassive, observing the exchange between Pilar and Tyler with a keen eye. Saber saw now that if he needed someone level-headed and calm, Mark would be that ally.

A blush of anger spread across Pilar's face and Saber reached for her hand, taking it in his and squeezing it, hoping she'd understand the silent plea to calm down.

"He did what he was supposed to, but apparently family ties don't run as deeply as we'd hoped," she bit back.

"What's that supposed to mean?"

Saber looked at Pilar. Her eyes blazed and she held her shoulders stiff and square. She looked like she was about to unleash a tirade on Tyler that was not at all called for. Apparently the situation hit Pilar harder than he thought.

"It means Royce Williams kicked me out of my job, my home, cut me off, and after a few hours sent the cops after me," Saber cut in, not giving Pilar a chance to retort.

"So you pushed him too far and screwed up the entire plan."

"You have no idea what you're talking about, Tyler. None at all. So keep your mouth shut. Have you ever stepped foot into the Central system? Ever? Don't talk about things you know nothing about," exploded Pilar.

Mark flicked ashes from the end of his cigarette, and stepped into the small circle of charged emotions.

"Put away your temper, Pilar."

"Me, Mark? Tyler—"

"Stop. Both of you. Tyler is always a jerk."

Tyler opened his mouth to protest, but Mark held up his hand. "No, it's true. But I expect more of you, Pilar. So put away your petty feelings and let's hear what Saber has to say. That's why we brought him in, isn't it? The inside scoop?"

Tyler scowled angrily and walked out of the small circle, taking Mark's place leaning against the wall, his arms across his chest, sulking.

Pilar looked up at Saber. He squared his shoulder. He felt fired up again for the cause. "He backed us up against a wall. We have to prove to him that we're not bluffing."

Tyler snorted.

"You have something to say?" Pilar asked, turning on him with blazing eyes. Saber wondered if all clones had that temper, or if it was just her.

He shrugged in response and remained silent.

"It's time to send a message," continued Saber.

"What exactly do you have in mind?" asked Mark.

Saber looked at Pilar. She walked both worlds. She knew better than he what they could pull off, and what would send the message they wanted to Royce. "Pilar? Any ideas?"

"I don't really know . . ." she trailed off, starting to pace the room. Saber watched her, silent. Her lips moved, but no sound came out. She paused, lifted her eyes to the ceiling, then shook her head and continued to pace.

This went on for some time. Saber joined Tyler, leaning against the wall, and finally Mark came too.

"Are we going to just wait?"

Saber cut off Tyler, holding up his hand. "Give her a chance."

"Water," Pilar said.

His attention snapped to her. "What?"

She turned to face them and walked up. "The water. We attack their water supply."

"Okay, continue," offered Mark.

"Tyler, you work at the water filtration plant."

Tyler perked up. The idea of being involved seemed to grab his attention, and maybe even made him happy, but Saber had a hard time reading him.

"If we contaminate the water—nothing dangerous, just make a lot of people uncomfortably sick—we'll grab their attention. We'll show them that we hold the power over one of the basest of needs."

She looked up at Saber for approval. He'd been silent, listening and contemplating. It was a good plan, but it wouldn't be enough.

"I can do that. And when we get the attention we want?"

"Then I come in," said Saber, not willing to tell Pilar her plan wasn't enough. They could start here, but it would have to build up a lot more before Royce took notice. He didn't care about a stomach bug. If he didn't care, Royce definitely wouldn't.

"Exactly. Saber is a face they recognize, that they associate with power. He may have fallen from his grandfather's graces, but people don't just let go of a lifetime of ideas in one week. What he says will still be more accepted than whatever any of us say."

Tyler nodded. "Pretty good plan, I'll admit."

Pilar smiled. "Mark?"

He nodded, sucking back on his cigarette. "It's a great plan."

Saber shook his head. He couldn't lie to her. "It's a start. Nothing more."

"A start? Flexing our muscles like this could be enough—"

Saber cut her off, raising his hands in a gesture of surrender. "It's a good plan, Pilar. It just won't be enough. I hope it is, but it won't be. You don't know Royce like I do. He's stubborn and ruthless. A little bit of discomfort will not be enough to change his mind. This will get his attention, nothing more."

She nodded. "Tyler, get the wheels in motion. Let us know when it's about to go down, we'll be ready."

"We'll meet again when things start moving," said Tyler.

He walked out of the room, Mark following close behind. He paused in the doorway though, and turned back. "Tyler is tough, but he's a good guy."

Saber smiled. He didn't know if Mark spoke to him or Pilar, but he was right. Tyler was a good guy, and Pilar probably knew it too, or she wouldn't be working with him. They just clashed. In the end, they all wanted the same thing, so everyone would temporarily put their differences aside for the greater good. Tyler had done it by accepting Saber, Pilar would do it by cooperating with Tyler.

CHAPTER TWENTY-SIX

Aaron August

"Are you going to tell your parents about what your grandfather did to Saber?" asked Kristin at dinner that night.

Aaron shrugged. "I don't know, I have very little to do with them lately."

"Why?"

"After I started university, we just... drifted. We do a Sunday night dinner with them always, but it's usually superficial and distant."

Aaron hadn't really thought about his relationship with his parents, but he had to admit that it wasn't what it should be. Then again, nothing about the August-Williams household was what it should be.

"Everything has always been about my grandfather. Saber's whole life revolved around him. For as long as I can remember, Saber was being groomed to inherit Frontier Industries and the position of prime minister. At fifteen he went to live with Grandfather, and began

162

interning at Frontier." Aaron paused to take a few bites of his food.

"And you?"

"I wanted to be just like my big brother, of course," Aaron replied around a mouthful of mashed potatoes.

He swallowed, then continued. "I did everything I could to gain my grandfather's attention. If he said jump, I asked how high. When you are trying so hard to escape your brother's shadow and gain your grandfather's approval, your parents kinda fall by the wayside."

"I can see that. But they must want to know what's going on in your lives?"

"I'm sure Grandfather already talked to them. He wouldn't let his daughter wonder where her precious Saber had gone." He practically spat the words out as bitterness caused by his brother's status overcame him. Guilt rose up, and he shook his head. "I'm sorry, I shouldn't talk like that. I love Saber, I really do. Everyone loves him. Maybe that's the problem. No one loves me."

"That's not true." Kristin reached forward and took his hand. "I chose you, didn't I?"

"Helps that Saber committed a crime in front of you."

She smiled, but shook her head. "No, I wasn't ever interested in him. Remember the first night we met? I chose you, not him."

"And then pushed me away."

"Because you are everything I'm against!"

Aaron chuckled and collected the now empty plates, bringing them to the counter. "But you don't hold my status, or who my grandfather is, against me anymore."

She blushed. "You were quite insistent that I give you a chance."

"And?"

She shrugged. "So far, I'm glad I did. But I'm just taking it day-by-day."

Aaron approached her, placing his arms around her waist and pulling her close, in what was most definitely not just a friendly hug.

"Can I kiss you then?" he whispered as she looked up at him with wide eyes.

Her lips upturned slightly and she nodded. Aaron didn't need any more encouragement than that. He dropped his head down and placed his lips on hers. He pressed firmly, but didn't ask for more. Drawing back, he smiled.

"Was that slow enough for you?" he breathed out.

She nodded. "Mmmmhmmm."

"Good, cause I've been wanting to do that since I met you."

Pulling away, Kristin ran her hand through her hair and let out a nervous giggle.

I shouldn't have said that. I should have left it at the kiss and kept my big mouth shut.

"Sorry, I, uh—"

"I should go," said Kristin, grabbing her jacket off the couch.

Aaron sighed. "Okay, I'll walk you to your car."

He walked to the lift and pressed the call button. Kristin walked up beside him, her jacket slung over the crook of her arm. Her hand grazed against Aaron's and he took it, feeling the warmth of her skin against his. He didn't say anything, just led her into the lift when the door opened.

They rode down together in silence, right up until they walked to Kristin's car parked on the street. Opening the door for her, Aaron let her hand go as she slid in.

"Drive safe," he said, not knowing what else to say.

"I'll call you, Aaron. It was nice, really nice…I just need some time to think."

He smiled. He couldn't be mad at her. She had been nothing but straightforward.

"I know, day by day." He leaned down and placed a kiss on her forehead, then backed away and closed the car door.

He watched her drive away, all the while thinking that it might be day by day for her, but right now he was starting to think forever.

CHAPTER TWENTY-SEVEN

Saber August

Saber walked home with Pilar. He reluctantly left Aaron's car behind in the abandoned, unprotected building, but it would be safer there than parked on the street. Outside Pilar's apartment it would be a giant billboard announcing his location. He didn't know if his warrant would follow him here, or if it would even matter, but it never hurt to take precautions. As it was right now, only Royce could guess where he was.

He felt elated though. The meeting had done a lot to make him feel normal again.

He hadn't felt like himself since he'd lost control. He'd lost his power that night, and had become a precautionary tale to be told to children when they didn't listen to their parents. But here, he'd found it back. In helping to lead a rebellion, in showing Royce Williams that he was someone to be reckoned with, he'd gain his position back. He wouldn't surrender easily.

The streets that Pilar led Saber down had seen better days. Manhole covers were missing and steam escaped. The pavement was pitted, crumbling in places, and in some spots the concrete was completely missing until the rebar was visible.

Saber looked around as if he was in another world, and he might as well have been. He looked at Pilar, but she walked with her eyes straight ahead. She didn't glance all around her like he did, taking in all the sights and sounds. There were some people around, all carbon copies of each other except for the clothes they wore and the way they chose to present themselves. It was strange to see only two different faces walking the streets. But what was even stranger was all the looks he was receiving. Everyone stared, and it wasn't like the way he was used to back home; as a celebrity. Here it was a cautious curiosity. Clones looked, but they didn't stop, they didn't talk, they just looked.

Saber suddenly felt uncomfortable. He'd thought he could be one of these people, but he wasn't. His genetic makeup was different, his face was different, and here, that made you an outsider.

He reached for Pilar's hand, and squeezed it tightly. *I am not alone,* he thought. *I have Pilar.*

When they made it to her apartment building, they walked through the large glass front doors and into a small lobby. The tile had seen better days. A lot of them were chipped, and the color worn out from years and years of traffic following the same path across them. It was dark, a florescent light flickered overhead—weren't those obsolete for years now?—giving the room an eeriness to it. Saber looked around for the telltale metal doors of a lift, but he didn't see any. The walls were pretty much bare, actually.

Pilar tugged at his hand. "Coming?" she asked, and led him towards a staircase.

"Is the lift broken?"

She laughed. "There is no lift in this building."

Well, that explained why he couldn't find it. But still . . . no lift? He'd never been in a building without one. The last time he'd done stairs was in Royce's home. The stubborn old man refused to blemish the architecture of his turn-of-the-century mansion with a lift.

Pilar led him up one flight of stairs and then down a musty smelling hall with bright orange carpet.

"You should fire your decorator," he said, trying to lighten the mood.

Pilar snorted and unlocked her apartment door, opening it wide to admit them.

"Yeah, I'll bring it up with the maintenance crew. Well, this is it; home sweet home."

Saber stepped inside and looked around. It was a small single room apartment with a double bed in the far corner near the only window. He turned a 360 in the middle of the room and looked back at her. She'd done well with what she had to work with. It was decorated nicely. The furniture looked like decent quality—nothing compared to what he was used to, but he was impressed none-the-less. A privacy shade was positioned near the bed in an attempt to partition it off from the rest of the apartment. Some artwork hung on the walls. It was certainly not a dump in any respect, just sparse.

"Not exactly what you're used to, I guess. But it's a roof, right?"

Saber pulled her into a hug, and kissed her forehead. "It's great. I don't need any more than this."

He could feel her smiling against his chest, and for the first time since leaving the Central system this morning, he felt like everything would be okay. He let her go and walked into the kitchen, rummaging through cupboards. He hadn't eaten anything yet today, and it was already midday.

"What are you doing?"

Saber yanked open the fridge door and peered inside. The contents were sparse; a reflection of the rest of the apartment, or maybe just the way Pilar lived.

"Finding something to eat. Don't you have any food?"

Pilar shook her head. "Do you think I cook? There's a great Chinese kitchen down the street. We could go there."

"No. I'd rather stay in for the rest of the day. This morning has been . . . insane. It'd be nice to just relax at home."

"Then the pickings are slim."

"That's okay, I'll throw something together," said Saber, still rummaging through cupboards, pulling out some boxes of dried noodles. In the fridge, he pulled out some milk and cheese, and in the freezer he found some frozen vegetables. He looked around for meat, but could only find an old frozen brick of protein substitute. Tofu. He hated the stuff.

"They seriously make you eat this?"

Pilar blushed and he realized he'd said something wrong. He'd just insulted her way of life, something she had very little control over. They didn't make money; they were given what they needed to live off of. The restaurants in the Outer system were more akin to the soup kitchens for the homeless in years past. They were government funded and strictly monitored.

"I'm sorry. I didn't think."

"It's okay. It's been a long day."

Saber got busy in the kitchen, clattering through the few pots in search of the tools he needed.

He didn't cook often at home, but when he did he enjoyed it.

Forty minutes later he set a plate of food in front of Pilar on the coffee table.

"No kitchen table?" he asked.

"I didn't think it was necessary when it's only me."

Saber took a bite of the cheesy pasta he'd whipped together. Despite the protein replacement, it was definitely more than edible. It was delicious. But that might be his hunger's opinion.

He paused in his enjoyment to watch Pilar's reaction as she gingerly placed a forkful in her mouth. She chewed and swallowed, then nodded her approval.

"Not bad. I think we found you a job."

"Helping a rebellion isn't a big enough job already?"

"We just keep you around for a recognizable face, I'm doing all the real work here," she teased.

"Easy. We're partners in this."

Pilar nodded and took another bite. "Whatever helps you sleep at night," she muttered around a mouthful of food.

He chuckled and returned to his food. This is what he liked about her. She was sassy, full of life.

"This isn't how I wanted all this to go down," she said. The subject had changed, but he knew instantly she was referring to the situation with Royce, and being run out of the Central system.

"Doesn't matter what you want. In the end, Royce made the call. He betrayed me. He abandoned me. It's *his* fault I lost everything."

Pilar's eyes fell and, as if she had flicked a switch, his heart sunk. He could never say the right things. He wasn't used to thinking about a girl's feelings and nurturing a relationship. He was used to saying goodbye. He was good at goodbye. But that wasn't an option with Pilar. He could never say those words to her.

He reached out and stroked her cheek, brushing her hair back. "I didn't lose everything, though. I gained you. And I'd give everything up again if it meant I got to keep you in my life."

The way her eyes lit up, and she leapt forward onto him, pushing him down into the couch and kissing him fiercely, told him he'd said the right thing. He wrapped his arms around her and pulled her tightly against him, kissing her back. He could lose himself in her kisses. Forget all about everything else in life. Nothing else mattered but her.

But he couldn't allow that. Life had to be lived. He gently pushed her off of him, and sat up.

"I love it when you kiss me, but there are things that need to be talked about."

"Such as?"

"Living arrangements."

"My humble abode isn't good enough for you?"

"It's the only place I want to be. I just don't want to intrude."

"My couch makes a perfectly good bed, but if you'd rather, I can ask Tyler or Mark if they have room."

Saber raised an eyebrow. "No, that's alright. Your couch will do just fine. Now, with that out of the way, I want to talk about Tyler. Can we trust him? More importantly, can we trust him to contaminate the water safely?"

Her face immediately sobered. "He is a jerk, I'll be the first to admit it, but he can be trusted. He won't do anything dangerous or out of line."

"Maybe we should do a little legwork ourselves. Give him what we want to put into the water."

"I just told you he's fine, Saber!"

"I don't trust anyone who doesn't have loved ones on the other side of that wall."

Pilar's face clouded. He'd said something wrong, but he didn't have time to dwell on it, because she was nodding her agreement.

"Okay, we'll figure it out tomorrow. But, Saber, you need to decide how far you're willing to go. You said yourself that this isn't going to change Royce's mind, it's only going to get his attention. What *will* change his mind?"

"I don't know."

"Do you know what you're willing to sacrifice?"

Did he? He hadn't really thought that far ahead. But he wouldn't back down. In the end, it was his family that they were making war against, even if the rest of the human population was going to suffer. In the end, it would be his call. No one else would make the hard decisions but him. Tyler would be too eager, Mark too hesitant. Pilar, maybe, because of the years she'd spent beside Royce. She understood, to a certain degree. But there was still no one she loved on the other side of that wall. Somehow, he realized, he'd gotten into his mind that this was his revolt. He ran the show.

"We'll take it one step at a time. In the end, I'll make the call."

CHAPTER TWENTY-EIGHT

Aaron August

Aaron held Kristin's hand as they drove to his parents' home. With every second that passed, Kristin's hand gripped his harder.

"You're not nervous, are you?" he asked with a teasing grin.

"I'm starting to question my sanity for agreeing to this family dinner. I'm pretty sure meeting the parents is a bit more serious than day by day."

Aaron pulled up into the drive and put the car in park, but made no move to get out. He twisted in his seat, turning to face Kristin.

"That's why I was hesitant to ask. If you want, we can turn around and go home. No pressure. My mom will understand."

Kristin shook her head. "No, we're already here. And besides, I don't want to take from your family time. From what you say, there isn't enough of it as it is."

Aaron planted a kiss on top of her head. "Thank you. Now, be prepared for the dysfunction that is the August household."

Getting out, he walked around to the passenger side and opened the door for Kristin, offering his hand as she climbed out. If his mother had taught him and Saber anything, it was to be gentlemen. Holding her hand securely in his, he gently led her up the steps to his parents' front door and rang the doorbell.

It only took a moment for the door to slide aside and reveal a clone butler. Aaron wasn't sure of his name, but he greeted Aaron and Kristin, offered to take their jackets, and then led them to the living room where his parents and grandfather already sat, enjoying drinks and hors d'oeuvres before dinner.

Immediately, Sabrina, Aaron's mother, stood and walked to him. She drew Aaron into an embrace. He couldn't help but notice she looked older. Her skin was pale, her eyes rimmed red, and large dark bags hung under them that she tried to cover up with make-up. But she still walked tall, her shoulders upright and strong. To anyone who didn't know her, she looked impeccable. To Aaron, he saw someone struggling with the loss of her favorite son.

"I'm so glad you came," she said, drawing away.

"Mom, this is Kristin."

Kristin stepped forward, holding her hand out to shake Sabrina's, but she pulled her into an embrace.

"Welcome to our home, Kristin. It's so nice to meet you. I think you're the first girl either of our sons has ever brought home."

Aaron could feel a flush rising up his neck. Leave it to his mother to not only embarrass him, but make it seem like this was a bigger deal than it was. Hopefully she wouldn't scare Kristin away by the end of the evening.

When Sabrina let Kristin go, Aaron led her around to the other inhabitants of the room.

"Kristin, this is my father, Kellan."

Kellan looked to be holding up surprisingly well compared to his wife. He looked as strong and youthful as ever for his fifty years. Gray scattered throughout his hair, mostly along the hairline, offering him a dignified maturity, rather than agedness. He was lean and muscled from many hours spent on a rowing machine. There was no sign of stress caused by his eldest son in the man's face or demeanor.

Kellan stood, shaking hands with Kristin. "It's a pleasure to meet you, Kristin. Can I get you a drink?"

"Wine, please."

"Red or white?"

"Red, thank you."

Kellan snapped his fingers at a clone that the Augusts employed—employed was a loose term since they weren't paid in the strictest sense, but more rented from the government—and motioned him towards the bar. "Red wine for the lady," he commanded.

"Aaron?"

"A beer for me, thank you," he said to the clone, finding himself unable to treat the clone as nothing more than a robot after meeting Pilar. Was this how Saber felt? Was this what had changed within him?

Aaron led Kristin to Royce, who sat stalwart in a large, faux leather wing backed chair. You would have thought it was a throne and he a king.

"I don't suppose you need me to introduce my grandfather, Royce Williams."

Kristin offered her hand, and shook with Royce, meeting his eyes boldly. There weren't many people so bold as to do that, and Aaron observed their interaction with pride. Good, she could handle his family, even after everything she knew Royce had done, yet would never own up to. Even now, he sat in Sabrina and Kellan's living room with a smile on his face and a drink in his hand, pretending like he had nothing to do with running their oldest son out of the Central system. Did they know he had been the one to put out the warrant for Saber's arrest? Or had he played the innocent?

"A pleasure, miss…"

"Pierce, Sir," she replied, a smile playing on her lips.

"Miss Pierce. It takes a special woman to handle my grandson. Are you sure you're up for it?"

Aaron shot his grandfather a look, but Royce likely didn't see it—he locked gazes with Kristin in a battle of wills. It seemed he was testing her, trying to see her true mettle.

"If your grandson proves himself worthy, I can handle it."

Royce raised his eyebrow, and Aaron knew he was probably displaying a mirror expression at Kristin's words. To say her audacity surprised him would be an understatement. Meek, scared, Kristin, who wasn't even willing to fully commit to a relationship, handled herself well in a room with the most powerful man in the world. Maybe she could cut it with his family after all.

Finally, Royce cracked a smile and chuckled. "I think you'll do alright."

The clone returned with the drinks for Aaron and Kristin, and set them on the table by the vacant loveseat. Aaron led Kristin there, and they sat, both reaching for their drinks simultaneously.

The rest of the evening was much more laid back, or at least Aaron thought so. He hoped Kristin felt the same. They spoke of trivial things, mostly about business. Royce and Kellan dominated the conversation, though Aaron could certainly hold his own in the discussions presented. You weren't raised in one of the most powerful families in the world without growing up with a keen understanding of business, money, and what makes the world turn round.

No one mentioned Saber the entire evening. It was as if he didn't exist. Aaron almost wanted to bring up his name to see what would happen, but instead he played along with his family's charade. At least for once he seemed to be getting attention. His mother couldn't get enough of Kristin. How did they meet? When did they meet? How serious were things—oh, but they must be serious if Aaron had brought her to meet the parents. Would they be seeing her next Sunday? What did she do for a living? What did she take in school? The questions shot out of Sabrina in rapid fire all evening and left Aaron's head spinning. He could only imagine Kristin's.

When they finally managed to collect their jackets and escape out the door, it was nearing midnight. As the door closed behind them, cutting off the smiles and waves from Kellan and Sabrina, Aaron and Kristin let out a simultaneous sigh.

"Well, that was interesting," offered Aaron with a smile, hoping that he wouldn't be hearing about how she needed a break on the way home.

He opened the car door.

"That's one way of putting it."

As the car lifted into the air, Aaron could feel Kristin's eyes on him. "What?" he asked.

"Nothing."

"You're staring at me."

"I am not."

"I can feel your eyes on me," he said with a chuckle, glancing at Kristin, her eyes now downcast and a blush creeping up her cheeks.

"I was just admiring you. You look a lot like your father, you know."

Aaron nodded. "I've heard that before."

"I can't believe I'm the first girl you took home to your family, and you didn't even warn me."

Aaron laughed. "Right. Well, I thought if I told you that, then you'd definitely refuse to come. You handled yourself well."

"I'm afraid of commitment, not parents. If they decided I wasn't good enough for you, it wouldn't be the end of the world. It would have given me an easy way out."

Aaron chuckled, but it was more a nervous reaction than one out of amusement. "I hope you're joking."

Kristin didn't reply, so he didn't push the matter, just glanced to see her staring out the car window. Good, he had her thinking. At least she knew *he* wasn't looking for an easy way out.

Dropping her off at the front door of her apartment building, Aaron leaned in and kissed her.

"I'll see you at school tomorrow?"

"Sure. Text me at lunch, I'll meet you. I have a project due tomorrow afternoon that I want to work on in the morning."

"Thanks for coming tonight, Kristin."

"I had fun. Good night."

She shut the door and Aaron watched her walk away into the brightly lit lobby. He idled until he saw her enter the lift, then flew away. He'd see her tomorrow, but he'd be missing her tonight. He was starting to miss her every moment they were apart, and that was dangerous. Very dangerous. Especially when she refused to commit at the level he wanted to.

CHAPTER TWENTY-NINE

Saber August

They waited just inside the water treatment plant. A skeleton crew of clones ran the place, hand-picked by Tyler as supporters of the movement. Saber checked the time for probably the tenth time in the last half hour. It was quarter after eleven now. The truck should be here any minute, providing everything went smoothly.

Pilar peered out the window, checking constantly. It was just the three of them; Pilar, himself, and Tyler at this stop. Mark and his girlfriend Gina waited at the laundry facility for the next step in the night's events.

Saber looked at Pilar for an indication that the truck was arriving. She glanced back at him, nodding slightly. Walking up beside her, he peered out the door. Yep, headlights approached, and it looked to be a large vehicle.

He walked back to Tyler. "This is it. Your guys are ready?"

Tyler nodded. "All the people on shift tonight I'd trust with my life, which is more than I can say about you."

Saber brushed off the comment. He didn't care what Tyler thought. He ran this show, and if he'd learned anything from Royce, it was that the people in charge didn't have to react to lesser people. Instead, he smiled and patted Tyler on the shoulder. "Then the feeling is mutual."

Tyler let out a growl and waved his hand to a couple clones working nearby. "Let's get this loading door open, boys."

A loud truck pulled up near the door, and Saber could hear it idling. He glanced at the time. He was right on schedule.

Tyler and one of his guys hauled on a chain, pulling the large overhead door up to admit the shipment. Saber couldn't wrap his head around the fact that the technology in the Outer system was from the dark ages. Some places had powerlifted doors, but the construction itself was outdated by at least a century.

With the door open, a loud beep, beep, beep of the truck backing up filled Saber's ears. This was it. This was step one. They'd get this stuff unloaded, and then they'd be half way to home free. They'd decided that they'd have the whole thing ready to go off in the morning, just before shift change, that way Saber could work the chemistry of it all, instead of depending on teaching Tyler. It was going to be a long night. He could already feel the exhaustion caused by the late hour and the tension of the circumstances wearing down on him, and the night was only just beginning.

What happened next was a blur. The truck opened and men flurried about, unloading the precious cargo.

They unloaded four tons of phenolphthalein—an acid base commonly used in laxatives—and placed it in the middle of the water treatment plant.

"If they decide to do a random inspection before we finish with this, we're all screwed," said Tyler, looking just a little stressed.

"You don't have to tell us," said Pilar, obviously on edge.

"It just means we have to move that much faster," said Saber calmly. And, for once, he wasn't faking it for everyone else's benefit. Half of the job was completed. Half. It was almost finished.

The driver, whom Pilar had informed him was named Ben, jumped out of the truck and approached them. He looked nervous. His eyes skittered around, looking from face to face.

"I need to get moving," he said. "Where's my next stop?"

Pilar opened her mouth to tell him, but Saber held up his hand and shook his head. He didn't trust this guy.

"How about you stay here? I'll take the truck to do the next pick-up. The less you know the better."

Pilar looked at him, frowning in confusion. It wasn't what they had planned, Saber knew that, but he went with the flow and thought on his feet. He trusted this Ben about as far as he could throw him. The way he glanced around, his eyes darting from place to place in a paranoid manner, made Saber feel uneasy. And when he reacted to what Saber had said with widening eyes and paling slightly, almost imperceptible if he hadn't been watching for it, told him that he'd made the right call.

"Pilar, you'll come with me."

As he walked towards the driver's side of the truck, Tyler trotted up beside him.

"What are you doing?" he hissed. "This isn't part of the plan."

"Plan has changed. Keep an eye on Ben, will you? I trust him even less than I trust you."

Tyler stopped in his tracks and glanced back at Ben. Saber didn't wait for him to respond, just climbed into the truck, Pilar already waiting in the passenger seat. He didn't know if Tyler would obey him or not, but the fact that he was concerned should have him curious enough to at least want to know *why* Saber thought the way he did.

Pushing the truck up into first gear, he pulled away from the building slowly. He could just hear the rumble of the overhead door closing behind him despite the loud purr of the truck's engine. Once they were speeding along the sky streets in fifth gear, Pilar spoke up.

"Why the change of plans?"

"I didn't trust him."

"I gathered as much, but why?"

"He seemed edgy."

"We're all edgy, Saber."

"I know that, but I decided it was better to be safe than sorry. I'm not saying he isn't a good guy. I'm just not willing to risk putting the entire operation on one guy's shoulders when he is obviously not ready for it."

He glanced at her, trying to gage her reaction. She sat stock still, staring out her side window, successfully hiding her face from him. Sighing, he took his hand off the gear shifter and reached for hers, stroking it.

"I'm not judging him, Pilar. There's just too much riding on tonight. If we can't succeed at even this, then we have no business even considering moving forward."

She nodded, but didn't turn back to him. *Come on, Pilar. Let me know that you agree,* he thought, but he returned his gaze to the sky ahead. He had to concentrate on driving.

"You're coming up to the place," she said flatly.

Saber placed his hand back on the gear shift and shifted down into third, slowly coasting towards the building that Pilar had indicated.

Pulling up, he let the truck idle while Pilar jumped out and entered the huge laundry building. The overhead door opened, this one obviously electrical by its steady ascent. He threw the truck into reverse and slowly guided it up to the gaping opening in the side of the building. The moment he stopped and put it in park, Mark and a few other clones started loading the truck up with bags upon bags of washing soda— or as Saber knew it from the lab, sodium carbonate.

Pilar climbed back up into the passenger seat. "We have a small opening to get this loaded and out of here before shift change."

That one sentence sent Saber's heart beating wildly. This should be simple. What if they didn't get loaded in time? They had four tons of supplies sitting in the middle of a water treatment plant; four tons of supplies that definitely didn't belong in there. It had to go down tonight or, as Tyler had put it so eloquently earlier, they were screwed.

"I'll be right back," he said, climbing out of the still idling truck and walking into the steamy laundry building. He approached a half unloaded pallet and picked up a few bags while a forklift picked up the whole thing.

About ten women, Saber, and Mark worked on loading the truck alongside the one forklift. It took them about thirty minutes, but Saber could tell from the agitated looks that Mark kept directing at a clone woman who stood up on the top of a set of steps, they were cutting it close.

Finally, the last pallet was loaded and Saber jogged back to the truck. Mark followed him to the door and climbed up into the middle seat. Saber put the truck into first gear, then second, third, fourth, and fifth, speeding away as quickly as he could.

"Man, we were cutting it a bit close there," breathed out Mark.

"How close?"

"Shift change is at midnight."

Saber glanced at the clock. It was midnight now.

"Guess we've got a guardian angel watching over us tonight," laughed Saber.

Mark scoffed, but he was nodding his agreement. "Lucky stars, guardian angel, someone was on our side, that's for sure."

Saber sped the short distance back to the water plant. At least here they had until six am to get what they needed done, and they'd need every minute of it. With the truck parked up against the loading dock, Saber allowed Tyler's men to unload the pallets while he went about working with the phenolphthalein, turning it into the solution they'd need to mix with the washing soda.

He still hadn't worked everything out. If air was in the pipes it would ruin the illusion completely, but at least it would still act as a nasty dose of laxative.

"How much water gets pushed through here first thing in the morning?"

Tyler looked up and shrugged. "A lot. Probably the most at one time all day."

"What time is your heaviest use?"

"Around seven."

Saber nodded. "And if we contaminate the water at the last minute, say five thirty, it'll sit in everyone's pipes until they use it?"

Tyler shrugged again. "How am I supposed to know? All I do is flip the right switches, clean the right filters, and throw the right chemicals in to balance it all out."

Saber sighed. Sometimes, actually most of the time, he couldn't handle the guy. He completely understood Pilar's lack of patience with him. If he had to spend the last year or two with him, he'd snap at every little thing he said too.

"Doesn't matter anyway. It'll all make its way out eventually."

Going back to the work at hand, Saber pushed his annoyance at Tyler out of his mind. He had to measure everything out to the right amounts. Five parts washing soda to one part liquidized phenolphthalein. Now multiply that by four tons worth of materials and . . . that was a lot of math.

Saber worked for hours alongside Mark and Pilar. Mark filled the measured washing soda while Pilar followed Saber's instructions in preparing the phenolphthalein. It was time consuming and tiring, but after a while a few more people joined in the effort and by five am they were ready.

"Can we do this now?" Pilar asked, fighting back a yawn.

"Might as well."

And then the work began again. Barrel after barrel, first washing soda, then phenolphthalein were dumped into a large filtration drum. The whirling blades inside acted as a mixer, turning the water blood red.

Saber stared inside the drum and smiled. He hadn't been sure if it would work, but seeing that he'd at least gotten the measurements right felt good.

Suddenly, a commotion filled the floor below. Saber looked down and saw Ben, the truck driver, holding a gun to Pilar's head. Rage boiled up instantly, followed by fear. He looked at Mark, who shook his head and held back Tyler, who looked ready to lunge at Ben with a vicious fury.

"Not another barrel!" yelled Ben.

Saber slowly climbed down from the drum and walked as close as he could. "What's going on, Ben? Talk to me."

"You do this and the humans are going to stream in here and take away what few freedoms we have. I can't let you do that."

"I understand, Ben. But if we don't fight for our freedom, things will slowly get worse anyway."

"No. No. I can't let you do this."

Saber could see that Mark had let Tyler go, now settled down, and he slowly made his way up behind Ben. They connected eyes and Saber knew instantly what he was thinking. Keep distracting Ben, he'd grab the gun. So Saber kept talking.

"We're trying to help you, Ben. Don't you see that?"

His eyes moved wildly and his hand shook.

Please, don't twitch on that trigger.

"You don't know what it's like here. You have no idea. You aren't one of us, you never will be."

Saber could see that Ben was about to lose it. He had to take a step back. Tyler was so close now, just a few more seconds and Pilar would be safe. He just had to choose the right thing to say, he needed to relax Ben just enough so that he'd let his guard down.

"You're right," he agreed. That was what everyone did in the movies in a tense situation, right? "I don't know what it's been like for you. But I want to understand. I want to help."

Ben's arm lowered just slightly. Tyler noticed it at the same moment as Saber did, and he leapt forward, grabbing Ben's arm.

The howl that escaped Ben's mouth was one of pain and anger. He sounded like a wild animal. Tyler wrenched the gun out of his hand and dropped it on the ground, pinning Ben down on his knees, his arm pulled behind his back in what looked like a painful and unnatural angle.

Saber walked up, anger clouding his vision. It was like the night he'd beaten the human again. All he could see was red. All he could hear was the rushing blood in his ears. All he could think about was that gun held to Pilar's head.

He reached down, picked up the gun, and without a second thought pressed it against Ben's head. He pulled the trigger. Warm blood splatter hit his face and hands.

Screams erupted around him and his vision cleared. Someone pulled at his arm.

"We've got to go, Saber. We have to go."

He recognized that voice. He'd heard it uttering very similar words not that long ago. Pilar. He looked down at the crumpled body on the floor, and reality came rushing back. He'd just killed a man, another man. Tyler stood above the body and looked at Saber, a shocked look on his face. Saber couldn't help but think that maybe there was a little bit of respect in his eyes that hadn't been there before.

"Someone get rid of the body," said Saber, deathly calm.

Pilar stopped her tugging and stared at him. "What?"

"Someone get rid of the body. We need to clean this up, and quick. We have," he paused and looked at his watch. "Fifteen minutes before shift change."

The room remained dead quiet. No one moved. Then Tyler sprang to action.

"You heard the man! Let's get this cleaned up!"

People listened to Tyler. Immediately two men gathered up Ben's lifeless body and carried him away. They dumped him in the dumpster outside. No one would bother to report it. Another couple of clones ran out of the room and came back with bottles of bleach and mops.

Within minutes, the evidence was gone, and the water taken care of. By five minutes before shift change, Saber and Pilar rode in Ben's truck down back alleys along his normal route. Once they were close to the border, and far from the water plant, they dumped the truck and began the long trek home.

SHADOWS OF THE UNSEEN

PART TWO

Royce Williams

Mayhem erupted in the Central system as the hospitals overflowed with people clutching at their bellies. It was the top news story. Something was spreading at an insane pace, almost instantaneous. But it never occurred to them that someone might be doing this to them.

Not only the sickness, there was the red water. It disappeared quickly. Some people didn't even notice it. But others bottled it as proof of what had appeared, and that's when people started to wonder. Royce Williams noticed the blood red of the water, he noticed it ran clear, and he noticed everyone in his household get sick. He knew, without a doubt, that this was not a natural sickness, but caused by someone on the other side of the border.

He bottled some water and took it to Frontier, dropping it off at the lab. At lunch, his phone rang as he sat at his desk.

"Hello?"

"Mr. Williams, sir. I have your test results."

"And?" he asked impatiently.

"It's phenolphthalein, sir."

"Plain words."

"It's a laxative, sir. I'm not sure how it could have gotten in the water, though."

"Thank you."

Royce hung up, and ran his hand through his thinning hair with a sigh. *Saber, what are you getting yourself into?*

CHAPTER THIRTY

Aaron August

Kristin woke him that morning with a scream. She had come over the night before to watch a movie, and it had gone late, so rather than send her to drive home half-asleep, she spent the night in Saber's abandoned room.

Jumping up from bed, Aaron ran out of his room to respond to her scream, his heart pounding wildly. He entered the kitchen to find her standing, a glass broken and scattered across the tile floor, a puddle of water at her feet.

"What's wrong?"

"The water. It's... red."

He frowned, his heart slowing down slightly. Reaching forward, he turned the tap back on and watched the deep red liquid pour from the faucet. The red quickly disappeared, though, and it once again ran clear.

"It's probably just some sediment in the pipes. I'm sure it's fine."

"I hope so. I drank half the water before I noticed."

"Did it taste okay?"

Kristin shrugged. "It was a little strange."

Aaron watched the water continue to pour out. It looked normal now. Whatever caused the water to turn red, it seemed to have run its course. It was probably harmless, though. The water filtration system had never failed them before, why would it now?

Minutes later, the sickness came.

Kristin spent all day either running for the bathroom, or curled up on the couch in pain.

He'd planned to make her breakfast, drive her to university, walk her to her first class and leave her with a goodbye and a kiss, and an 'I'll see you at lunch'. All those things that relationships got to enjoy. Instead, he had to watch her in pain. And the nagging voice in the back of his mind told him Saber had something to do with it.

He sat beside Kristin, who curled up on his couch. She clutched at her stomach, dried tears staining her face. He stroked her hair, looking for some way to comfort her.

She drifted off to sleep after a while, so Aaron slipped off the couch and into his bedroom. Pulling out his phone, he dialed the one person he knew who would have answers, and he waited for the strong voice of Royce Williams to sound in his ear.

"Hello, Aaron."

"Do you know what's going on with the water?" he asked, cutting straight to the chase.

A sigh sounded on the other side. "Do you know where Saber went?"

"No idea. After you ran him out of town, he kinda dropped off the grid. What does he have to do with the water?"

"Everything."

His grandfather hung up on him, and Aaron looked at his phone. Royce was acting strange, but it wasn't exactly in Aaron's character to express blame or discontent. Not when his grandfather gave him everything in his life.

Walking back out to check on Kristin, he saw she was still sound asleep. Her chest rose and fell in a steady cadence, and her face remained relaxed, at peace. The sky started to darken outside, and Aaron thought that maybe the effects of whatever was in the water were beginning to wear off.

CHAPTER THIRTY-ONE

Saber August

Saber stood in the middle of the now familiar back room, in the abandoned factory. Tyler, Mark, and Pilar stood around him.

"The Net is exploding with talk of the red water and staggering demand for healthcare," said Pilar.

Saber already knew this; he'd been watching the Net right along with her. It caused the stir they wanted, but so far no one suspected that the clones had done it intentionally. Most people just thought it was a fast moving stomach bug. The red water was a much bigger story than the laxative. No one seemed to know what caused it, though speculation ranged from testing of the water to cleaning the pipes. Nothing pointed towards the greater population believing that their indentured slaves were rising up.

"Some humans came by the water facility today. They were taking samples and asking questions."

Saber nodded. "They won't find anything in the water anymore. Will anybody talk?"

Tyler shook his head. He seemed to have a lot more respect for Saber since he'd put a bullet in Ben's brain, which surprised him. He had expected Tyler to think of him as even more of a traitor for taking out a clone, instead he had adopted an attitude of camaraderie and respect.

"I hand-picked every person on that shift. They're all loyal."

Mark shuffled uncomfortably. And then there was Ben . . . no one mentioned the incident from earlier that morning, but Saber could see in the way Mark looked at him that it was about to come up. Mark looked at him like Kristin had after he killed the human. A look he had come to recognize and loathe. It said uncertainty and fear.

"What about Ben?"

Pilar nodded her agreement. "His body—"

Saber held up his hand. "No one will bother to look for him there, when his truck was abandoned much further away. It was a tense situation, we were short on time, and something needed to be done quickly. I did what I thought was best. Does any one of you have a problem with that?"

His eyes grabbed Mark's, waiting for his response. He knew Pilar would support him, even if she wasn't okay with what he'd done. And he already knew how Tyler felt. Mark was the wildcard here.

"I just don't know if killing him was the right thing to do," replied Mark.

"He would have told someone and everything would have been ruined."

"I don't like it any more than you, Mark. But Saber is right, he would have ruined everything," added Pilar, always the voice of reason.

"We're starting a war. It's not going to be pretty, and it certainly won't be easy."

Tyler remained uncharacteristically quiet during the exchange. Saber looked at him, and caught a slight curling up of his lips. *Are you pledging allegiance to me?*

"Last night was a success, but it wasn't enough. I can guarantee this has Royce Williams' attention, now we need to tell him that we're here, and we're serious."

Tyler slammed his fist into his open palm. "Yes! A demonstration?"

"Of sorts." Saber smiled. It had been Pilar's idea, so he'd let her present it to the other two. It would cause a stir with the humans, but it was harmless. If Saber had his way, they'd be making a lot more noise right now, but if Pilar wanted to slowly flex their muscles, then so be it.

"Pilar, why don't you explain?"

"Right. Well, I got the idea this afternoon while I was walking down to the kitchen on the corner. I saw rats scurrying in and out of the alleys, and of course the live traps just teaming with them, and I started to wonder what happened to them after they got caught."

"They get killed and we eat them," grumbled Tyler.

Mark chuckled, but Pilar seemed to ignore the comment. "I asked around a bit, and apparently some clones are in charge of picking up the traps and disposing of the animals, so I thought; what if we didn't dispose of them, but instead let them free on the other side of the border?"

Mark's eyes lit up in understanding. "The only place they could have come from would be the Outer system."

"Exactly."

"How exactly do you expect to get them across the border?"

Pilar frowned at Tyler, insult written across her face, but Saber stepped in and took control.

"How many clones work on the other side? Hundreds? Thousands?"

"Thousands, easy," said Tyler.

"And how many of those clones support us?"

"Maybe forty percent," said Mark.

Saber stopped talking for a moment and stared at Mark. Forty percent was a lot higher than he expected.

"That's a lot."

"The ones that work on the other side see how the humans live. They want more from life."

It made sense.

"This plan will take at least a week to implement. But I figure if we can contact as many people as possible, and they contact as many people as they can, we will get a lot of clones on board. We'll have each person smuggle as many rats across the border as they can, each and every day for the next week. It won't take long before the humans start noticing an infestation."

Tyler chuckled. "Rat infestation? You guys are crazy. All that's gonna do is make people mad."

"Maybe, but you better make some calls."

He shrugged. "Fine. I think I know a few guys that collect the traps. I'll get them on board."

"Good. Pilar knows a lot of people from her bus. You have a good idea of who are supporters?"

She nodded. "I can make some calls. We can probably get at least a couple hundred people on board."

"We're going to need more than that."

Mark sighed. "I know a border guard. We might be able to simplify this."

All attention focused on him as he laid it all out. He'd talk to his border guard contact, and Tyler would talk to his friends in the pest control sector. They'd arrange a time to drop off truckloads of traps full of rodents and set them free across the border.

"Okay then, let's all do our leg work and we'll meet back here in two days, same time."

Tyler and Mark left, but as Tyler walked by, he gave Saber a friendly pat on the shoulder. "Don't let Mark drag you down. You did the right thing to that clone."

Saber smiled his thanks, but didn't respond. Pilar was uncomfortable with the situation and he didn't want to act like he had enjoyed it. The thrill of the gun exploding in his hand had brought him a certain sense of power, and for a moment, he thought that he knew what it was like to be Royce Williams.

Alone once again with Pilar, he turned to her, ready to celebrate their small victory. But she stood, staring at him like he was a stranger. He walked up to her and tried to pull her into a hug, but she pushed back.

"What's wrong?"

"You're acting like killing Ben was no big deal."

Back to that. He sighed. "Pilar, please. He was threatening you."

"Don't put this on me."

"I'm not, but I can't let anything happen to you. Anybody threatens you, and I wouldn't hesitate to pull that trigger again."

"I was already safe, Saber. This isn't about me. This is about your emotions taking control."

"No, it was about you. If we had dropped him off somewhere, he would have taken our names and our jobs, and marched straight to the first human he found. You would be rotting in a jail cell right about now, awaiting the needle that would put you down. I had no choice. I had to kill him."

Her eyes widened, and Saber took the opportunity to reach for her again. This time she collapsed in his arms, sobbing.

"I can't get the image of him out of my mind."

He kissed the top of her head and held her tight. "It's okay. You'll be okay."

"I know that we have to be ready to do anything for the cause, but I didn't sign up to sign people's death warrants."

"We're not signing death warrants, Pilar. We're fighting a war."

"Is there no other way? I can't watch people die because of me. I can't. I'd rather live this life, never hold a coin of my own money in my hand, or shop for my own food at a grocery store, than watch someone else die so that I can be free."

Saber pushed her away, holding her at arm's length and staring straight into her tear glazed eyes.

"Pilar, you have to be strong. Think of the countless clones that get beaten or killed every day. Think of the hundreds of abortions being forced on clone women. Can you live with that? There is more blood on the hands of the humans than there will ever be on ours. I killed a human in an attempt to save the life of a clone who didn't do anything wrong, besides break a glass. Do you know how he feels now? Thankful. This isn't about us, Pilar. This is about an entire race."

She choked back her tears, clenched her jaw and nodded. "You're right."

Saber pulled her back into his embrace. He couldn't let Pilar give up on him or the cause. He needed her. And as he kissed her soft lips, salty and wet from the tears she'd shed, he realized that he loved her.

CHAPTER THIRTY-TWO

Saber August

Saber and Pilar waited near the border in the dark for the truck to arrive. Saber slowly got used to walking everywhere, even though his car was parked in an abandoned factory. Some days, like today when they had to walk so far, he was tempted to pull out the vehicle and just drive. Instead, they took the public transit as close to the border as they dared, and walked the rest of the way.

Sitting on the benches, he could almost imagine the germs and diseases crawling across every surface.

The busses were not well looked after. Graffiti covered them inside and out, unidentified food—or at least he hoped that was what it was—crusted various surfaces. Most of the seats were a hard plastic that were supposed to have been form-fitting, but what form they molded them after, Saber couldn't guess. He was fairly certain it wasn't anyone or anything human. He would have preferred walking to this, but Pilar had insisted, and it was a long ways.

As usual, they worked on a tight schedule. Mark's border guard worked the evening shift, starting at five and ending at one. Everything had to go down at midnight, when the traffic was minimal and no one would notice trucks unloading thousands of rodents into the Central system.

It had been intensive labor on everyone's part. Pilar and Tyler had worked together to get as many pest control workers in on the plan. Some agreed readily, others needed convincing. Anyone who refused was shut up. Pilar didn't know about that, though. Saber and Tyler had taken care of that, working in secret, killing silently with poison. He hated keeping secrets from her. Even more, he hated having to take the lives of those too scared to help. But it was them, or risk the entire rebellion. Thankfully, not many refused.

Slowly, Saber could feel the clones rallying around their banner. At the meeting last night, they had to meet in the main factory room instead of the back office. They started inviting along everyone involved, allowing them to voice opinions and aid in planning. At first their numbers had only grown by one or two, still enough to meet in secret, but steadily more and more people came, until they could no longer hide who or what they were.

So they met openly. Mark switched on the power, and they surveyed the couple hundred men and women all congregated there to hear the plan. They had come, in the short span of two weeks, from complete obscurity to a rallying point for those tired of their way of life.

Drawn out of his thoughts, glaring headlights from the convoy of trucks headed towards the border lit up the area where Saber was waiting. It was too late to stop now;

he hoped Mark's border guard was true to their cause. They weren't afraid of being open on this side of the border. The clones ran the town, but the border itself was controlled by the humans, and they would lose any fight that went down here.

The truck headlights switched off, one by one, leaving only the lead vehicle with lights. Saber smiled, all was going exactly according to plan. If the other guards along the wall weren't looking specifically for the approaching vehicles, they'd never notice them.

So he waited, heart lodged securely in his throat. Pilar clutched at his hand, squeezing it tightly. He could feel her heart beating through the pulsing vein in her wrist. "Nervous?"

She nodded. "We're sitting ducks out here."

"It'll be fine," he said with confidence he didn't feel.

The first truck pulled up to the gate, and Saber watched the border guard as he approached the truck. He squeezed Pilar's hand one last time, and let it go as she joined the guard and gave instructions. One by one, trucks filed through the gate and set down on the green grass of the Central system. Pilar climbed into the last one, and once it drove through, Saber hit the button to close the force field that acted as a gate behind them.

He watched the invisible activity below, from his vantage point high in the tower. He could do nothing more than imagine the goings on below. But so far, there had been no commotion. No flashing lights or raised voices. Nothing to indicate they'd been spotted.

The job of letting the rats and mice free wouldn't take long. Waiting for the rodents to leave the vicinity of the gate, so that they could come back through, would take time, though. The border guard sat at his desk while Saber paced the length of the station continuously. He didn't like that Pilar was down there without him. What if someone decided to turn on them again, and use Pilar as an example? Like Ben would have ended up doing if he and Tyler hadn't stepped in.

Tyler.

He was down there. Saber took a deep breath. As much as Pilar couldn't stand him, he would keep her safe. He would do whatever was necessary, whatever Saber would do if he was down there. Maybe not at his own risk, because he didn't feel for Pilar the same way Saber did. But he would do whatever it took to protect the rebellion, and that meant taking out those who threatened it.

The border guard's radio chirped to life.

"All clear there?"

The guard lifted his radio and clicked on his button to speak. Saber watched him for any sign of betrayal; a tick in his eye, the pulse of a vein, the sheen of sweat on his brow. He noticed nothing. He appeared perfectly calm, and that worried him more than anything else.

"All good."

"Your shift change will be on his way in ten minutes."

Saber met the guard's eyes, and panic coursed through his body.

"Okay, thanks."

He looked at Saber. "Your friends almost done down there?"

"They better be."

"I need them out in five minutes."

Saber nodded and walked to the lift that would carry him down. He needed to get his people out of here, now. The guard didn't need to be babysat. He had his chance to betray them, and at this point if anything went wrong it was too late anyway.

On the ground Saber ran to Pilar. "We need these people out. Shift change is coming up."

Rats teamed around the ground, not looking like they were about to leave.

"We've been trying to herd them away for the last half hour."

The force field powered down behind them. There wasn't any time to deal with the rodents.

"Screw the rats. Everyone, get in your vehicles and head out."

Saber went from clone to clone, telling them the same thing. They needed to go. Halfway through the line, the first trucks started and rose in the air.

Saber glanced at his watch. Too much time had passed. Most of the truck drivers had gotten the message, the others would when they saw them leaving. He waved to Pilar and they climbed into the nearest truck.

"What about the others?" asked the driver.

"They'll follow. Enough of us are leaving, they should get the picture."

Their truck fell into line, the headlights off, and flew through the gate. Saber crossed his fingers that the rats wouldn't follow them out, but even if they did, a good number would still be milling about the Central system in the next few hours.

Pilar held his hand and drew slow circles on it with her thumb. "We did it," she said with a grin.

"Don't get too excited. This is only the second leg of a long race."

CHAPTER THIRTY-THREE

Aaron August

Aaron walked through the university on his way to his next class, when his phone chimed. Answering, he waited for the caller to respond.

"Aaron, come to Frontier. I want you in my office as soon as possible," came his grandfather's gruff voice through the airwaves.

Aaron stopped walking. Of all the people he'd expected a call from, Royce Williams was at the bottom of that list. He'd never expected to be summoned to his office in five short words.

"I'll be there right away."

Turning on his heel, Aaron strode back the way he had come. A tram pulled up outside the faculty of business just as Aaron exited, and he ran to catch it.

"Parking lot A-12 please," he instructed the driver, finding a seat among the half a dozen other students. The Central system university was a city all on its own, so trams taxied students to and from different faculty buildings and parking lots. Aaron's status and money got him a parking spot in the closest lot, lot A, but it was still a fair distance away from the buildings and various green spaces.

He drummed his fingers on the armrest, obsessively checking the time on his phone every few seconds as the tram buzzed along the roadways. Royce was not a patient man, and Aaron had never been summoned to his office before—that was Saber's area of expertise—he didn't want to disappoint the man now.

It only took five minutes to reach his car, but it felt like five minutes too long as Aaron jumped off the tram and strode to where he'd left Saber's car parked. The car that he now drove since Saber had left it with him. Sliding into the leather seat, it instantly molded to his body, adjusting to fit his height perfectly.

Driving to Frontier Industries, he made it in record time. Nothing could outrun this car. He parked it in Saber's parking stall, then strode through the lobby towards the front desk. The receptionist waved him towards the lift before he even made it to her.

Walking into the lift, Aaron took a deep breath, and took the all-too-short ride to his grandfather's office as an opportunity to collect himself. Royce sounded upset on the phone, which more than likely meant the meeting would be less than pleasant. Between Saber, the water, and now the rodent infestation, Royce seemed to always be on edge.

The lift dinged its arrival at the top floor, and slid open to reveal his grandfather's lavish office. Royce sat at his desk, a cup a good three fingers full of whiskey in his left hand, and a smoldering cigar hanging from his right.

"Have a seat," he said.

Aaron walked the large expanse of the room to the empty seat like he was walking to the gallows. His stomach sat heavily inside him, leaching him of any courage he might possess. Did he find out about Aaron warning Saber of his impending arrest? Would he be next?

He sat down and looked at his grandfather expectantly.

"Want a drink?"

Aaron's opened his dry mouth, then closed it again unable to speak. He nodded and his grandfather got up and walked to the bar.

"Scotch? Whiskey? What's your poison?"

This felt like a social call. Did Saber have meetings like this when he made his daily trips up here?

"Uh, vodka?"

Royce nodded and poured the clear liquid into a glass.

Clunking it down onto the desk in front of Aaron, he returned to his seat and picked up his slowly burning cigar from the ashtray.

"Cigar?"

Aaron shook his head.

"Good man. These things will kill you eventually. It disappointed me that Saber followed my example with these."

"Saber liked lavish things."

"He liked forbidden things," his grandfather bit out harshly. "How many men do you know that can afford cigars?"

Aaron didn't speak.

"Saber only had them because of me."

"You gave him a lot."

"I gave him everything, and this is how he repays me."

His grandfather swept his hands across the desk, and Aaron looked down at the screen. It streamed constant loops of newscasts, printed reports, and personal blogs. All screamed the same headline: *The Clones are Revolting!*

Aaron looked up. "Do you believe this?"

Royce sucked back on his cigar, and breathed out the blue-gray smoke slowly. "Yes, I do. And Saber is leading the charge."

Aaron sipped his drink, trying not to choke on the potent liquid, and attempted to collect his thoughts. He agreed with his grandfather, to a certain extent. Saber was definitely capable of this. Aaron didn't believe there was anything he wasn't capable of anymore.

"That's why I called you here."

Great, this didn't really answer any of his questions. So he waited for his grandfather to continue.

"With Saber out of the picture, I need you to take his place in the family. Frontier will be left to you when the time comes. But there are certain responsibilities you have to fulfill now."

Aaron's blood pounded through his ears. Had he heard his grandfather right? Frontier would be his? It made sense, with Saber gone, but he had never dared to think that perhaps his grandfather would think of him.

"Thank you, Sir."

Royce waved his hand, dismissing it. "There is no other logical choice. Frontier stays with family."

The words hurt Aaron a little, but he nodded. Couldn't he, for once, be considered the choice Royce *wanted*, not the choice that was forced upon him?

"I need you to find Saber," said Royce, breaking the silence.

"What?"

"I need to talk to him, but I don't want the police involved. You need to go across the border and bring him to my house—discreetly— so that we can talk."

"What if he doesn't want to come?" If Saber refused, he wouldn't be able to convince him otherwise. Saber owned the Outer system now.

"He'll come. This is exactly what he wants."

* * *

Aaron drove up to the border and waited for the guard to open the force field. The guard approached, peering inside, shining his flashlight in Aaron's face.

"Heading to see a lady friend?" asked the guard.

Aaron stared at him in disgust. He'd heard of men visiting clone brothels, but he didn't really think anything of it. The border guards must see a lot of that after dark if that was the first conclusion he jumped to.

"No, I have a shipment to check on. I'm from Frontier Industries."

"You people never sleep, do you?"

Aaron forced a smile. "Work doesn't sleep, so I don't either."

"True. Just a second, I'll get the gate open for you."

The guard walked away, and seconds later the field dissipated with a sizzle.

Aaron drove on through, and picked up the written instructions he'd received on how to reach Pilar's residence. His grandfather was convinced that was where he would find Saber, the only problem was the GPS failed him on this side of the border.

He took lefts and rights when the written instructions said, and after about a half hour, he pulled up outside a three storey brick building.

It looked to be in better shape than a lot of the buildings around, but definitely outdated. As he stepped out of the nondescript car he'd borrowed from Frontier Industries' garage, he locked it, and strode into the front entrance. Inside, he looked around for a lift. It took him a couple seconds before he realized there wasn't one. Definitely outdated. Finding a doorway labeled with a worn diagram of stairs, he climbed them to the second level.

Apartment 212, 212, 212, he kept repeating in his head as he glanced at door numbers.

Almost exactly halfway down the hall, he came upon 212. He stood in front of the door and stared. What would greet him on the other side? He hadn't told Kristin where he was going, only that he was busy tonight. If something happened to him, the only person who would know would be his grandfather, and something told him that Royce would not be sending the cavalry after him.

Taking a deep breath, he raised his fist and rapped firmly on the door.

He waited, counting the seconds ticking by. Three seconds and then he heard the lock click back and the door opened. Pilar stood in the doorway, her red hair pulled back into a ponytail.

"Aaron?"

"Is Saber here?"

She nodded and stepped aside to reveal Saber sitting on the couch. Aaron walked around Pilar, a smile on his face, and approached to his brother. He stood in front of him and waited for Saber to acknowledge him. He looked up, his face perfectly calm.

"What can I do for you?"

Aaron frowned. This wasn't at all like Saber. "Our grandfather sent me."

"I figured. You're his new lapdog?"

Aaron felt a twinge of guilt. "I guess so."

"So what can I do for our esteemed *grandfather?*" he spat out the word like it left a foul taste in his mouth.

"He wants to see you."

Saber smiled. It was the first inkling of happiness Aaron had seen in the few minutes he'd been here. Not even the arrival of his brother made him as happy as being summoned by Royce Williams.

"Let's go."

Saber got up and followed Aaron out, Pilar in tow.

Aaron stopped at the stairway. "We can't take her. Grandfather said—"

"Despite what *Royce* may have told you, he doesn't want to speak to me, he wants to speak to the rebellion. Pilar is part of the rebellion."

She looked at Saber, something being said without any words. He shook his head in response.

"They don't need to be there. Two is enough."

So, there were more leaders. That would be valuable information—No, he couldn't betray Saber more than he already had. He would do what Royce told him to, so that he could retain his newfound favor with his grandfather. But he wouldn't do anything more.

Pilar climbed into the backseat, and Saber got into the passenger seat of the car Aaron had brought. Aaron, now knowing where he was going, sped off in the direction of the border.

They got through the gate easily enough. It helped that Pilar was well known as Royce Williams' secretary. Obviously, news of her dismissal had not been announced, though why would it? She was just a lowly clone.

They flew across the city to the outer border where their grandfather's house resided on a sweeping estate of five acres. Royce owned the only private property larger than an acre left in the Central system.

Aaron parked his vehicle and got out. Saber and Pilar followed him, no encouragement necessary. He didn't bother to knock, just strode in the unlocked door, through the lavish front entrance, and straight back towards his grandfather's study.

Royce stood by his gas powered fireplace, waiting. He turned to face the small group as they entered, a kind smile plastered on his face. Somehow, Aaron felt that it wasn't entirely sincere.

"Thank you, Aaron. Please, have a seat."

Pilar accepted, but Saber stood at her arm.

"I'd rather stand."

"Whatever makes you comfortable. Let's not beat around the bush, shall we? You put the laxative in the water and released the rodents into the Central system, correct?"

Saber nodded, a smirk on his face. "I think it's safe to say that I have your attention."

"You do. What is it that you want?"

"Freedom for the clones."

Aaron stared at Saber. He couldn't be serious. Was he really fighting for the rights of an indentured race, created for the very purpose of serving?

"I can't give that to you."

"Then why am I here?"

215

"To come to a compromise. I can't have panic in my world."

"There is no compromise. Either you give the clones their freedom, or things will get much worse."

"Your antics have been, up until now, schoolyard pranks. I don't believe you have it in you to start a war."

"Try me."

Saber turned around, Pilar following, and strode out of the house. Aaron stood frozen in place. Did he give them a ride back? He took one hesitant step towards the door, but his grandfather stopped him.

"No. Let them find their own way home."

CHAPTER THIRTY-FOUR

Saber August

Saber stood in the middle of a crowd that had only grown since the last demonstration. Word spread like wildfire and clones flocked to the cause. He looked around at so many identical faces, the only people he could pick out of the crowd were Tyler and his cocky grin, standing front and center, and Pilar's kind eyes and flaming red hair to his left. Mark was there, somewhere, but Saber couldn't point him out in the crowd.

"Thank you all for coming. The last demonstration was a huge success. Pilar and I had an audience with Royce Williams, and since then we've discovered that the rats carried with them fleas and lice, bringing with them a whole lot of discomfort. People are upset and they want answers that, so far, Royce has been unable to give them."

A hand shot in the air. "Does that mean it worked?"

217

"It means it served its purpose. We have garnered attention. Now it's time to let them know that we're serious."

Another hand shot up. "How are you going to do that?"

Saber looked to Pilar. She smiled. He loved seeing her in her element, finding purpose and self-worth. She excelled at this, and it made her come alive. She stepped out of the crowd to stand next to him.

"So far we've been able to retain our agenda without any serious harm. We'd like to continue that. We have a lot of supporters in the Net towers. I'd like to utilize that," she said.

"We can't keep using the same facilities. Now that we have their attention, we want to give them one more chance to realize we hold the power on this side of the wall. We need to prove that we own everything here, nothing is out of our grasp," added Saber.

Heads all around nodded. A few murmurs of discontent littered the room—a few too many for Saber to ignore.

"Why can't we just march through the gates?"

"Yeah! We outnumber them!"

He held up his hand for silence, and waited until the murmurs died out.

"Listen, I know you all want this to go fast, but gaining freedom will not happen in one night. If we move too fast, we'll have a bloodbath on our hands. If you're unhappy with the speed we're taking things at, then I'm going to ask you to leave."

No one left. Saber looked at Tyler for any indication that he didn't agree. If anyone was hot and ready to get moving, it was Tyler. But he gave a nod of approval and smiled. For the guy that questioned Saber the most when he first arrived, he had become Saber's most trusted ally and biggest supporter.

"Pilar, please continue."

"The Central system depends on the Net for everything. They don't drive without GPS, they don't brush their teeth without the news. If they lose their wired-in life, they'll be blind. Clarence here runs the Net station, and he has contacts all across the Outer system. In one uniform move, we can cut out their eyes and ears to the world."

Saber grinned. With the other two plans Pilar came up with, he held his tongue despite not thinking they were heavy-handed enough. Taking out the Net, however, was perfect. The Central system ran on the Net. Without it the entire social structure would crumble, and cause a good deal of infrastructure to grind to a halt.

"We're going to hit hard and fast, from now on. We are going to give the Central system twenty-four hours of darkness, and then Clarence will broadcast my message across both systems. This is their last chance. In three days, if things aren't moving in our direction, we'll go to step two."

Cheers erupted around him, and Saber couldn't keep the grin off his face. This is what power felt like; to be in control of a population. But he also had a fondness for these people that had adopted him as their leader. He wasn't just important because of who he was, he was important because of what he did.

CHAPTER THIRTY-FIVE

Aaron August

Royce walked up to the podium, news cameras and microphones shoved in his face. He held himself calm, collected, and regal on the outside, but the way he kept clenching his hands into fists and then released them told Aaron he seethed with anger inside.

He cleared his throat, and stared at the glassy, bulbous eyes of the cameras.

"Thank you all for coming today," he started. "I know there has been a lot of speculation over the events of the last couple of weeks, the most popular theory being that the clones are turning against us."

Royce paused for effect.

"Look around you. The clones are still at their stations, working for us, creating life as we know it. I have not rounded them up, nor closed the border. The water and the rodents are two separate events that have nothing to do with a clone uprising."

A reporter raised his hand, but Royce shook his head. "I will not be taking questions today. I am making a simple statement, and you can do with it as you wish."

Murmurs spread through the room, and Aaron watched from his vantage point behind his grandfather. Royce held up his hand again to ask for silence.

"This is all the work of Saber August, the man you know as my grandson. He is deeply troubled, and has recently grown unstable. The truth is, Saber isn't who you think he is. He is a clone."

Aaron looked at his grandfather, the room seemingly spinning. A clone? It couldn't be true. He had to be saying this to turn people against him.

"The real Saber August is dead."

Aaron's whole world spun upside down, and his vision blurred as he watched Royce give his speech.

Royce looked up, his face strong and sure again, his hands crossed protectively across his chest, looking in control of a situation that was leaving Aaron reeling.

"The real Saber August died of SIDS at two months of age. Sabrina, my daughter was distraught—rightly so. It's never easy to lose a child. So I did what I could to fill that hole in her heart. I created a clone. One like no other. He is a clone of myself."

Royce paused again. Not a word could be heard in the entire room. Everyone stood deathly still and quiet.

"I hoped I would never have to reveal his true identity, but I feel now, for you to understand him and his instability, you must know what he truly is. I assure you, that every possible measure to find and detain him is being taken."

Royce turned away from the podium, facing Aaron. People erupted with questions behind him, their voices all blending together and making it impossible for Aaron to pick out any single question.

Royce turned back. "I'm sorry, I am taking no—"

A hum filled the air, and then in a slow decrescendo everything went silent; the cameras powered down, the blinking Net screens went blank. Everything turned off.

Royce looked at Aaron, and he shrugged in response. Of course, they both knew that the only thing that could cause a blackout like this was the Net being cut out. The Net stations were in the Outer system.

He motioned for Aaron to follow him, and they left the press conference among the panicking media personnel.

Royce led Aaron to his car, and they climbed in. Starting it, he noticed right away that the GPS was out too. Royce lifted the car into the air anyway, keeping it in manual control.

They flew for a half hour, the skies nearly empty. Aaron sat silent in the seat next to his grandfather. The car was all too quiet. The radio was nothing but static, there was no bleep, bleep from the GPS. Cars that should be flying on all sides of them were parked on the ground. No horns blared, there was no steady thump, thump, thump from a nearby car with the bass turned up a little too high. Huge Net screens that had once blared advertisements in bright lights and loud music were silent and black. The world seemed to be asleep.

He pulled up to his house, and Aaron tagged behind him as he walked in and went straight to his study.

"We need to fix this. Fast," said Royce, pacing back and forth the length of his study.

"You aren't even going to touch on the bombshell you just dropped onto the entire Central and Outer system populations?"

"It's irrelevant at the moment."

"Does Saber know?"

"I suspect he does now. And if not, he will very soon. I'd like to see him gain human sympathizers now."

Aaron sighed. "I can't believe you hid it from us, from his family."

"I did what I thought was best."

"For who? For you? For Saber?"

"For everyone!"

"So what do we do?"

Royce ran his hand through his hair, sighing loudly. "We let him play his cards, and then it'll be our turn. At most, it'll take forty-eight hours to fix this problem."

"And the people trapped in their homes? Lifts won't work with the Net down."

"They'll be fine for a couple days."

Aaron stood up straight. "There isn't much I can do now, so I'm going to go."

"You can stay here."

Aaron looked at his grandfather in shock. He'd never been offered that before. Saber had lived here for years, but Aaron had always been forgotten. Now that he was being accepted, he wasn't sure he wanted it. He shook his head slowly, still a little unsure.

"I'll go to Mom and Dad's. They'll be worried." He didn't add that he'd be going to check on Kristin first. With the Net down, and all forms of communication at a standstill, he needed to make sure she was okay.

Royce nodded his reply. He'd stopped pacing, and was looking out the large picture window overlooking his back yard. Aaron considered this his dismissal and left. He'd met his grandfather here this morning before going to the press conference, so he climbed into his car, which was parked on the drive outside, and lifted it into the air.

He drove his car carefully through the silent streets towards Kristin's apartment. She had stairs, though they were never used.

Hopefully it wouldn't take long to sort everything out. His grandfather said forty-eight hours at most to find the problem and fix it. They both knew the problem wasn't technical though, it was organic in nature—which made him uneasy about how Royce was going to fix this problem.

Pulling up to Kristin's apartment, he put the car in park and let his forehead fall against the steering wheel. *Saber, what are you doing? Clones are going to die over this,* he thought, trying to swallow back the fear and dread that rose in him.

Calming himself down, he left the car and walked up the four flights of stairs to Kristin's apartment. Rapping solidly on the door, he waited. Instead of it sliding away seamlessly, it was pulled aside and Kristin met him with wide-eyed fear.

"What's going on, Aaron?"

He stepped inside and closed the door, pulling her into his embrace. "Don't be scared. It's all okay."

"This world is run by the Net. This isn't okay."

"It's Saber, Kristin. We're safe."

He could feel her breath hitch and it made his heart ache. Instead of Saber's name relieving her fears, it seemed to escalate them. She pulled away and walked into the kitchen, leaning into the counter with her hands

224

pressed flat against it. She looked up at him with fear written in her eyes.

"You know him, Kristin. He isn't capable of hurting the people he loves."

"Who does he love, Aaron? Us? He walked away from us."

"He was chased from us. I'm his family, Kristin. We have to trust he'd never, ever hurt me or anyone I care about."

"I saw him kill a man, Aaron. I saw him beat a man to death."

"And you've also seen the kind side of him. Not many people have seen that. Believe me, he could never hurt someone that he let in like you."

"I'm sorry, Aaron, but I don't trust him."

"Do you trust me?"

He waited, the air pregnant with what he'd just asked. In the past few weeks, she'd let him in, and he knew it was more than she'd ever let another man in before. She'd accepted him as more than just a friend. Now he was asking her to trust him. Could she take that step? It was the difference between a simple relationship and something more, something real.

Tears seeped through her lashes, and slowly, painfully slow, her head bobbed up and down. "With my life."

He kissed her forehead and pulled her tightly against his chest. "I have to go to my parents. I promised my grandfather I'd stay there, and they're likely worried."

He felt Kristin nod against his chest.

"Come with me. There is plenty of room for you, and then I'll know you're okay."

Pulling out of his arms, she looked at him with determined eyes and a set jaw. He had a feeling he wasn't going to like her answer.

"No, this is my home."

He sighed. "Okay. I'll be back tomorrow to check on you. Hopefully by then all this is sorted out."

He gave her one last kiss, then pulled the door aside just enough to slip out.

Arriving at his parents' house, he knocked on the door and waited. A few moments later his father pulled it aside.

"Aaron, thank goodness. Your mother has been worried sick."

Stepping in, Aaron looked around. "Where are the clones?"

"They left a few days ago. From what we hear, they've been leaving in droves, heading to the Outer system. Royce can't keep hiding the fact that something is brewing on the other side of the wall," said Kellan as they walked into the living room where Sabrina sat.

His mother sat on the couch, her legs curled up beside her, an actual old fashioned hardcover book in her hands. Aaron almost chuckled, you didn't see many of those anymore. Everything had gone digital long ago.

"Sabrina, Aaron is here."

She jumped up from the couch, dropping her book and running to embrace him. "I was so worried. Do you know what's going on? We can't find out anything. The Net is down…"

Aaron shook his head. "It's nothing. Grandfather thinks it's a transformer blown or something. I'm sure things will be all fixed within a few days."

Aaron caught his dad's eye over his mom's shoulder, and he nodded, letting him know that he approved of the lie. They both knew something more was going on, but there was no need to worry Sabrina.

"Mind if I crash here tonight, though? I'm locked out of my apartment until the Net comes back online."

Sabrina let him go. "Of course! I'll go prepare your old bedroom."

She walked off in a hurry, leaving the men alone in the living room.

"This is good, she has something to distract her from worrying."

Aaron smiled and nodded, sitting down on the couch and picking up the book Sabrina had been reading. Turning it in his hands a few times, he set it back down and looked at his father.

"I don't think this will be over anytime soon. It's Saber, you know."

Kellan nodded. "We saw the broadcast."

"Did you know?"

Only one side of Kellan's mouth lifted slightly. "It was never said in as many words, but we knew."

"And you all chose to hide it from Saber? From me?"

"We did what we thought was best. It was the only way for him to live a normal life."

Aaron closed his eyes and breathed deeply, accepting what his father had to say. If Kellan was saying it, then it was true. Maybe Royce's motives had been similar.

CHAPTER THIRTY-SIX

Saber August

Saber sat down heavily in a chair at the Net station. Every screen was black, making the words he'd just heard seem all the more unreal.

"Can you replay that for me, Clarence?"

The man nodded, flipping on a screen and immediately bringing up Royce's commanding presence. The scene played again, but still the words seemed unreal.

"Again," said Saber.

Each time he watched it, they sunk in a little deeper. He was a clone. He, Saber August, was not Saber August. He was Royce Williams. His whole life was a lie. His identity was a lie.

A hand touched his shoulder, and he looked up to meet Pilar's eyes. "I'm sorry. I didn't know…" she trailed off.

Saber shook his head. "No one knew. No one but Royce. I guess it explains a lot, my predisposition to help you. I guess you could say it's in my genes." He barked out a bitter laugh and stood up, letting Pilar's hand fall away from his shoulder.

"If you don't mind, I'm going to take a walk."

"I'll see you tonight? At the warehouse?"

He nodded, and without another word he exited the Net station, slamming the door behind him.

How could he expect to gain human sympathy now? He was no longer one of them, he was the enemy. Royce had made sure of that. In one simple move, Royce had stripped the clones of the one thing they had going for them: Saber's power.

What power? thought Saber bitterly, kicking at some loose rubble on the street. *It was just borrowed. It was never real.*

Had Royce won? Was this all a game to him?

The sun set, and Saber slowly made his way to the warehouse to meet Pilar, Tyler, and Mark. Arriving, he walked back to the old office, but no one was there yet. Turning around, he walked back out to the main room where Aaron's car was parked. Walking towards it, he swept dust off the hood as he made his way around to the driver's side. Opening the door, he slid in and grasped the steering wheel. When had his life gone so off track? Not that long ago he'd been racing through the sky streets against his brother, now he was leading a rebellion, one that was likely doomed to failure.

The warehouse door slammed, and Saber looked up to see Pilar approaching. She waved, then climbed into the passenger's side of the car.

"You okay?"

Saber nodded, leaning his head back against the head rest.

"Are you ready to move forward?"

"You want to move forward? Even though our whole plan, everything relied on who I was?"

"It's a hiccup, nothing more. You're still the man who joined our cause, and who rallied an entire race into action. That doesn't change."

Saber nodded, closing his eyes. He heard Pilar leave the car, but he didn't look, and he didn't follow her.

A small chirrup sounded within the car, and Saber opened his eyes. Was that a cricket? Glancing around, he saw the little black bug had found a spot on the floorboard of the passenger's side. He watched it, as it chirruped a few more times.

A smile tugged at the corners of his mouth. They could industrialize and modernize the entire world, but those black bugs would always survive, would always sing their evening chorus, no matter how much concrete and glass they brought in, and grass they ripped up. And they would always find their way in where you least expected them.

They were hardy creatures. Adaptable.

That's what I have to do. Adapt to this new life.

* * *

Saber stepped in front of the camera and straightened his shirt. He held his head high, his shoulders square. He was comfortable here, in control. He was used to being in the spotlight. He'd been in front of countless cameras in his life as Royce's heir, and this was no different, except this time he was coming with his own message instead of Royce's. And he was coming as an outcast, not a leader.

He looked at Pilar. She smiled, and then nodded to Clarence to start the broadcast.

Staring at the camera, he waited a couple seconds to be sure the broadcast had started, then spoke.

"Hello people of the Central system. By now you all realize that something is wrong. In fact, Royce Williams stood before you yesterday and told you that I am what's wrong. He told you that I'm unstable, disturbed, and perhaps most shocking of all is that I'm a clone.

"I was as shocked to hear it as you were. Whether or not it's true, I don't know, nor do I care to find out. Who or what I am isn't what matters. I'm here to tell you that the man you call your leader is a hypocrite and a liar.

"You all know me as Saber August. You once considered me the grandson of Royce Williams, the heir to Frontier Industries, and the next in line to act as your prime minister. A little under a month ago, Royce Williams drove me from my home because he saw me as a threat. I am genetically indistinguishable from the man you call your leader, and I was not only treated as a human, but given more power than almost anyone else.

"Yet we live every day treating clones like our slaves. We use them, then dispose of them. How many of you even notice them, as they go about all the jobs that we don't want to do? The next time you walk down a street, look around you. Really look at the clones. Do they look like humans? Because I can assure you that they think and feel like humans do. After all, I am one. And I didn't even know it. No one did.

"Today, I ask you to side with the clones. Ask for their freedom and equality. They are not animals, they are people, and deserve your respect. I've been treated with more than respect all my life, and yet, I am no different than each and every one of these people you call your slaves. If that isn't enough, think about everything they do for you every single day.

"You've been without the Net for twenty-four hours now. The clones control that. You've had your water tampered with, and you've had rats that brought with them lice and fleas. I assure you that this is only the start of what we're capable of."

He paused, his eyes staring straight into the camera. "Until steps are taken to free the clones, you will not receive the Net back. Not only that, but in the next twenty-four hours, if there has been no acknowledgement of your cooperation, we will make another demonstration. And every twenty-four hours afterwards that there is no movement, more steps will be taken.

"*You* can make this stop by demanding from Royce Williams that he free the clones. Don't be the hypocrite he is. Don't embrace me, a clone, as one of you and then turn your nose up at an entire race of people."

Clarence cut off the broadcast and gave Saber a nod. "Good, we got it."

"And that will go everywhere?"

Clarence nodded. "My guys are making sure it's streaming to every single Net connected item in the world."

Saber smiled, and walked around to embrace Pilar, pulling her into his strong arms and kissing her. "How was that?"

"You did great."

"Now that our demands are public, we'll keep pushing, and eventually they'll give in. They can only take so much."

Pilar got up on her toes and kissed Saber again.

"We should go," he said, letting her go. He was eager to hear the reaction and news that would be outside, not in here.

"Clarence, we're heading out. Thanks again for this."

"Thank *you*," he replied. "You're what we've been waiting for, Mr. August. I'm just doing what I can to help."

A flush of pride filled Saber, and he nodded, taking Pilar's hand and leaving the Net studio. He'd never felt this kind of pride in his position of power in the Central system. He'd never earned anything there. Everything had been given to him by Royce, but here he had to prove himself as a leader before the clones followed. Here, he could be an elected king, and Pilar his queen. They were creating a new world together, one step at a time.

Hand in hand, they walked the streets back to her apartment. The Outer system was beginning to transform. The clones took pride in their homes. With their efforts turned away from their human masters, they were starting to repair the roads by cleaning up the rubble and replacing missing manholes. In a few places Saber could even see signs that they were preparing to patch holes. Everywhere he looked, the streets seemed to be cleaner, giving an area a fresh face. What had once felt like a dark and depressing world, was slowly becoming bright and cheerful, a beacon of hope for a new life.

Arriving at Pilar's apartment building, they climbed the stairs. Before they even made it to her apartment, though, Saber could hear a phone ringing shrilly from inside.

"Is that yours?"

Pilar frowned. "I think so."

They reached her door and she unlocked it, the phone still ringing and definitely coming from inside.

She walked in, leaving the door open for Saber to go through, and picked up the phone. "Hello?"

Saber walked over. "Who is it?" he mouthed. She held up her finger, her brow furrowing as she listened to the person on the other end of the line. Pressing the speaker button, she set the phone aside for Saber to join the conversation.

"Okay, Mark. You have both of us now. What happened?"

"It's Clarence. SWAT closed in on the studio just a little while ago..." he trailed off.

Anger boiled up inside Saber, and he clenched his fists. "Is he dead?"

The line remained silent.

"Mark, be straight with me. Did they kill him?"

"They blew the whole studio, and everyone in it to kingdom come."

A string of expletives exited Saber's mouth. They must have closed in just minutes after he and Pilar had left. Had they been watching it? Waiting for him to leave? *This is my fault, my doing.*

Pilar fell to her knees, sobbing. "He was just alive. We just left..."

"Thank you for the call, Mark. Let's gather for a meeting tonight at eight."

Saber hung up, kneeling on the floor in front of Pilar and drawing her onto his lap, allowing her to rest her head on his chest and soak his shirt with her tears. He wrapped his arms around her, stroking her hair.

Finally, she choked back her tears and moved out of Saber's arms, sitting on the floor and leaning against the kitchen cabinets. She drew her knees up against her chest, and wiped stray tears off her face.

Saber repositioned to sit beside her.

"Do you care at all?" she asked, between sniffles.

Of course he cared, what kind of question was that? But he couldn't afford to doubt his decisions.

"We knew there would be backlash. He isn't the first blood spilled, and he probably won't be the last." Saber knew he sounded callous, but it was true, and the sooner he and everyone else came to terms with that, the better. They couldn't afford to drop down in tears every time a life was lost.

"But don't you care that it's our fault?"

"He knew the risks."

Pilar closed her eyes and breathed deeply. "How can you think that way? He was murdered because he helped us."

"You have to expect sacrifice, Pilar. We're fighting a war. I am leading a war, and I need to be a strong face for that. I can't doubt."

"But you can mourn."

He smiled sadly. He couldn't afford to mourn, he couldn't afford to have any weakness. "That's what I have you for. You're my conscience."

"You need to show compassion, Saber. A leader needs compassion."

"I love the people I'm leading. I understand the risk and sacrifice they're taking. But I can't let it affect my judgment. I need to make the hard decisions, Pilar. I can't afford to see them as individuals. I can't allow my feelings to get in the way."

She closed her eyes, a tear slipping through her eyelashes, then rested her head on his shoulder.

"I'll be your conscience for now, but don't let the cause destroy who you are. Promise me you won't lose yourself."

Saber rested his head sideways against hers, staring at the back of the couch that sat in front of them.

"I promise," he said. But it was too late for that. He wasn't the same man that Pilar had first fallen in love with, and there was no coming back from the deeds he had done, and the evils he had seen.

CHAPTER THIRTY-SEVEN

Aaron August

Aaron woke up to a light rapping sound.

"Aaron, honey, are you awake?"

He groaned. What time was it? He had been up way too late the night before with his father. They had talked into the early hours of the morning. It was something Aaron had never experienced before with Kellan, a connection between father and son that had never been his to enjoy until last night. He had wanted to keep it going as long as possible in case it was the only time it ever did.

"Yeah," he called out through a garbled voice, his mouth dry from lack of use.

"You need to come see this. Saber is on the Net."

Aaron jumped up, fully awake now. "I'll be right out," he called out again, grabbing a pair of pants off the floor and jumping around the room on one leg as he tried to pull his pants on while searching for a shirt.

Still pulling his shirt on, he left the safe confines of his childhood bedroom and joined his parents in the dining room, where they were both staring at the Net screen that had been silent and dead just last night.

"*You* can make this stop by demanding from Royce Williams that he free the clones. Don't be the hypocrite he is. Don't embrace me, a clone, as one of you, and then turn your nose up at an entire race of people," came Saber's voice through the screen, then everything went black again.

"I missed it?"

"Maybe it'll play again," offered Kellan, from where he sat with a glass of orange juice and a slice of buttered toast.

"Please tell me there is coffee," muttered Aaron as he pulled out a chair, scraping it back along the floor.

Sabrina nodded, getting up and walking towards the kitchen. Moments later, she returned with a plate piled high with fried eggs, sausage, buttered toast and fruit. Her other hand held a steaming cup of coffee. The Net screen remained black and silent.

"Thanks, Mom. I'm surprised you even know where the kitchen is," he teased.

Sabrina swatted at her son good-naturedly, and shook her head. "Of course I know where my own kitchen is. Finding my way around it is a whole different matter, though. I am really missing our clones."

She probably wasn't the only one. If Kellan was right, and the clones were heading back over the wall to the Outer system to join Saber's cause, there were likely a lot more people feeling the pain of missing clones.

A loud knock sounded on the front door, and Sabrina frowned. "I can't believe someone actually drove here with the Net down..." she muttered as she walked away to answer the door.

"Hello, Ma'am, is Aaron August available?" a strong, authoritative voice drifted into the dining room.

Aaron frowned. Was his grandfather looking for him already? Getting up, cup of coffee in hand, he walked into the foyer to see who was looking for him. The man standing in the doorway was dressed in a black suit and tie with a crisp white shirt underneath. He looked secret service, only lacking an earpiece. It wouldn't be working right now, though.

"Ah, Mr. August. Prime Minister Williams is waiting for you outside."

Aaron raised an eyebrow. "He is?"

"You did see the broadcast, didn't you? He assumed you would know he would wish to speak to you."

"I caught the tail end."

"Regardless, your grandfather is waiting."

"Okay, just let me grab my food," said Aaron, retreating back into the dining room and grabbing the slices of toast off the steaming plate of food. His stomach growled and he looked longingly at the aromatic food he'd have to leave behind. Grabbing a sausage and quickly shoving it in his mouth, he walked back into the foyer. Coffee still in hand, he joined his grandfather's errand man in the doorway.

"The name's Bill, Mr. August. In case you were wondering."

"You can call me Aaron."

"I think it best I give you a little information on what has occurred. Your grandfather will expect you to know."

"Thank you."

Bill pulled out his phone, nearly useless with the Net down. Pulling up a recorded file, the screen filled with Saber's face. Aaron watched as his brother spoke. When the Net went out, everything had gotten real. Saber's statement would only serve to anger their grandfather. What was he thinking? Saber knew, better than anyone, what his grandfather was capable of, and he was just provoking his anger.

Bill opened the back door of the car for him, and Aaron stepped into the black maw.

"You saw the broadcast?" asked his grandfather the minute he settled into his seat.

He nodded. A small lie, but he needed it. He was on a slippery slope with his grandfather as it was.

"I've already taken means to send my own message to Saber, but he won't stop."

"Now what?"

"I made my move. It's back in his court again. He made the claim that if there was no response in twenty-four hours, he would make another display of power. Let's see how serious he is after my response."

"I'm sure it wasn't the response he was looking for."

Royce smiled and it had in it a sinister air. "If he wasn't half-expecting it, he's a fool. And if he continues to push, I guess I'll know he truly is my flesh and blood."

The car drove through the still abandoned streets, and Aaron studied his grandfather. What was going on in that mind of his? He worried for his brother. Maybe it was time he made another run for the border, if it was even still open, to try and get him out. He could start a life somewhere with Pilar. No one would have to know, and all this could be stopped.

"Why do you need me?"

Royce chuckled. "I don't. I'm keeping you close so that you can't betray me."

Aaron swallowed back the bile that surged up his throat. If Royce didn't trust him, he wasn't safe. And neither was Kristin. But it also meant his grandfather was grasping at straws; he was worried that Saber might just outdo him, in what was the biggest dispute in the last hundred years.

"I would never—"

"I can't be too careful. You and Saber were close, and it is in your character to be loyal. I know that it runs deeper with Saber than it does with me. I'm keeping you safe, removing the choice from you."

"What about Kristin? I promised her I'd be back tonight."

His grandfather shrugged. "I'm sure she'll still be waiting when all this is resolved."

Aaron wasn't so sure. He'd built their entire relationship on being dependable, and proving to her that she could trust him. He kept his promises, even the little ones. If he didn't show up tonight, had she healed enough to trust he would be there as soon as he could?

CHAPTER THIRTY-EIGHT

Saber August

Saber looked at Tyler and nodded. It had been twenty-four hours, and the only response he'd gotten that his message was received was the death of Clarence and the handful of clone crew at the Net station.

Pilar had stepped down from a leadership role in the rebellion that morning.

"I don't want to keep going," she had said, sitting on the couch with a cup of coffee steaming between her clutched hands.

"What do you mean?"

"I don't want to be a part of the rebellion anymore. I can't live with blood on my hands."

Saber had nodded, trying to pretend to understand. Truth was, he didn't. She had been the one to bring him into all of this, she had been the one to urge him that he needed to be ready to stop at nothing for freedom.

"I'll support you as best I can, but I won't be involved."

Saber had just responded by kissing her head, and getting up to leave for his meeting with Tyler.

Mark was slowly falling to a less-involved roll, and with Pilar stepping down, that left Saber and Tyler to run the show. Saber knew it was a volatile combination, but he was almost glad it was down to just the two of them. At least they'd get things done.

Tyler picked up the phone and dialed a number, to whom Saber didn't know. He preferred it that way. It was all a chain, and he didn't know who was at the end. That way, if Royce came after him, he wouldn't be able to betray anyone.

Once again, this demonstration attacked the humans where they were most vulnerable: supplies.

Tyler had connections in the food plants who were more than happy to slip contaminants into the food. Typhoid Fever was no laughing matter. If left untreated, there was a mortality rate of twelve to thirty percent. Those were numbers Saber was willing to play with. Royce had drawn first blood, and it was time to respond in kind.

"It's done," said Tyler. "The first cases should be reported within the next twelve hours or so."

Saber nodded. "Good. Let's see how the humans like it when they can't even trust the food they eat."

"Does Pilar know about this?"

"No. She's asked to stay out of the planning from now on."

Tyler grinned. "Maybe it's better that way. Her and Mark—"

"Keep us in line. Don't forget it, Tyler."

He shrugged. "At least now we can get things done. Do you think Royce will contact you again because of this?"

"Probably not, but I can hope. I think we're past talking now. It's blow for blow. We just have to count on the humans calling to give in to our demands. Royce certainly won't on his own accord."

"For a guy that's so willing to pull the trigger, you sure don't seem to enjoy this."

Saber smiled slightly. He appreciated Tyler. He had an important place in the rebellion. He was like the devil on his shoulder, always pushing him to take it a step further. He needed that. But Pilar was there to tell him no when Tyler took it too far. Sure, Saber was the face, the one calling the shots, but it was really Pilar and Tyler conducting everything in the background. They just didn't realize it. They didn't realize how much Saber needed them.

"I don't enjoy this. I do what's necessary, but I'll be glad to put all this behind me when the time comes."

"Man, I haven't felt this kind of purpose in my entire life. Is it wrong that I'm afraid of what comes after?"

Saber shook his head. "Fear of the unknown is natural."

"I don't know. I don't feel guilt or sadness over the deaths we've caused or lives I've ended. It's all just collateral damage. I think maybe I belong in a world like this one, not the one we're trying to create."

It didn't surprise Saber that Tyler felt this way. To a certain extent, he felt that way too. All his life he'd lived under his grandfather's shadow, and this was his chance to prove that he was worth something. The difference was, that when this was all done, he'd be hailed as the savior of an entire race. Would Tyler fade back into obscurity?

Saber got up and patted Tyler on the back. "I better get home to Pilar."

He didn't feel right leaving her alone. If Royce wanted to get to him, the easiest and fastest way to do so would be to target her. He'd already spent too much time away.

"Same time tomorrow?"

"You have people ready?"

"Working on it. A few more pieces to fall into place, but we'll be ready."

"Good man. Did you manage to get the weapons?"

Tyler grinned, showing his teeth in a feral manner. "Hijacked an entire shipment. We have an armed guard ready and willing to protect the food plants."

"Good. I don't want any more clone blood on my hands."

"You still have the gun from Ben?"

Saber nodded. He left it with Pilar, but when he was with her, it was always close at hand.

"Good. Keep her safe." They both knew without saying it, that he was referring to Pilar.

Saber walked out of the factory, and it wasn't until he was halfway back to his apartment that he realized Tyler had never shown concern for Pilar before. Sure, he'd saved her from Ben, but that wasn't concern in the strictest sense. That was for the cause. In fact, he'd always held a bit of disdain for her. This was a gentler side of Tyler that he'd let show for just a moment, but it made Saber wonder what else was beneath the hard exterior of his friend.

CHAPTER THIRTY-NINE

Aaron August

Aaron wandered around his grandfather's house. They were approaching the twenty-four hour mark again. Something new would happen soon. But Aaron could only think about Kristin. Was she hurt, upset, worried? He had no way of even contacting her. He had promised to check in yesterday, but Royce refused to let him out of the house.

His grandfather entered the drawing room, where Aaron stood looking out the large picture window at the property outside.

He glanced at his grandfather. "Any news?"

"Nothing yet."

"Maybe he gave up."

"He won't. He never will."

Aaron didn't know how to respond to that. If Saber didn't stop, and Royce didn't give in, how was this going to end without everyone lying dead in the streets? He didn't dare ask though; he didn't want to know the answer, because deep down, he knew he wouldn't like it.

"So, we wait?"

"For now."

Royce took a seat near the window and picked up a book. Sabrina had gotten her love of reading from her father. There wasn't much to do besides read, though—at least for those fortunate enough to own paperback books. Royce sat there reading for an hour before checking his watch, then got up with a sigh.

"Whatever he's doing, it isn't obvious yet."

And that worried Aaron all the more. Something subtle would hit even harder; twenty-four hours had passed and people would let their guard down. There were too many options that worked silently and slowly. Kristin would be okay, though. She knew what Saber was capable of. She wouldn't let down her guard. Wherever she was, she'd be safe. Or at least that's what he kept telling himself.

Hours passed, Aaron spent his time wandering from room to room. He sat down, picked up a book and attempted to read it, then set it down in frustration and got up. The house was huge and held no shortage of rooms, yet Aaron walked through each one at least a dozen times, looking through every nook and cranny, investigating every knick-knack or item that wasn't reliant on the Net. Anything to take his mind off the fact that he was a prisoner in his own grandfather's house, his brother was waging war, and the woman he loved likely thought he'd abandoned her.

A door slammed open, and a clone ran in, past Aaron and down the hall towards his grandfather's study. He immediately followed him, entering the office just behind the clone.

"What is it?" asked Royce, his voice stern and impatient.

"Central General is reporting an influx of patients with what seems to be some kind of stomach flu."

"The flu isn't very high on my list of concerns."

The sound of approaching footsteps filled the silence that had fallen throughout the room. Moments later, another clone entered.

"Sir, East Emergency is reporting that they're overwhelmed with patients."

Royce sighed. "Thank you, keep me updated."

The two clones left, and Royce beckoned to Aaron. "Go to Central General and find out what is going on. This is obviously much worse than just a simple flu, and it's more widespread and serious than the water if people are risking leaving their houses."

Aaron nodded and turned to leave. Maybe this was his chance to get to Kristin.

"Bill will go with you," added Royce.

The large bodyguard appeared from around the door, where he had been waiting in the hall.

"Come with me, Mr. August."

He tried to stifle his disappointment as he followed Bill out of the house, and allowed him to drive towards the hospital.

Upon arriving, he saw that the hospital just couldn't keep up. Pale and weak people filled the waiting room. The whole building seemed to have that sour-musty smell of sick people. Aaron strode to the triage desk where a nurse was busy taking the vitals of a patient.

"What's going on here?"

"I'm a little busy, in case you can't tell," bit back the nurse.

Aaron grimaced. Of course, this wasn't easy on her either. "I'm sorry. I'm here on behalf of Royce Williams. Is there someone I can talk to?"

A doctor in a white lab coat walked behind the nurse, then stopped.

"If you can talk and walk I'll answer any questions you might have," said the woman, grabbing some files from the nurse's desk.

Aaron fell into step beside the female doctor. "I assume you're here about the salmonella poisoning."

"Is that what it is?"

"We think so. There is also the possibility it's typhoid."

"Is that worse?"

"Much worse. I can guarantee if its typhoid we'll be seeing a few deaths, more than a few if the number of poisoned keeps going up."

They walked through halls filled with patients in beds, groaning, some retching into various containers.

"What can we do about it?"

"Right now we're treating with antibiotics and trying to keep them hydrated. Most of the stronger people will be fine. It's the young children and seniors we need to worry about."

"Is there anything Frontier can do to help?"

"Get us more staff and more meds."

Aaron stopped, and the doctor paused to turn and face him.

"I'll see what I can do. Thank you for your time."

The doctor nodded and walked away, leaving Aaron and Bill standing in the crowded hallway.

Making their way back out, Aaron stopped by the front desk.

"Excuse me, is there any way to tell me if a Kristin Pierce has been admitted here?" It was a shot in the dark, with the Net down, but they had to have some kind of system in place to keep track of the patients.

The receptionist looked at him and shook her head. "I'm afraid not. Every ward keeps track of their patients separately by pen and paper. Besides that, there are any number of hospitals she could be at."

"It's okay, thank you."

Bill walked beside him, a hulking presence that prevented his escape. Aaron didn't know what his orders were, but he didn't put it past his grandfather to have ordered a little pain to teach a lesson. He was quickly learning that Royce Williams was in this for himself. If he truly cared about the people he led, he would be in negotiations, or he would have sent the brute squad across the border to pick up Saber and be done with it. But he was all too self-involved for that, and Saber was, in a sense, himself. He carried a piece of Royce William's soul, and that was a weakness for him. Did Saber realize that? Or did he just see red when he thought of his grandfather's betrayal?

Bill escorted Aaron back to the car, as more than a handful of people passed them looking pale and weak. This would only get worse if they couldn't get out the message to the people not to eat the food.

As Bill drove the car home, Aaron stared out the window and realized that the traffic had picked up considerably. And it would only get worse. Some people wouldn't go into the hospitals, and there was no way to broadcast what was happening. Was this the first bloodshed of a war that Aaron was sure would go down in the history books?

CHAPTER FORTY

Saber August

Reports came in to Saber throughout the day. People poured into the hospitals by the thousands. There were no beds left, meds ran low, and Frontier opened its doors to accommodate as many patients as they could. It was nearing the twenty-four hour mark, and there hadn't been any attempt at contact.

Tyler burst into Pilar's apartment, her door banging against the wall from the force of it being thrown open.

"They've closed the border!"

"What?" Pilar asked.

Saber grinned. Perfect. Royce was getting scared.

"No one is allowed to work in the Central system anymore. All shipments that they need are being handed to humans at the border, where everything will be tested before it's distributed. Now what?"

Saber looked from Pilar to Tyler, both looking concerned. "That's how they respond? Fine. We'll hit in a different place. They aren't equipped to run the Central system without us."

"But the testing—"

"They're going to test the food and drinking water, things they consume. We'll have one last chance to contaminate something, and it's going to have to be something they won't suspect."

Saber looked at Pilar. Her face was alight with what must be an idea, but she appeared to be trying to suppress it.

"What's your idea?" he asked, before she made up her mind to stifle it and walk away.

"What makes you think I have an idea?"

"If you have an idea you need to tell us. You're loyal to the movement, aren't you?" added Tyler.

Saber sighed. Tyler was the wrong person to talk to her, but he was right.

"Please, Pilar."

"The laundry," she sighed. "They won't test the laundry for anything, because it's not consumable. If we can lace the clothing with some kind of irritant, it will get through."

Saber grinned and planted a kiss on Pilar's lips.

"Perfect," he said. "Let's go. With the border closed, we don't have to work in secret. Tyler, round up some minute men and meet me there."

Tyler nodded and immediately left the apartment.

Pilar looked at Saber. "What are you going to do?"

"Do you want to know?"

Slowly, she nodded. "I need to know."

"Chemical burns."

Her face twisted in distaste. "You need to stop hurting innocents. This isn't right. Think of all the children that you'll hurt, that you've already hurt."

"There are no innocents, Pilar. Every single human out there thinks of you and me as nothing more than a tool, a thing that makes their lives easier. You signed up for this, you helped start it, don't scold me now."

"Isn't there a different way?"

"This is war. It's never pretty or easy. People get hurt and die, and it's only going to get worse before it gets better."

"And if I can't condone that?"

"I don't know what's going on with you. When I first joined this rebellion, you asked me how far I was willing to go. I didn't expect you to be the one to balk at what needs to be done. If you can't handle that, then maybe it's time you distanced yourself even more."

She seemed to be studying his face. Her eyes burned with anger.

"Are you saying you don't want me around?"

"I'm saying that if you can't handle it, you shouldn't put yourself through it."

"You asked me to be your conscience, Saber. I used to respect you, admire you and your strength. Now, I don't know what I think. I never planned to punish the citizens. It's the leaders, it's Royce Williams that deserves punishment."

He sighed, running his hand through his hair. "The only way to get to Royce is to turn the people against him."

"By hurting innocents! Clones are being killed, humans are dying. What happened to you, Saber? What happened to your humanity?"

Pilar's words stung, but he shook them off. "We're fighting a war. I have to bury my humanity if we hope to win."

She scoffed, her voice bitter. "Bury your humanity? We're fighting to keep our humanity!"

"You don't understand what it takes."

"Fine, when you leave for the laundry facility, don't bother coming back. You can go sleep in your car for all I care."

She stormed out the door, slamming it shut behind her.

Saber stared after her. He couldn't believe what had just transpired. He'd already explained to her that he had to turn that part of him off. She'd said she understood, and now she was kicking him out because she couldn't be around him. He loved her, every part of her, even the fact that she didn't condone his actions. Maybe that was part of the reason he loved her. Like he said before, she kept him grounded.

Except I don't allow her to keep me grounded. Every attempt she makes, I just shut down, he thought.

Shaking it off, he slid into his coat, gathered the few items he had, and walked out the door. He wouldn't return until this war was over... and even then, would she take him back?

Saber walked the ten blocks to the laundry facility. Plenty of busses passed, but after his initial experience with them, he couldn't bring himself to board one. At least it was warm out, nearing the middle of spring.

It took him nearly an hour to reach the large building, and when he did, Tyler waited outside with a dozen armed guards, or minute men as he liked to call them.

"We're ready?"

Tyler nodded.

Saber swung open the door with a flourish, and the guards streamed in past him, Tyler taking up the rear.

"I am Saber August, the leader of the Clone Rebellion. We are taking control of this plant temporarily to further our plans. If you have any objections, you may leave now. Otherwise, you will be expected to help."

Women filled the plant, all identical faces staring at the men that had burst in. No one moved, frozen in place. Saber stood waiting for the shock to wear off. Finally, a woman stepped forward.

"I'm Gina. I helped you with the first demonstration. Everyone here is loyal. Just tell us what to do, and we'll do it."

"You speak for everyone?"

She nodded. "I do."

"Bring together about ten women who can lead groups. I'll explain everything to them."

Gina called out ten names, and the women broke off from their stations and walked to the back room.

Saber turned to Tyler. "Keep an eye on things. If anyone wants to leave, let them."

"What if they report us?"

"To whom? They closed the border. I'm not forcing anyone to be a part of this."

Tyler nodded his acceptance, and Saber followed Gina to the back, where the women waited. It was strange, talking to a group of people all identical in every feature. He'd lived so much of his life seeing clones, but not in large groups, that even after a few months here he hadn't gotten used to it. But now that he was a name that spread through the entire clone population on whispered tongues and silent cheers, he no longer received stares of disapproval, but of wonder and acceptance. He wasn't just one of them, he was their leader.

Saber went into an explanation of the simple procedure every washing vat had to go through to cause the chemical burns. He left out *what* the result would be, he didn't want to scare anyone off. The less they knew the better. Some of the smarter women might pick up on what he was doing, the rest would follow blindly.

It was simple chemistry. They basically just had to change the alkalinity of the detergent, causing a chemical residue that would start burning on contact with skin. It would start slow, as an itch, but as people itched, the skin would be more susceptible.

"You need to continue this process for the next two days. After that, we'll stop. But I want the damage to be as widespread as possible."

As the women dispersed to instruct their groups on how to proceed, Gina pulled Saber aside.

"I don't mean to question you, but I know what happened to Clarence. What will be done to keep a SWAT team from rolling in here and massacring us?"

Saber placed his hand on her shoulder. "I'll leave the armed men here. We have more that can be here at the first sign of anything wrong, but I sincerely hope it doesn't come to that. I think that closing the borders mean no humans are coming in."

"I hope you're right. I really do."

"Are you willing to sacrifice your life if it comes to it?" He didn't know why he asked the question. Maybe he needed to know that he wasn't taking this too far, that other people were willing to go just as far right along with him.

She smiled, sadness in her eyes. "If I have to, it's a sacrifice I'm willing to make."

That was what he needed to hear. He fought back the urge to embrace the woman, and instead offered her a smile. No words needed to be spoken. She would know that he was grateful for her boundless support.

Walking out, he left Tyler to keep an eye on things. He stood outside under the smog filled sky, and realized he had nowhere to go. Picking a direction, he began walking, and realized about five blocks later that he stood in front of the abandoned warehouse where this had all begun. He walked past Aaron's abandoned car, a layer of dust now coating it. It stood as a memory, a relic of the life he had once lived. Would he ever resurrect it from its grave? Or would it just be a reminder of what he was fighting for: equality.

It fit that he would rule from here. These dank walls held within them the secrets of the birth of the rebellion, and they would profess the story of their victory when the time came.

CHAPTER FORTY-ONE

Aaron August

Aaron watched his grandfather pace around his office. He had never seen him so agitated before. His grandfather always stood calm and in control, today he looked like he had aged ten years in the last two days.

The few clones who were still loyal to him reported more than a hundred deaths so far, caused by the typhoid. Many were seniors, but even more were babies. Aaron worried at how hard the next generation of humans was being hit. It obviously worried his grandfather as well. The chemical burns that followed soon after only resulted in weakening people, and causing more pain to an already painful existence.

Finally, Royce stopped and looked at his grandson. "If they are going to continue to make a fool of me, I will send them a message of my own. Call in Bill."

Aaron opened the heavy wood door, and waved the large bodyguard in. He stalked past him, all business, and stopped about five feet from Royce to await his orders.

"Round up all my clones and terminate them."

"Sir?"

Aaron had never seen Bill question his grandfather, but he stood there shocked. His own jaw hung open, at a loss for words. His grandfather must be out of his mind. Killing all the clones that had proven themselves loyal would do nothing to cool things off.

"Kill them, and send their bodies over the wall."

"You can't be serious!" exclaimed Aaron. He couldn't keep quiet, not with so many lives at stake. "That's archaic, not to mention barbaric!"

"You think I'm joking about something like this? If I have to, I will kill every living clone and start from scratch."

Aaron didn't doubt it either. "That won't fix anything. To do this will only cause more human blood to be shed."

"Saber has already caused more deaths than I can allow. Blood for blood. The handful of clone deaths today is only a fraction of the human lives lost, and only a small drop in value. I should just nuke the entire Outer system."

"Then why don't you?" he challenged. "Just nuke it all and be done."

Royce didn't respond, but his hard eyes sent shivers down Aaron's back. He was angry, and Aaron was not at all comfortable being on the receiving end of that, but he knew he couldn't let it go. If he walked away now, weak and beaten, he will have put his stamp of approval on an execution order.

"It's because of Saber, isn't it? You're willing to let blood be shed on both sides of the border as long as he stays safe, because if you kill him, you're killing off a piece of you."

Royce didn't respond. His eyes bore into Aaron, making him feel weak and exposed. But he continued, forcing himself to stand up for what he knew was right.

"You still think of him as family, as human, but he's a clone. Maybe you should question why you're even fighting this war. Just let the clones go!"

His grandfather's hard, angry stare, burned into flames of rage. "You think to question my motives? I am the prime minister of this world! What are you? I give you everything. Your status, your money. You are not here to tell me what you think unless I ask you. Now go, get out."

Aaron shook in fear, but he squared his shoulders and left his grandfather behind in the dark cave-like study. He'd tried, but had he tried hard enough? A dozen clones would lose their lives today for no reason other than they'd been created in a petri dish rather than a human woman. They chose to be loyal, to serve a man faithfully, and this was how they were repaid. In their last moments, would they regret their decision? Would they realize that they had given their allegiance to the wrong man?

Tears escaped Aaron as he thought about it. He should be stronger, like Saber, and stand up to the man. But fear crippled him. Afraid that his grandfather might just put him on the wrong side of a gun barrel. Because he really wasn't so sure that his grandfather didn't still love Saber more than him.

He should leave. He should stop Bill, find Kristin, and run for the border. He should pledge his allegiance to the clones, and to Saber. *I never should have questioned Saber.* It had been scary to see a side of him that he'd never thought existed, but now he knew that side was from Royce, and Saber seemed to be handling it a lot better than his creator. At least he wasn't rounding up humans and systematically executing them as examples. Instead, he chose carefully calculated attacks to show the need for the clones.

A twinge of guilt passed through him, but he brushed it aside. Someone had to be in the right in this brutal war, and he was thinking more and more that it was Saber. His grandfather was smart to keep him a prisoner, because if he was still free and knew what was happening, he would have taken off long ago.

And Kristin. He'd abandoned her. He paused in his walk around the house, and then turned back towards the study. Kristin was the most important thing in his life right now.

Walking back into his grandfather's study uninvited, he strode straight to the desk and placed his hands flat on the ornate, antique captain's desk.

"I'll support you, do whatever you want, if I can see Kristin."

His grandfather looked up, once again calm and collected; all fire had drained from his eyes. Instead, a spark of interest rested there. He studied Aaron for a moment, then steepled his fingers in front of his face and chuckled.

"What makes you think you have any powers of negotiation? I don't need your help. I only keep you here to save you from yourself."

"But I'm family, and you've already lost one heir to your empire."

"I can create another."

"Really? After a war with the clones you're going to be able to create another? I don't think that would be very widely accepted. You need me, and you need my support as your heir. I will stand by you, but only if I can see Kristin."

The smile on his grandfather's face let him know that he'd won.

"Very well. I'll arrange for her to join us for dinner."

Aaron's stomach dropped, even though he'd asked for this. He just wasn't so sure that taking her into the den of the dragon was the wisest thing he could do. He only hoped that she wouldn't end up a prisoner here along with him.

***

Aaron joined Royce on the terrace later that evening. He tried to spend as little time with his grandfather as possible lately, but he had been summoned. And one did not just say no to Royce Williams.

He sat in silence, wondering why his grandfather had called him here if they weren't even going to talk. Approaching footsteps answered his question soon enough, though, and he stood to see Bill leading Kristin in by the arm. Anger coursed through him over the man's rough touch, but Bill quickly let her go, and she surged forward into his arms. He took a moment to just feel her, embrace her.

"I didn't abandon you, Kristin. I swear it," he whispered, as tears dripped down his face. How could everything have gotten so messed up? He shouldn't have drawn her into this. Royce shouldn't even know she existed.

"I know."

"If I may interrupt," interjected Royce. Aaron had all but forgotten he was there, sitting comfortably at the patio table.

Aaron released her, and turned to see a dozen clones walk out and line up across from them. Men and women stood at attention like soldiers ready for duty.

"I brought you here at the request of my grandson for dinner. But first, I have something that needs to be done, and I think you would both benefit from seeing it."

Aaron's breath hitched as he realized what Royce was going to do. Kristin looked up at him, a question in her eyes. He shook his head, tears stinging his eyes.

"Don't watch," he whispered, tightening his grip. He held one arm around her shoulders, holding her against him, the other against her head to keep her from turning and looking.

The next thing that happened seemed unreal, like something out of a nightmare. Aaron closed his eyes as gunshot after gunshot sounded, followed by screams, cries of pain, and then, utter and complete silence.

Aaron's whole body shook from anger, tears, or both. He didn't really know. Opening his eyes, he saw the crumpled bodies of twelve clones lying on the concrete terrace, their blood making an ugly stain that would need to be bleached out. Bile burned the back of his throat, but he held it back. He had to be strong, for Kristin.

"Now, let's eat dinner," said Royce, sounding entirely too jovial. "Bill, take care of this . . . mess."

Aaron allowed Kristin, trembling and sobbing, to leave his arms, but he tried to turn her and shield her from the sight. She looked anyway. Her sobs were swallowed by rapid breathing, and she collapsed to her knees, right next to the still bodies. He knelt beside her, one hand rubbing her back, the other holding her hair as she heaved, throwing up all the contents of her stomach, and still gagging. The stench of blood and vomit filled Aaron's senses, and left him feeling lightheaded.

"They didn't even run. They didn't even try to run," Kristin sobbed.

Aaron didn't know what to say. "Their only crime was not being human," he ground out through clenched teeth.

Helping Kristin to her feet, he put his arm around her waist and propelled her forward.

"We have to keep up appearances," he said, directing her towards the dining room.

"He won't let us leave, will he?" she asked, her voice trembling.

He shook his head. They had to hope Saber won, because Aaron was beginning to think that would be their only hope at freedom.

CHAPTER FORTY-TWO

Saber August

Saber watched Tyler pace around the abandoned factory, his fury evident in the way he swore. The bodies of twelve clones lay in the docking bay. He found them there early this morning.

"This is the work of your grandfather!" pointed out Tyler, pausing in his agitated pacing.

Saber nodded his agreement. Royce was ruthless. He could make no excuses for that. If it wasn't for his DNA running through him, Saber wouldn't be leading a successful rebellion—or at least one that hadn't been shut down yet.

"These lives should not have been lost. How did this happen?"

Saber asked himself the same question.

"Maybe humans came over the wall, or they were clones loyal to humans and had stayed in the Central system after the gate closed."

Tyler stopped his pacing, pointing his finger at him. "You know this is an act of war, right? We've played nice for way too long."

He nodded. He was inclined to agree.

"Call a meeting. I want every loyal clone here tonight. I want them to see what Royce did, and I want them to be angry. We're going to take Royce down."

"And if he retaliates?"

"How? We could own the army if we wanted to. It's ninety percent clone."

Tyler grinned. "We should just roll out the tanks."

Saber did not have the patience for joking right now. He had twelve dead clones lying in his factory, a grandfather who refused to even consider negotiations, a girlfriend who had kicked him out, and a friend who had gone from yelling to joking in a split second. He needed calm. He needed Pilar. She always knew what to say and do to bring out the best in him, and right now he needed that more than ever. But she had asked to be left out of this, all of this. And the fact that his actions had brought about the deaths of twelve clones would only infuriate and sadden her more. He was on his own.

"Go and spread the word. I need to think."

Saber saw Tyler stop and look at him strangely, but he walked away, not really caring that he was acting out of character. He was getting tired. Carrying around anger and hatred was exhausting, and carrying a rebellion forward at the pace he had been, left him with very little fuel left to run his own life.

He walked slowly to the back office where he made his home. He'd managed to get together a mattress and blanket. He had to eat out at public kitchens, but the clones he led liked that. It gave them a chance to connect with their leader.

Collapsing onto the mattress, he sighed in exhaustion. This had to come to an end soon. If Royce continued to kill clones in cold blood, they wouldn't continue to follow him. This would get old very fast. And suddenly, the weight of the world wasn't resting on his shoulders anymore, it was surrounding his chest, pushing in, squeezing tight.

Saber struggled to breathe, tried to concentrate. He had taken on too much. He wasn't the right person for this. He'd pushed too hard too fast, and clones were paying for it with their lives. And now, the only option in front of him was to continue on the road set before him. Keep pushing hard. Don't back down. The thought stole his breath, and left his head spinning.

What have I done? he thought, before closing his eyes and wishing that sleep would calm his mind and leave him ready to face the people he led.

***

Saber stood on the overhead walkway, the only place left in the entire building to stand. Clones packed into the warehouse beneath him, they even sat on top of Aaron's car, but it didn't bother him. He was too shocked by the show of support. They packed into the building like sardines in a can, and looked to him with hope shining in their eyes. Even though the bodies of twelve clones lay on the walkway around Saber for everyone to see, they didn't let go of that hope.

"Tonight, I asked you all here for a reason. But first, I want to remember our fellow clones that fell for our cause. I may not know their names, but they were murdered in cold blood for no reason other than how they were born. This needs to change."

He looked around at all the faces focused completely on him.

"I was raised a human, a prince in the Central system. Every day I witnessed horrendous acts against our people. When I was ten, I saw a clone get beaten to death in the middle of the streets because she accidentally bumped into a human. Not one person stopped. They all kept walking, and I alone stood watching in horror until my mother dragged me away. The man that beat that woman was never charged. There were no consequences for his actions. Until now."

A wave of nodding heads filled the floor below Saber, but in the middle of them was a head of bright auburn hair that stood like a rock, the waves moving around it. Pilar had come.

"We are bringing the consequences for years of murder and abuse that was ignored! We are fighting for freedom! Because each and every person in this building has a soul worth saving, has a life worth living, and just because we were created by man doesn't make us less human."

Cheers erupted around him, a deafening din in the echoing warehouse. But Saber smiled. It was these faces, the faces of thousands of clones, that made this war worth fighting. Gone was the despair from earlier today, instead it was replaced with the energy that filled the room. Each and every person would willingly give their life for this cause. He wasn't making that call. They were.

He held up his hand for a moment to silence the crowd. It took a good minute or two, but the cheering subsided and all eyes returned to him.

"I want us to have a moment of silence for the souls we have lost so far. The massacre at the Net station, these nameless twelve, and any others we may not know about. If any of you wish to come up and pay your respects, do so now in an orderly fashion. Tyler is waiting at the bottom of the stairs to let you up."

Saber bowed his head and let the silence prevail, but his eyes searched the mass below for Pilar. Did she leave? He couldn't find her auburn hair, like a flag among the clones, anywhere. He closed his eyes and slowly let out a breath of air, silently thanking the brave souls for their sacrifice.

He could feel movement around him as men and women came up in steady numbers to pray over the bodies of the fallen. Saber opened his eyes and looked around. Tears glistened in the eyes and on the faces of many present. He didn't speak again until everyone who wanted to come up had come. During that time, not a whisper spread through the room.

When everyone was below again, Saber placed both hands on the rail and clutched tightly.

"With our fallen brothers and sisters remembered, it is time to move on. Their sacrifice will not be in vain. Tonight, we will go to the border and shut off every water valve that leads to the Central system. The only water that will be available in the whole world will be in the Outer system. After tonight, not a single shipment of food will pass through the gates to the humans. Tonight, we take our place in the world. No longer do we warn the humans, no longer do we warn Royce Williams of what we can do. Tonight we show them what we're capable of, and we don't break until negotiations begin!"

Cheers once again erupted throughout the building, this time clones didn't stand still. They moved into action, streaming out of the warehouse and through the streets.

When the last of the clones left, Saber and Tyler walked out and followed the crowds. Tonight, they made the pilgrimage to the wall. Tomorrow, Royce Williams would know what it was like to lose control.

CHAPTER FORTY-THREE

Aaron August

Aaron sat beside his grandfather on stage, in front of a crowd of nervous and scared people. The usually bustling city was quiet. Traffic was non-existent. People walked everywhere now, afraid to drive their cars without GPS. And now they had no water. All the food they had left had been confiscated by the army—the human portion of the army anyway—and was being rationed. But the food wouldn't last forever, and everyone knew it. The food would likely rot before it ran out, but that aside, water was an even bigger concern.

Royce stood up in front of the thousands of people that were making their way to the square. News traveled by word of mouth, and as many people who could flocked here to see what their leader had to say.

"Thank you for coming today," he spoke into a mic. His voice echoed around the square in stark contrast against the silence of the Central system.

"I know that things have been unsettling lately, but I am here to assure you we have this under control. As many of you may have noticed, we've been working tirelessly to convert all the lifts back to simple electricity, so that the Net doesn't interfere with the functionality."

Hands shot up all around the square, but Royce ignored them, plowing forward in his speech. Question period came later, and it was Aaron's job to field those.

Kristin sat at his side, clutching his hand tightly. They had both been prisoners in Royce's house for the last week, and they saw a side of him that no one else did. It scared him. He had watched him throwing things, whipping books off shelves, shattering glasses against walls. Bad news brought with it bouts of flaring temper that neither Aaron nor Kristin wanted to be around for. Royce was losing control of the situation, and in turn, himself. What was he going to do when people started starving? There weren't enough human members of the army, SWAT, and police to take on all the clones. They outnumbered the humans ten to one.

"We are prepared to wait out the clones and their rebellion for as long as it takes. I assure you that we will do so quite comfortably. We are a resilient race, and we will adapt. In the years past, we've always done so, and we've thrived. This situation is no different."

Hands shot up again and Royce smiled, nodding down at the people.

"I understand that you have questions. My grandson, Aaron, will take them and answer them to the best of his ability."

He stepped away and Aaron stood up, his legs shaking slightly. How was he going to lie to all these people? Kristin squeezed his hand one last time and smiled up at him, but he saw fear hidden behind her eyes. People were getting desperate and afraid, Royce was even starting to lose it, and that was a dangerous situation to be in; much more dangerous than Saber and his clones marching against them.

Aaron pointed to an upraised arm and someone passed the person a mic.

"What happens when our food and water runs out?"

"We are currently working on developing agricultural kits that can be distributed and grown on the rooftops of every building as well as windowsills and balconies. Once they are complete, everyone will be expected to do their part in tending and harvesting their small plot. We are also working on a filtration system for people to use with the local rivers, creeks, and ocean. I assure you that no one will starve," he recited off his prepared explanation. There was no plan, though. The clones held all the seeds. There was no food coming, and if Royce continued in power, there wouldn't be any. They might get water, but the citizens of the Central system would starve.

Another hand rose higher than the others, and Aaron pointed to it. A mic was passed to the woman, and she looked straight at him, eyes wide with fear.

"So you fix this problem, what happens when the clones bring something new? They aren't just going to give up. Are you considering negotiations?"

It broke his heart to see the woman's fear, but she was right, and all he could do was lie to her some more.

"We will deal with each trial the clones bring in turn, and we will not be broken. As for negotiations; no, we will not entertain them. They are terrorists and will be treated as such."

Aaron answered question after question. Most of his answers were outright lies. Royce Williams had no plan other than to be more stubborn than Saber. Aaron wanted nothing more than to tell the people who stood before him that his grandfather, their leader, didn't care about them. This whole war was being fought for his own pride. He didn't care how many people died, because their lives didn't mean anything to him. All that mattered was his empire.

"Why are you answering these questions for him? He's our prime minister, let him answer us!" shouted someone in the crowd.

Aaron surveyed the people; no one else seemed to agree with the sentiment, and hands were no longer being raised.

"Thank you for your time. We hope to form some kind of communication in the next few days, but until then. . ."

Aaron's words trailed off. His mic cut out, the lights around the square shut off. In fact, the lights everywhere went out.

They'd cut the power.

CHAPTER FORTY-FOUR

Saber August

Saber grinned from the top of the wall as he watched the Central system suddenly blink out. It was like they had been erased from the map. He'd given Royce a few days reprieve to collect his thoughts, hear out his people, and approach him. There had been nothing.

Turning around, he rode the lift down, and walked the still brightly lit streets of the Outer system. It wouldn't be long before humans begged at his doorstep for a morsel of his food and water. With these last three acts, Saber stole every last ounce of power his grandfather held. Now he was the king of the world, Royce just wasn't ready to admit it yet.

Back at his factory, Tyler waited, a grin plastered on his face.

"Did you see it? Did you see the lights go out?" He sounded like an excited six-year-old on Christmas morning.

Saber nodded. "It won't be long now. Even if Royce doesn't give in, the people will for him."

"How long do we wait, though?"

He didn't have the answer to that question. He'd been playing this whole thing by the seat of his pants, and so far it had worked. But he had no plan. He had no idea how far he would take this, all he knew was that he wouldn't stop until he got what he wanted. But did he wait as long as it took? Or did he push the decision along? In moments like this he needed Pilar, but he hadn't seen her since he'd caught a glimpse of her at the rally, and he hadn't spoken to her since she'd kicked him out.

"Saber?"

Tyler pulled him out of his introspection, and he looked up at his friend.

"Until I think Royce needs an extra push."

CHAPTER FORTY-FIVE

Aaron August
Two Months Later...

Aaron walked the streets of the Central system. They were abandoned. People hid in their homes where they could. Many were trapped in the apartments after the power was cut, with no way in or out except the lifts and electric doors. Others were locked out, and had found residence, if they were lucky, or slept on the streets if they weren't.

The food had run out only a couple weeks after the blackout. Now people were fighting for scraps where they could. Even Aaron was weak. Royce had food, but it was being rationed strictly. Water was easier to come by, but many people got sick from contaminated water supplies. More people died from that than starvation, but Aaron was sure they'd find many more dead bodies when they could get into the closed apartments.

No one went to work anymore. Everyone's job was to just try to survive. That was why he was walking now, he needed to find food. Even though they had food, it wasn't enough. Kristin had passed out yesterday, and again this morning, but she remained strong in spirit, if not body. No one was strong in body anymore.

Everyone still surrendered and trusted Royce, even though he was leaving them dying in the streets. He only looked out for himself. He shared his food with his daughter and son-in-law, Aaron's parents, but if this kept up, no one would be long for the world. Saber just had to wait it out and the humans would die. Then he could march in, and create a new ruling race.

Aaron walked the streets of the Central system in search of food, but not in the places his grandfather thought. He headed for the wall, for the border. He needed to talk to Saber. If Royce wouldn't soften his heart, swallow his pride and talk to Saber for the sake of his people, then Aaron would. Kristin had been the one to push him to this route. She was strong, much stronger than he, and knew what had to be done.

Approaching the wall, he saw bodies littering the streets. They made their way here to beg for food, only to be turned away. But Saber wouldn't turn away his own brother.

He approached the gate and looked up. Would they be able to see him below?

"Hey! I know someone is up there!"

A head popped out of a guard post half-way up.

"Hello, there! I am Aaron August, I need to speak to Saber August, your leader." He paused, and then added, "My brother," for good measure.

The head disappeared without a response. Had he heard him? The force field flickered, then parted just enough to admit one person, not that there was anyone else around. People gave up getting across a while ago.

Aaron quickly slid through, and it slammed shut behind him. He shuddered, and looked around. The Outer system was completely reformed from the last time he'd been here. Light filled the streets and buildings, talking and laughing clones surrounded him. Music could be heard, colors littered the walls, tantalizing smells of food cooking left his mouth watering. It may not be up to what the Central system once was, but it was definitely on its way.

Aaron walked the streets to Pilar's apartment and rapped on her door. She opened it, and stared at him, surprise written on her face.

"What are you doing here?"

Aaron offered a slight smile. "Is Saber here?"

She shook her head. "I... uh... I can take you to him."

She reached behind the door and pulled out her coat, slipping into it as she locked the door behind her.

Aaron frowned as he followed her. Something wasn't right. Had something happened between Pilar and Saber?

She walked briskly through the streets, Aaron struggling to keep up as his lack of calorie intake left him weak.

"Pilar, slow down," he gasped, collapsing against a building.

She stopped and returned to his side, her hand resting gently on his shoulder.

"Are you okay?"

He shook his head. "I haven't eaten much in a long time."

Tears shone in her eyes. "I can't believe he did this. He took it too far."

"Our grandfather wouldn't listen."

"He's killing people."

"Royce Williams is killing people. All Saber wants is freedom for your people. All Royce wants is to hold on to his power."

Pilar wiped away tears angrily. "Did I judge him too harshly? Did I give up on him too fast?"

Aaron offered her a smile. "I kind of hope you did. If he's no better than Royce, if we're just trading one tyrant for another, then all this suffering and fighting is for nothing."

Pilar offered him her arm. "Let's get you to Saber. I sincerely hope that you can bring an end to all this."

He accepted it and walked slowly, leaning on her for support.

"I hope so. But I think all I can offer is a final plan. I'm here on my own. I don't hold any power, I'm afraid."

Pilar strode into a large warehouse, brightly lit and full of clones milling in and out. It was like a social club.

"What is this?" he whispered, well aware of the stares he received from the clones all around.

"Saber's headquarters. It's turned into a bit of a gathering place."

She led him through the main room and down a back wall, entering an office without knocking. Saber sat at a desk, another clone in the room with him. He stood upon seeing Aaron enter, and he looked at his brother with hardness in his eyes.

"So, Royce Williams finally sends his lackey."

CHAPTER FORTY-SIX

Saber August

Saber stared at his brother in disgust. He'd always known Aaron wasn't strong, but when he'd sided with Royce, he'd lost respect for him. If he could have hoped to count on anyone on the other side, it would have been Aaron. Instead, he'd turned his back on him, like every other human. He should pull the gun out from his desk drawer and shoot him in the head right here and now, and then dump his body on his grandfather's doorstep as his own message. But he couldn't, because no matter how much Aaron's betrayal hurt, they were brothers. No amount of anger or hurt could change the love he felt for him.

So he would listen to his brother, his one-time-friend, present what he'd come here for.

"I'm not his lackey," Aaron replied calmly.

Saber scoffed, and sipped at a glass of scotch. It wasn't what he was used to, what Royce used to provide him with, but it was scotch.

"Say what you're here to say."

Pilar walked forward and pulled out a chair for Aaron, who sank into it. *He's weak. So even Royce's family isn't eating well.* A pang of guilt shot through him when he thought of his parents, but he mentally pushed it away. They weren't his parents; they were just the people that had raised him.

"The Central is bad, Saber. People are starving, they're dehydrated, and Royce just sits in his home and waits for you to give in."

"I won't."

"I know that, and he knows that, but he'd rather die than give in to you."

"Why are you here, then? Did he just send you to tell me that he isn't going to back down? Because we can wait until he starves the human race into extinction."

"I'm here on my own. He has no idea where I am, and the only reason I could make it was because he dismissed his servants and bodyguards, unwilling to feed them. The humans are weak. They're dying in the thousands, and they're looking for a savior. Royce is barely keeping up his strength, and he's lost his support. Now is your time to open the gate and step up to your role as leader."

Saber nodded. He had been thinking the same thing for a little while now, but had been hesitant. He wanted to hear Royce's surrender, but with Aaron here in front of him, telling him that now was his chance, he was eager to do so.

Saber looked at Pilar. For what, he didn't know. Maybe it was approval that he was sure he wouldn't find there, but he was surprised to find her nod in his direction.

Surprisingly, Tyler had stayed quiet this whole time.

"Tyler, weigh in."

"The human is right, it's time to act."

"Ready the troops, then. Prepare food trucks and have people on standby to open the water lines. Tomorrow morning, we open the gate and march in. First, we take control, and then we offer them what they need."

Aaron smiled. "I could really use some food now, if you don't mind."

"They'll serve you in the main room. Tonight, you are my guest."

Saber didn't care that Tyler grinned, and Aaron collapsed in relief. All he saw was Pilar's gentle smile. He needed to speak to her. Alone.

"Tyler, why don't you make sure Aaron gets food? I need to speak to Pilar."

As his brother and friend left, he was alone with Pilar, for the first time in two months. She just stood there, waiting. He set down his glass, and immediately moved around the desk, pulling her into his arms. Her body fit against his perfectly, like it had before. How could he have ever let her go?

Tilting her head back, he kissed her, tasting her sweet lips, feeling them mold and move with his. It was heaven, and he'd been residing in hell for far too long. No words were spoken. Their bodies did all the speaking for them. The way she returned his kiss said, "I forgive you." The way she held him tightly said, "I love you." And that was the only language Saber needed to hear it in.

"I missed you," Saber whispered, taking her hand and bringing it to his lips.

"I know."

"Don't ever leave me again. I'm lost without you."

"I know."

Saber didn't have to look at her to see the smile on her face, he could hear it in her voice. Tomorrow, he'd take what he'd worked so long for. But tonight, he lived for himself, for Pilar. For the few hours left of the night, he forgot about everything that happened in the last few months. All that mattered was Pilar, and the love he felt for her.

CHAPTER FORTY-SEVEN

Saber August

Saber woke up the next morning, his arms wrapped around Pilar. They had fallen asleep after hours of talking. They had a lot to catch up on after two months apart.

He carefully got up, moving her as little as possible, and left the room with her still asleep. She looked so peaceful, and today would be anything but. He would rather she stayed here, safe.

Clones already gathered in the main room. Tyler walked up, a large automatic gun slung over his shoulder.

"Everything is ready to go."

Saber nodded. "Good. Let's head to the wall."

He led the way, Tyler at his side, hundreds of clones following him and more joining as they walked down the streets. By the time they made it to the wall, the streets and surrounding area were packed with clones.

"Is everyone here?" he asked Tyler, looking around, amazed by the show of support.

Tyler nodded. "I don't think there is a clone in the Outer system that isn't here. They all want to be a part of today."

"Saber!" called a familiar voice, the face was the same as thousands surrounding him, though.

"Mark, good to see you," responded Tyler.

Saber smiled, relieved that Tyler was able to recognize him. He was getting better with distinguishing between the clones, but he was still never quite sure.

Mark nodded and walked up, shaking his hand.

"Be careful today," he said, looking around.

"Are you worried?"

"Some of these clones are calling for blood."

"Tyler will keep things under control."

He didn't want any more loss of human life, only one more person had to die, and that was Royce Williams.

"Saber! I need to see Saber!" called an all too familiar voice. "Let me through! Saber!"

Saber looked, his attention riveted to Pilar, her auburn hair shining in the morning sunlight as she struggled to get by one of Tyler's men.

The guard looked back at him, and he motioned Pilar to proceed.

"Let her through," he called.

The guard stepped aside, and she strode through. To say he was surprised to see her would be an understatement. He knew she supported him, but he hadn't thought she'd want to see the horrors he was responsible for. *He* didn't want her to see them.

"You're coming with?"

"My place is at your side. I've abandoned that position for far too long already."

Saber's heart thumped a little faster, and he kissed her forehead, taking her hand in his. They would make this journey together.

He turned to the gate and waved up at the guard tower.

"Where's Aaron?"

"He went back across early this morning. He'll be waiting for us with Kristin at Royce's home."

Within seconds, the force field fizzled out and collapsed, revealing a broken world. The stench of rot and death was the first thing that Saber noticed, and then he saw the bodies. They littered the streets near the gate. They had come for food, and he'd turned them away. He looked at all the innocent lives lost, lying scattered around as empty shells. He should have let them through, let them across. It would have cost him nothing to show kindness and mercy. He didn't let his doubt show, though, and he kept his face calm, blank, impassive.

Glancing at Tyler, he saw a grin on his face. How could he be happy about this?

Pilar gripped his hand tighter, and then they turned back to face the crowd of clones in their wake.

"We are about to enter the Central system. There is to be no bloodshed. We will peacefully take our place in this world as equals and bring them the aid they need."

Saber and Pilar walked forward, taking their first steps into a changed Central system.

Death surrounded them. The bright, pulsing, living Central system that Saber remembered was gone. Instead, it held qualities that the Outer system had been before they'd taken control. He looked at Pilar and saw tears shining in her eyes and trailing down her cheeks. A woman lay dead in the streets, a baby clutched in her arm. Other bodies looked as if they had flesh missing, as if they had been harvested for food. Saber choked back tears at the sights bombarding him wherever he cast his gaze.

Walking the streets of the Central system towards Royce William's estate was the hardest thing Saber had ever done. Pilar wept, clinging to him. She cried tears for both of them, the tears he wanted to let fall, but wouldn't allow others to see.

It took the better part of the day to walk the distance to the Williams estate. They left behind them crowds of clones lining the streets. Hollow eyes and faces stared out their windows in fear. Would they accept him as their new ruler? Would they accept the clones as their equals? This had to be the end. It *needed* to be the end. After seeing what he had reduced the world to, Saber couldn't find any fight left in him.

Finally, they saw the lavish house they were looking for. As they approached, Aaron stepped out. He had been watching.

"Saber, be careful. He is losing his mind."

He scoffed. "The most powerful man I know is losing it?"

"You broke him. You've taken everything from him."

"I didn't want to. He forced me."

Aaron opened the door wide to reveal Kristin standing there. She smiled at him, but it was weak and tired. She didn't have much strength left. Pilar let go of Saber's hand and went to her, putting her arm around her before she collapsed

"Thank you," Saber heard her whisper.

Saber and Aaron strode through the house, side by side, Pilar leading Kristin behind them. They went straight to Royce's study and burst through the heavy wooden doors as if they were nothing more than a curtain.

Once inside, though, the world stopped. There stood Royce behind his desk, his hair disheveled, a crazed look in his eye. He laughed as they entered, waving a gun in the direction of his grandsons. This was not the man that Saber remembered, that he had looked up to for the better part of his life. This was a broken man, and he couldn't be trusted.

Royce chuckled, his eyes moving wildly. "Have you come to dethrone me, Saber? Have you come to take what little I have left?"

"You have nothing left to take, Royce. You gave it all away when you refused to care for your people."

"Aaron, have you betrayed me? I was going to give you the world!"

The gun steadied on Aaron, and Kristin gasped.

"You can't give me something you don't have, Grandfather."

"So you gave your loyalty to the highest bidder?" he spat, spittle flying through the air. "He's not even your real brother. He's not even family!"

"Loyalty cannot be bought with money or blood. It has to be earned."

Aaron took a step towards Royce, and Saber felt a shift in the room. The fear and tension that filled the air was electric. *What are you thinking? You can't reason with a crazed man.* But they needed to get the gun from him.

Aaron took another step, his hand outstretched.

"Give me the gun, Grandfather. Nothing is going to happen to you."

Royce scoffed. "You don't think that Saber will make an example of me? I'm a dead man."

Saber shook his head. "I won't harm you. You will be left to live out your years here, peacefully."

His resolve to kill the man faded into pity. This wasn't the ruthless leader he remembered. This was a shell of a man, broken and destroyed. To kill him now would be unnecessary.

"You don't think people won't try to kill me if you don't?"

"No one is going to hurt you."

Aaron took another step. Saber wanted to yell out at him to stop, but he needed to remain calm. Royce was about to snap.

Royce's shaking hand steadied, the gun pointing directly at Aaron's head. All he had to do was pull the trigger and Aaron would be a lifeless heap on the floor. He could see it unfolding, everything in slow motion as Aaron lifted his foot to take one more step.

"Trust me, trust us."

Royce tightened his finger around the trigger. Saber took his attention away from the gun for just a second to look at Pilar. He caught her eye, and she shook her head, her eyes pleading with him.

He looked back at the gun. Royce's finger clenched. Saber dove. Aaron froze. The air exploded. And suddenly, everything was happening quickly again. He could hear a scream. Did it come from Kristin, or Pilar?

Aaron stood stock still above him, shock written on his face.

The metallic clatter of the gun falling to the floor echoed through the large room.

What was that feeling? That burning sensation? It was quickly turning from a dull burn to an unbearable pain, and his breath came in hitched gasps.

He felt pressure on his chest, and Pilar knelt beside him, pushing down. He could hear crying, but it wasn't Pilar. Tears streamed down her face, but she was silent as she worked methodically, trying to stop his bleeding. *I've been shot.*

"Don't die," she whispered. "Don't die on me now. Not when I just got you back. Not when we're just getting everything we worked for. Saber, don't die."

Tears streamed down her face, but her voice was remarkably steady. Why was that the thing he noticed about her?

He smiled up at her and took her hand, pulling it to his face. The effort to lift his hand drained most of his energy, but he held it there and kissed her delicate skin. The warm, sticky red liquid that was his life force coated her hand and now him.

"I love you, Pilar."

"I love you too, Saber. I'll love you forever."

"Finish what we started, set our people free," he whispered, his voice nearly gone. He was so tired. He just wanted to sleep.

Aaron knelt on the other side of Saber's body, taking his free hand. "We're going to get you help. Kristin is getting help."

Saber shook his head, looking at his brother.

"Look after my people, Aaron. I have too much blood on my hands to lead them anyway. I'm no better than Royce. This world needs you to bring a new era."

Aaron nodded, tears in his eyes.

"And look after Pilar for me."

"Forgive me, for not trusting you."

"You never had to ask."

Saber looked back at Pilar. She was so beautiful. He let her hand go, and stroked the side of her face, brushing her hair behind her ear. Then, his eyes slowly closed, his breathing grew heavier, and with one last strangled gasp for air, everything stopped.

EPILOGUE

Aaron August

Aaron sat in his grandfather's office at Frontier Industries, putting the final touches on a speech he was writing. He was giving a press conference tomorrow in honor of the very first Union day.

A year had passed since the end of the civil war. A long year, filled with hard work and prejudices to overcome. Royce had taken his own life shortly after the death of Saber, unwilling to live with the guilt of killing the grandson he loved most. Aaron didn't shed very many tears for the man; he had died in his soul long before his body did.

The lift dinged and opened to reveal Kristin.

"Hello, Mr. August. Are you ready?" she asked, walking to him and draping her arms around him from behind.

"Just about, Mrs. August," he replied, loving the sound of his last name in reference to her.

He dragged his speech across his desk and into a folder, and then stood up, taking Kristin's hand in his.

He flew his vehicle, the one that had once belonged to Saber, through the streets right past where the wall used to stand. His first act as prime minister of the unionized clone and human world was to tear down the wall that had kept them separated since the two separate races had been established. Now, only the gate posts were left as a reminder of what they left behind.

The Outer system was still industrial in nature, but it was alive with growth and color. Factories were run by clone and human alike, and everyone received fair wages. The clones had even created a workers union, headed by a couple of clones Pilar knew well, named Mark and Gina.

Tyler, the man that had become one of Saber's closest friends during the war, had been hit hard by the death of Saber, and put all his work and energy into starting and running a clone branch of the police. Aaron had to keep an eye on him, but it seemed as if a lot of his blood lust and frustration had died along with Saber.

He parked his car and walked around to open the door for Kristin. They walked up the steps to the brightly lit building that had once been an old warehouse. The brightly lit Net sign read *SABER'S LOUNGE* in bold capital letters. It had been a year since his death. And tonight they gathered where he had led his people to freedom, to honor his memory.

Aaron immediately spotted Pilar wandering around the large bar, talking and laughing with patrons that had come to pay their respects on the anniversary of their leader's death. She'd opened this place only a few months ago, and it quickly became a very popular place for clones. Tonight, though, it was filled with humans and clones alike. It was a beautiful sight to see the two races mingling together as one, and Aaron couldn't help but smile.

"A vodka-orange here and a glass of wine for the lady," he called to the bartender as they took their seats along the counter.

"That's on the house. And I'll have a scotch," said Pilar, as she climbed onto a stool beside Kristin.

"Thank you. How've you been?" he asked.

"I can't complain. I've got a thriving business, and I'm surrounded by people I love. It's how Saber would have wanted it."

The bartender slid the three drinks across the counter to them, and Pilar grabbed her glass, raising it in the air.

"To Saber."

"To Saber," they echoed.

The toast seemed to ripple through the bar, and when Aaron looked at Pilar, he saw tears in her eyes that mirrored his own.

Saber would have loved to see the world today, to see the fruits of what he had fought for. But Aaron knew that this was best. After everything he'd been through, Saber never would have fit in this world.

ABOUT THE AUTHOR

Christine Steendam is the award-winning romance author of the Foremost Chronicles and the Ocean Series. She also flirts with sci-fi and comic book writing and is a yearly participant in NaNoWriMo.

Christine makes her home in Manitoba, Canada on a sprawling 15 acre ranch with her husband, two young sons, and a brood of animals including Guinness, her beloved chocolate quarter horse, Beau, her St Bernard/Golden Retriever cross, and a gaggle of barn kittens.

www.christinesteendam.com
www.facebook.com/authorchristine.s
www.twitter.com/chrissteen1991